TIME BLADE

Age of Jeweled Intelligence

P. Christina Greenaway

ISBN-13: 978-0692133590
ISBN-10: 0692133593

Age of Jeweled Intelligence

GLOSSARY

Ruberah [Ru'be'rah]	Land of the Ruby Kingdom on ancient Earth
Jeweled Spheres	The astral spheres of the jewel kingdoms
Astral Command	Communication control for the spheres
7 Jewel Kingdoms	Ruby: creation
	Emerald: power
	Gold: love
	Sapphire: mental acuity
	Amethyst: volition
	Diamond: intuition
	Pearl: illumination
Rube	A force derived from the astral energy of rubies
Mt. Rube	Jeweled mountain through which Rube flows to Earth
Time Blade	Weapon used to cut, reverse, or stop Time

EmFire	A force derived from the astral energy of emeralds
Planet Miron [Meer' on]	Home of the human family prior to Earth
The Sun Kingdom	The next universe
The Master	Spiritual guide for Earth during Time of Ruberah
The Witness	One who observes and records the Master's meetings with the Lords for Earth
Dark Master	Collective conscious of man's lowest nature
Time	Mastermind that oversees the evolution of the human family
Sacred Future	A promise thrown into the River of Life
Astral Disk	Hand computer to access astral forces
SunVision	The astral disk of the Sun Kingdom
The Cycles of Time	The recorded history of everything that's ever happened on Earth

I would not wish
any companion
in the world but you

— William Shakespeare

for Earth

BEFORE EARTH

CHAPTER ONE

Streams of silver-gold light flow in from the next universe, holding the remains of the space station intact. *Diamond Fire* stands posed for takeoff—the last craft to leave for the Jeweled Spheres. Rae Blue gulps back grief, and waves and smiles at his family as they mount the boarding ramp. His facial muscles ache from the effort, and the bitter taste of fear lumps in his throat. He takes himself to task. A man without a planet to live on must keep his thoughts on the moment at hand—the breath taken. The next is the future. It may not come, but eternity rides in the space between the breaths. Rae Blue shifts his glance inward to the sparkling blue orb lodged between his frontal lobes, and bows mentally to his sapphire wisdom. *I come to serve.*

The visionary plane opens—shears of clear light—reaching as far as the eye can see. Rae Blue inhales a deep breath and pictures everyone in transit to the Jeweled Spheres finding happiness, no matter the galaxy of their final destination. He exhales slowly, imprinting his vision on Time. *It is so.*

Hope evokes gratitude, a welcome relief from sorrow. He glances back to his family. Mother ushers his younger siblings inside *Diamond Fire*. Father hesitates at the door, rubbing his temples. Tears have been wept, farewells said, and his father is not a forgetful man, yet he descends the ramp, and strides back to Rae Blue. His gait is purposeful and the nuances of his character, valor and integrity, hang palpable on the air, descending on Rae Blue like a lofty inheritance. "What is it, Father?"

"Do whatever Master asks of you. His quest for the human family is of the highest order."

"Do you think I doubt that?"

"You are used to questioning Master. It is a path of learning for you, but you no longer enjoy the safety of the classroom."

"What are you not telling me, Father?"

"You showed great bravery during the Rescue, my son, but it is sometimes easier to risk your life for your fellow man than it is to accept a truth that goes against the grain of your nature."

Rae Blue searches his conscience. His first duty is to Master, the great Sun Lord Luca. It has been since his seventh birthday, when he began studying the astral energies of jewels with him. The Sun Lord had come back from the Sun Kingdom to help mankind evolve. Rae Blue aspires to win the Sun Heart and follow in his footsteps. That's the grain of his nature. "I don't understand your meaning, Father."

"Just consider my words." His father spins around and returns to the spacecraft, never looking back.

The door to *Diamond Fire* closes, and the sleek silver craft sweeps into the cosmos, nosing through the gaseous brilliance of the afterlife of the fallen sun.

Astronomers had kept close vigil on the depleting star. Just this morning, teleported intelligence indicated core collapse should not happen for at least another five days. Fleets of spacecraft stood ready for the mass evacuation of everyone on the planet. Earth, the new home for the human family, was expected to be ready to receive them within the next two days. The plan was tight, but well rehearsed and revered in the hearts of the people.

Master arrives on the dock—striding toward Rae Blue. His crystal-beaded hair clangs about his shoulders. The Sun Crown rests on his head—ten thousand whirls of silver-gold light—their dazzle so bright they dim the stars, yet fall softly upon the human eye. Rae Blue wants to run into his teacher's arms like he did as a boy, when Luca would tousle his hair and ask him if he'd done his homework. He always had. He'd never let Luca down.

"Thank you for your brave efforts today," the Sun Lord says.

"Am I the only one left?" Rae Blue asks, his voice soft as a whisper.

"All survivors have returned to the Jeweled Spheres, where they will transform to the astral and be assigned to other galaxies in need of their talents." The Sun Lord squeezes Rae Blue's shoulder. "We must move on. We have work to do. Connect with your jeweled intelligence, and follow the beam of my vision."

Traveling the cosmos with Luca is a part of everyday life for Rae Blue. He glances at his astral disk—a glow of shimmering icons on his left palm—and taps the double sapphire. His orb beams brightly. *My astral body, please.*

Transformation happens with the asking, and once inside his sapphire form the tensions of mortal life recede. He follows Master, as he slices through space in his body of silver-gold suns. The debris of planet Miron soars by on a solar wind—rivers of dust and rock. Giant asteroids tumble one over another, urchins of the universe now.

Master swerves around the spheres of the jewel kingdoms—seven brightly colored globes, each with its own galaxy of stars and towering crystal city. He keeps his left hand raised, palm forward, in recognition of the goddesses. Although they will be busy relocating survivors today, each goddess will sense Master's presence. In the cosmic hierarchy, a Sun Lord ranks higher than a goddess, but Luca is careful not to slight them—six very powerful women. Gold, Lord of Love, is male. Rae Blue directs rays of gratitude from his heart to the beloved Lord. Gold has returned to his astral sphere after living inside planet Miron for billions of years, radiating love to all who had lived on her.

The Curve comes into view—an arc of radiance that marks the divide between this universe and the next. On the other side of the Curve lies z27, the black hole that forms the entrance to the Sun Kingdom. Luca heads south, picking up speed. Rae Blue's light body quakes under the pressure of converging forces. He amps up the fire of sapphires flowing from the orb into the veins of his astral form, and catches up to Master.

Earth floats inside a luminous hologram. In the making for hundreds of years, her geography fills slowly in. Rae Blue treads air next to Luca at the top of the glowing circumference, while Master leans his ear to its light. He listens to the womb of creation, fondly named Adora by the Mironese. The lords of love, angels of the divine feminine, and legions of celestial beings have all assisted Adora with the creation of Earth.

"Focus on your double sapphire," Master says, straightening up. "Loan me the full attention of your highest awareness."

"It is so, Master."

The Sun Lord raises his left arm above his head, palm forward. Silver-gold flames shoot through his fingers and pelt into the cosmos. A blast of orange plasma erupts, and Earth's sun star explodes to life. Rae Blue would dance from one end of the universe to the other, proclaiming the news, except the birth of the planet holds him spellbound. The hologram melts away, and Earth rotates in space, her landmasses, mountains, and oceans similar in every way to the late planet Miron.

Giddy, ecstatic, and humbled, Rae Blue bows to Earth. *I will love you and defend you for all the days of all the lives I shall live.*

Master speaks, addressing the cosmos at large. "Everyone who died on planet Miron today will, in time, reincarnate on Earth, and the Age of Jeweled Intelligence will begin anew."

The news buzzes around the universe at the speed of light, and galaxies and planets blaze with goodwill toward mankind. Earth's Cycles of Time light up, two giant wheels spinning slowly, filling space for as far as the eye can see. One wheel will hold the events of the past. The other the future—a reflection of probabilities that could result from past actions, and the all of Earth's history will be recorded there, saved forever in the astral. Behind Earth's Cycles, the wheels of the Mironese era fade into the far regions of dark matter, closed but never forgotten, at least not by Rae Blue.

The sight of a girl tumbling backward out of the black hole jolts the beat of Rae Blue's heart. His chest tightens, as a knot of feelings settles in, tangled and unfathomable. The girl leaps over the Curve, dives into Earth's Cycles of Time, and offers her Sun Intelligence to help rebuild the human family.

The extravagant generosity of someone coming back from the Sun Kingdom to serve Earth, ignites Rae Blue's passion to offer the all of himself. He bows into Time—the mastermind that oversees the evolution of the human family. Before entering the mortal world, every soul deposits an atom of its highest awareness in Time. These luminous masses swirl around Rae Blue, revealing the perfect pattern for humanity—man at one with his Sun God. Rae Blue falls to his knees. "Use me," he says. "Show me how I may help mankind resume his quest for a place in the Sun Kingdom." A gleaming instrument falls into Rae Blue's hands, a knife studded with gems. Time Blade, the most powerful weapon ever held by man. Rae Blue curls his fingers around the steel-rimmed handle, and pledges his life to wield the Blade upon the call of Time.

The Sun Lord's hand falls heavily on Rae Blue's shoulders, yanking him back from Time. "Think carefully about accepting the Blade," Master says. "Time would be your master—Time blends souls to suit evolution. It does not recognize the feelings of the mortal heart, such as yours."

Rae Blue stands tall, shoulders squared. "My soul has already accepted custody of the Blade and my heart will follow its command."

The pause is long before Master speaks again, but Rae Blue does not consider rescinding his pledge. His heart will just have to grow to accommodate the needs of Time.

The Sun Lord speaks. "If that is your decision, then I shall teach you the laws of the Blade."

Master has carried Time Blade through all the ages on planet Miron. He has used it to cut, stop, forward, or reverse Time, correcting deeds that could destroy the human family. That Rae Blue feels worthy of taking his place seems incomprehensible, and yet he does. He bows deeply to the Sun Lord, hoping to assuage any arrogance on his part. "Thank you, Master."

The Sun Lord pats Rae Blue on the head, a habit of consolation. "I am empowered to ask something of you. May I proceed?"

"I am yours to command."

"I came to planet Miron to lead her people into the Sun Kingdom, and I did not complete that job. I shall endeavor to do so on Earth. Your father served as my Witness in sessions with the Council of the Lords for the planet. He listened to and remembered all that passed between the Lords and myself. I will need a new Witness on Earth. Will you, Rae Blue, fill this position?"

A chill runs through Rae Blue. The job is hard, but he doesn't shy from challenge. His thoughts trail back to his father. *Do whatever Master asks of you. His quest for the human family is of the highest order.* Why did he think Rae Blue might doubt that? The answer dawns on him. Master had created the SunShield to cover the space station—to ensure the safety of those departing for the

Jeweled Spheres. Why did he not cover the whole planet? The SunShield could abate any force this side of z27. He could have held everyone safe until Earth was ready for human life. A slow rage gathers in the pit of Rae Blue's stomach. "Why did you let millions of people die?"

"No one asked me to save them. Man is a lord god born into a physical body. His Sun God waits for him to awaken. What man brings about himself is what he needs to develop that awareness. It is not for me to alter that."

Rae Blue's jaw drops. He could have asked Master to spread the SunShield over the entire planet and keep everyone safe. Anyone could have—except Rae Blue's father, serving as Luca's Witness, but most fell into fear and forgot. Others, Rae Blue included, sprung into action. He forgot the rule he learned at Master's feet when he was seven years old. The Sun Lord must be asked for help.

It feels to Rae Blue as if his heart will burst from his chest and hurtle into space and seek a better soul to inhabit. The law of the Sun God seems trivial against the loss of so much human life. Anger rages—white-hot—burning all his senses but one: anger. Just or unjust, he cannot dismiss it and he does not want to. Anger will keep a space between him and Master—a space where he will never forget what took place on planet Miron and never let it happen again.

He meets Luca's gaze. "I will be your witness on Earth."

TWENTY-FIRST CENTURY EARTH

CHAPTER TWO

Waves double up, rising some thirty to forty feet high. Sky paddles toward a wall of towering green water and leaps on his board, cutting sideways into the wave. Crouching, he strokes the air, smoothing the way, then tears it up, shooting the curl. The sparkle of foam spits in his face, speed whooshes by, and time draws him in. Time, as he finds it in his sleep—beyond the measure of minutes and hours—a crisscross of filmy substance, tunneling back and forth through the cosmos.

"What do you want me with me?" Sky yells.

He hits a sudden bump in the ocean—something hard like the fin of a whale. The leash snaps from his ankle, and his board spirals away. Whitewater engulfs him. He fights the onslaught, kicking and thrusting his body up, up, up. Surfacing, he catches a quick breath then gasps for another, but the roiling waters drag him back down. Undercurrents hammer and thrash him. He's been here before—dozens of times, but he's always been too busy battling for his life to be afraid. Not now. Fear grips him. Death stalks the horizon, threading its needle, looping time—his time—snapping it short.

Sorry, Mom. Don't miss me too much. You always say nothing dies.

Dad, what can I say? I wish I hadn't fought you at every turn. I ...

Light happens—oceans of it, waving around Sky—a thousand shades of white and silver—bright but soft on the eye. Sky surfaces in his body of blue light—the body he wears in his dream travels. A tall, angular man with golden eyes walks toward Sky. Long, crystal-beaded hair sways about his shoulders.

"Get back into your Earthly form," he says. "You have much to do in this life."

Sky's nerves jangle and fuse together. "What do I have to do?"

"You know."

The man starts walking away. Sky sprints after him, running across the ocean. He latches onto the man's arm. "I know you from somewhere. Who are you?"

"Take your life back now. This opportunity will not come your way again."

The man disappears, but his words sink into Sky's memory like destiny carved in stone. His physical body drifts in the undertow, leaden as a corpse. Sky dives back into it, and the blue light of his dream body kick-starts his pulse. A surge of optimism rushes in, tremendous, as if coming from the whole world.

Sky surfaces the ocean, and heads back to shore, swimming for his life and for all that he has to do.

CHAPTER THREE

On the beach, Sky joins some friends, celebrating freedom from high school and whatever comes next. He sits close to the shore, taking stock of her for the first time. Cameron, brown hair, brown eyes, pointed chin, high forehead, small, square-shaped glasses. Sky caught Cameron staring at him several times in class, but she always flipped her hair forward, hiding her face. Sky figured she was just checking guys out, as she'd recently moved to the area. Still, something about her disturbs him. Does he desire her? Not really, but he wouldn't say no if she came on to him. He laughs beneath his breath. Not a big threat.

Cameron wades into the sea, carrying a beginner surfboard, a big clumsy thing designed to float an elephant in a storm. The waves are mellow, and an instructor tries to teach her to mount the board. She keeps wobbling and falling off. However, she doesn't give up. That interests him. He opens the camera on his phone and takes shots of her, trying to catch the spirit of her effort.

Marco, Sky's main surfing buddy, taps him on the shoulder. "Sorry I missed you earlier. How was the surf?"

"Epic." Sky recalls the man with the golden eyes, thinking he might never have met him if Marco had been there. His timing would have been different. Marco runs late for everything.

Marco grunts, "Luck seeks you out, Sky Hunter."

"Yeah? Where were you? In bed with Rosie?"

"Dude, you've gotta be there for your girl when she needs you." Marco grins. "We're off to play volleyball. Coming?"

"I'll catch up with you." Sky holds the camera steady, keeping Cameron in sight. She finally gets both feet on the board, rides a wave for a few seconds, then crashes. Sky is about to leave, when she emerges from the ocean. She tosses her hair, laughing, looking radiant and powerful. He snaps shot after shot of her, catching the waves crashing around her and the wind blowing her hair every which way. Cover-girl hot.

What girl wouldn't want a great photo of herself? Sky selects the best picture, and finds her number in the class directory. He hesitates. Unease prickles the back of his neck. He doesn't know her, except for those awkward moments when he caught her staring at him. What the heck, it's just a photo. He hits SEND.

He drives up the dirt lane, and nudges his truck into a clearing beside the studio, Valhalla, as his Great Grandfather Leo had named it. Valhalla means hall of the slain, of those who died in battle, and is watched over by the Nordic god, Odin. That fits Sky. He's pretty sure his spirit has been in Valhalla, perhaps is even still there—well, part of it anyway—that which got left behind as the rest of it veered over the blue skies of Istanbul. His way of seeking life on Earth, according to his mother, who happened to be there at the time with his father, madly in love, her speak for making out in some park. As she tells the story, she was gazing into bluest of blue skies, and felt his spirit. It shone like blue fire, and so she named him Sky Blue. Annoying as it is be to constantly asked how he got his name, he can only be grateful that his mother wasn't in country-naming mood at the time of his conception as she has been with his three younger sisters: Peru, Himalaya, and Thailand. Otherwise he would be called Turkey Hunter.

Wind whispers through the river birch trees surrounding the studio, and night shadows the land. Sky slides the patio door open. Home greets him, the cool calm of the solitary. He kicks off his shoes and treads on the paint-splattered concrete floors, squishing his toes against cerulean, vermillion, and yellow ochre, paint that overshot Leo's canvasses.

Moonlight shines through the tall, iron-framed windows, casting shadows on the bed—a mattress on the floor, close to the earth. Sky sits at the old captain's desk left over from Great Grandfather Leo's days, the cubbyholes that once held charts and maps now jammed with random articles about foreign lands—places where chance might take Sky—one week from today when he sets out to see the world.

Sky opens the top drawer of the captain's desk, and fishes out his wristwatch, also left by Leo. It's a manual wind from the 1940s, trimmed with yellow gold. The only numeral on the face is the twelve. The quarter hours are marked with a dash and the other numbers by square-shaped dots. Sky had it brought back to working condition and purchased a new tan leather band. He slips the watch on, tucking the end of the strap through the leather loops. Having time on his wrist brings a feeling of being in control—time in its own encasement, ticking because he winds it up every morning.

All we have to do is decide what to do with the time given to us. – Gandalf – *Lord of the Rings*

He glances at his iPhone. Two new texts: one from Zara, a girl he dated for a while. *We should talk.* He can't think why. Things ended amicably between them, well, for her. Zara Bosche was *the* hot girl in his class: dewy violet eyes, long, sharp cheekbones, and thick, chestnut hair, falling plumb straight to her jaw as if lopped off with a paper cutter. Sky would never pursue a girl like Zara—no need to invite rejection. But when she called one Saturday asking if he could partner her in a tennis tournament, he scurried right over to her house.

The Bosche mansion towered into the skies like a French chateau. Lushly landscaped, it came with two swimming pools and two tennis courts, one of each for the sole use of Zara's dad Simeon Bosche, billionaire real-estate magnate. Zara was a first class tennis player, and Sky could hold his own. Eager to impress Zara, he put aside the question, *what is time*, which occupies most of his time, and gave the game his full attention. Meaning he used the orb.

The orb has been with Sky since birth, a circle of sparkling blue light about the size of a dime lodged inside his brain. Sky can use it to scan the contents of books and highlight answers to questions, or to ace a serve, which is what he did that Saturday when he played tennis with Zara. He visualized the shot, directed blue fire down his arms, and then smashed his racquet down, driving the ball along the centerline. He aced every serve, and Zara played a killer net game. They won the mixed doubles, after which Zara ran around the court waving her racquet above her head, yelling like a wound-up cheerleader.

"Where have you been?" Zara jumped on Sky, wrapping her legs around his waist. He almost had an orgasm right there, on the court in front of the applauding crowd. He didn't have to wait long for the real thing. Zara led him into the pool house, where with one hand on Sky's back and with one extraordinary leap, she drove him across the room and onto the bed. Then she straddled him, dipped her hand into a goldfish-type bowl stuffed with condoms and rolled one onto his cock. Sky wondered how much practice it took to execute such an Olympian move. He had a few slick moves of his own, if sex was in the offing, but nothing so finely tuned as Zara's leap to fuck.

It lasted a couple of weeks. Zara mostly summoned Sky to her house for pool parties and games: tennis, croquet, pool, darts, poker, Scrabble, Trivial Pursuit, Ping-Pong, miniature golf, and fucking. It ended as abruptly as it began. "Well, goodbye," Zara said one day, leaning against her gleaming silver Porsche. "It was fun. Okay?" He all but dissolved on the spot, feeling hurt, tossed out like a piece of moldy cheese.

We should talk. Could she want him back? He cuts that fantasy short, and ruffles his fingers through the travel articles on the desk, thinking of the man with the golden eyes. *You have a lot to do in this life.* The wallop of having a mission excites him. What could it be?

The second message is from Marco, wanting to surf early tomorrow.

Ding! A text from Cameron arrives. *Shall I come over?*
Sky whistles a breath and stretches his arms above
head. He hadn't expected the photo to bring this result.
Cameron could look up his address, but then she'd arrive
at the main house, a definite no-no at this time of night.
Valhalla is hard to find. Sky texts her: *Need directions?*
I'm here.

The glow of headlights pierces the darkness on the
dirt road outside. Sky dashes outside to meet Cameron.
She parks behind his truck. An owl hoots, a haunting
echo fading into the night. Cicadas croak. Wind whispers through the trees, lazy like sleepy breath. Cameron
rounds the bend by the olive grove, and saunters toward
Sky. She wears jeans and a tank top, her hair swept back
in a ponytail. No jewelry. No makeup. Eyes big behind the
square-shaped glasses. She barely resembles the girl Sky
framed in the photo, but that's the beauty of photogra-
phy. The camera froze her in a moment of triumph. Time
befriends the camera.

"How did you find the place?" Sky asks.

"I called Zara."

"You did?" he says, thinking that strange. "Why not me?"

"I wanted to make sure she was over you. I mean ...
that's what girlfriends do."

Sky finds it hard to believe Zara would talk to Cameron about him, let alone give her directions to his studio. Zara thought Cameron was weird, crafty, a witch
bitch. Sky directs Cameron inside the studio and gestures
to the futon, the only piece of furniture other than the
bed. "Beer, Kombucha, Coke?"

Cameron reaches over the low square table and yanks a joint from a pot filled with sand and incense sticks. "Let's get stoned."

"That's Bomb Weed." Sky opens a small black box. "Try these for starters."

Cameron hits his hand away and sticks the Bomb between her lips. He sparks her up. She takes a long drag, holds the smoke in her lungs, then puffs it out slowly, blowing it in his face. She holds up her phone. Her glamor shot fills the screen.

"You get me," she says. "No one else has ever truly seen me before."

He drags on the Bomb. "That's just what happens when you take lots of shots of someone."

Cameron lifts the joint from him, takes a couple of hits and glances to the ceiling. She points to a sculpture hanging above his bed, the symbol of infinity made out of welded steel. "What's that?"

"Just something I made a couple of years ago."

"Huh?" She frowns. "Cool. You know," she says, still squinting at the sculpture, "it never appeared as if you studied in school."

Sky gets a sinking feeling, the sensation that she had spied on him. "What are you talking about?"

"I watched you," Cameron says. "When you arrived in the classroom, you just opened the assigned homework, closed your eyes for a while, then filled stuff in, like without any thought."

"Yeah, and I got the grades to go with that."

"You graduated with straight Cs. Did you aim for that?"

He feels caught like a thief with a stash of secret documents. "Why would you think that?"

She shrugs. "I think you're smarter than you let on."

Sky chuckles, rolling laughter in the back of his throat, scoffing good-naturedly like Grandpa Max does when questioned about his visits to the raunchy strip clubs in downtown L.A. "Thanks, I guess."

Cameron shrugs, and takes another drag on the joint. Sky has devoted years to being average in every way, except for when he showed off for Zara, and he's not about to play true confessions with this girl. The weed takes hold, and Sky fondles the watch. Time, according to quantum theory, cannot be measured to infinite accuracy. Time is fractious and fuzzy. He digs his fingers into his left palm, pushing and tilting his ear to his hand. There should be something there—like a computer—a link to some super intelligence.

"I like you." Cameron traces a finger down the bridge of his nose. "You're different."

"How's that?"

"I come up here to see you at midnight and you haven't tried to take me to bed yet?"

That's a come-on, if ever, but Zara left Sky feeling empty, like a sham of himself. Connection. That's what it's all about. If only life could be like when Monica drops by to run lines with Sky. Monica, his next-door neighbor, has a part in an online soap, and she sets up scenes for Sky, telling him who wants what and why. Recently, they rehearsed a love scene. Sky balked at first, because Monica was like a sister. Once she explained the stakes, the lovers would never see each other again, that this would be their last kiss ever, Sky got into the character. Monica directed him to gaze into her eyes and touch her cheek as if she were a priceless porcelain vase so delicate she could break beneath his fingers. The feel of her skin swept through Sky like a flurry of fire, and he was like a man in love.

Sky drags on the joint, playing it cool. Cameron might be a tease, or on a dare from another girl.

"You've got the bluest eyes I've ever seen," she says. "I want to lose myself in them."

He taps the face of his wristwatch, wondering if he should go for a soap-opera-type kiss with her.

Cameron raises her cell phone, and snaps a shot of the two of them. The flash breaks Sky's train of thought. She aims for another shot. He ducks. "Don't do that."

"Why not?"

Sky wrestles her phone from her and lays it aside. *Don't get stoned and naked and take pictures of yourself,* one of the rules his dad had set when Sky moved into Valhalla two years ago.

"I noticed the pool on the way in," Cameron says. "Let's go skinny dipping."

"Can't. The pool is on family ground."

"I'd like to meet your family."

Her eyes brighten as if lit from behind—glowing like glazed caramel fudge.

"I think your mom is *a m a z i n g*," she says, dragging the word out. "I want to take her *Find Your Inner Goddess* course. She's got over three hundred thousand followers online."

Something about that is way weird. He says, "Her followers are mostly middle-aged women, divorced, or broken by some other rotten life experience. What's your story?"

"Oh, I don't know. My mom's a nurse, and my dad's not around, he hasn't been for years." She sighs, and changes the subject. "What happened between you and Zara?"

He drags on the Bomb. "Nothing much."

"She told me you didn't fight for her."

He blinks, wondering where that came from. "She broke up with me."

"Yes, but she's Zara. She's movie star beautiful. Boys fight over her. So when she told you goodbye she expected you to keep calling, to beg her for another chance."

That's insane, but if the breakup had been a scene in Monica's soap, Sky would have understood why Zara thought the way she did, and then there could have been all sorts of snappy conversation, which would have made them laugh. Then he would have stroked her cheek and gazed into her eyes and—

"Hello!" Cameron snaps her fingers in his face. "What are you thinking?"

"Huh? Nothing."

Cameron snatches his hands and clasps them against her chest. "I won't let you go," she says. "Not ever."

She's in his face, eyes bright and intent, her breath whooshing in his nostrils, smoky and hot. He inches back a little. "You should know, I'm leaving town in a week and I'll be gone a long time."

"In a week!" She frowns as if having to recalculate her entire life, then takes another hit on the Bomb. "Well ... okay." She perks up. "Cool. Where are you going?"

"Europe, to start. I'm taking up life on the road, working odd jobs to support my travels."

"Why?"

"Why not?"

"What about college?"

"Later." He's got that down to a one-word answer, due to his dad's constant hounding on the subject. "What about you?" he asks. "What are your plans?"

She touches his cheek, and the scent of vanilla morphs off her fingers. He reconsiders the soap opera kiss, setting the scene. He loves her, but it's a love that cannot be. She rises from the futon and flops onto the bed.

"Get over here, Sky Blue Hunter. Hunt me down."

Sky stumbles into the bathroom, still groggy with sleep. He sloshes his face with cold water. His glance falls on a duffle bag on the floor stuffed with red thongs, t-shirts, a toothbrush and body lotion. *Cameron!* He peers back into the studio. She sits outside on the patio smoking dope.

He hauls on jeans, picks up the duffle, and joins her. "I've got a surfing date."

She glances at the bag and then at Sky, eyes bright behind the clear-framed glasses. "Why don't I leave that here?"

"Let's play things by ear."

"You're leaving in a week. We should make the most of that."

"We will." Sky walks her to her car, an old Honda Civic scarred with dents and scratches. When she opens the door, he slides the duffle onto the passenger seat.

"Okay, if that's how you want it." She glances back at him as if checking for sure.

"Keep it handy," he says.

"Want to go to a party with me tonight?"

"Sure. Text me where to pick you up."

She holds her phone way out in front of her, leans her head against his shoulder, and takes a couple of selfies. "This is me looking sad, parting from the boy I love."

"Yeah, right."

TEENS DYING FOR LOVE

ENTER NOW!

BE A CONTESTANT IN THE NEW
GROUNDBREAKING REALTY SHOW

If you've met him, and you know you couldn't live without him, log in, create an avatar, and tell us your story.

SKYCAM

I'm eighteen, and I've met him! I knew he was coming. I felt a rip in my heart, a tear that will soon drive me to take my life. OMG. Dying is on my calendar! It'll happen within the next week, because he's leaving town after that. I can't stop him, but he's mine until DEATH DO US PART! We made out last night. Amazing!!! If you select me for the show, I will tell all. He's the son of a celebrity with a huge online following. I'm a goddess to him. He took the attached photo. I don't look that glam most of the time but I feel like that when I'm around him. I will shine as a star in the heavens soon. I would love to be a star on Earth too—a light for all the other girls who just can't live without the boy they love.

TDFL: How old is your boyfriend?
SKYCAM: 18
TDFL: Congratulations! You have been selected as a contestant for *Teens Dying for Love*. You have been sent an email outlining the rules for blogging your story. Read it carefully. Take special note of rule #1: Do not use anyone's real name. Upload four photos of yourself. We will choose one as your profile shot.

Rock thunders through the house, and people dance, slithering against each other, some of them naked. Cameron dips her head to a table and snorts a line of coke. "C'mon," she says. "Get up here with me."

Sky does a line, and then they both do another. The drug lifts Sky into a light kind of wildness. The beat of the music vibrates through his body, and the rhythmic alphabet of drumming tingles the tips of his fingers. He draws Cameron into the throng of dancers. "Whose party is this?"

She thrusts her pelvis against him and drapes her arms around his neck. "Don't know."

"We're crashing?"

"There's no such thing for us. Everybody wants to be with us. We're OTP."

"What?"

"One true pairing, Skycam."

He fluffs a laugh, but a shiver of unease pricks his skin. The man with the golden eyes crosses his thoughts, and he feels a shift in his brain chemistry, sort of like the click of a door closing. He tanks down from the high.

Cameron shouts above the music, "Wouldn't you like to be famous?"

"No."

"Why not?"

She wobbles on the stilts of her shoes. He steadies her. A couple of naked dancers bump into them. Cameron laughs. "Let's strip."

"Hey, Sky!"

Dean Bosche, one of Zara's brothers, worms his way between Sky and Cameron. He's big and burly and his pupils are dilated, big as the bullseye on a dartboard, and his breath reeks of gin. Dean had goaded Sky at every chance during the time he dated Zara, demeaning him for flipping burgers. "Make mine a whopper," he'd say, fondling his crotch. Sky cracks his knuckles, the heat of rage flaring up. He slams his hand on Dean's shoulder and pushes him away. "You're crowding my space, Dean."

"Who the hell do you think you are?" Dean staggers back. "And who's the slut with you?"

"Fuck off!" Sky thuds his fist into Dean's gut.

Dean doubles over, but recovers and charges at Sky. "You're nothing," he says, ramming a fist into Sky's ribs. "You think you can come up to my house, win at everything and fuck my sister? Well you can't." Dean raises his arm as if to drive his fist into Sky's face, but Sky ducks and pummels Dean to the ground.

"Stop it," Cameron shouts.

"Fight," someone yells. Others join in—crowding around and yelling at Dean, "Fight. Get up and fight."

Sky hauls Dean off the floor. "You heard the people. Hit me."

"Fuck you." Dean dabs his bloody nose with the back of his hand, recoiling from Sky. "My father wants to talk to you," he says, eyes bulging. "And it won't be pretty."

A chorus of boos goes up as Dean slinks away. Sky drags Cameron off the dance floor.

"Who the fuck was that?" she asks, seething air through her front teeth.

"No one. Let's get out of here."

Cameron drags on his arm, but Sky keeps moving, shouldering his way through the crowd. What did Simeon Bosche want with him? *We should talk.* The dreaded thought arises. Could Zara be pregnant?

"Sky, wait for me."

He slows down, and they walk outside together. Salty air blows off the sea. Sky inhales, taking deep breaths, cooling down.

"Who was that guy?" Cameron asks, climbing into the truck. "He looked at me like I was dirt."

"Don't pay any attention to him. He's a jerk."

"He sure got you riled up. You were brutal to him, but I like that. He called me a slut, and you defended me."

Sky starts the truck, and Justin Bieber's voice booms over the radio.

"Oh, I love this song." Cameron turns up the sound. "*Die in Your Arms.* This is our song." She hums along, chiming in with the lyrics. "I'd like to die in your arms," she whispers, nuzzling Sky's ear. "What do you say to that?"

He nudges her away, and pulls the truck into the road.

"Oh my god! That guy was one of Zara's brothers, wasn't he? I recognize him from TV."

Sky turns right, driving onto Cameron's street. "I'll take you home."

"No. Let's go back to your place. I want to fuck."

He pulls up outside her apartment house. She looks ruffled, like a girl after a hard night of partying. "Not tonight. I've got to work for my mother starting early in the morning."

She folds her hands in her lap. "What does Zara's father want with you, Sky?"

He drums his fingers against the steering wheel. "I don't know."

Cameron takes his face in her hands. "It doesn't matter. I love you."

TEENS DYING FOR LOVE

In her profile shot, Cameron wears a black push-up bra and cut-off jeans. She bends over at the waist, placing her hands on her thighs. Her hair falls forward, hiding her face. Traces of a red thong show through the fringed bottoms of the shorts.

SKYCAM: He had another girlfriend before me, and she was perfect in every way, beautiful like a movie star, model tall, thin, and super rich. I think she may be pregnant by him. What if she wants him back? I don't care. I won't let him go. He's mine. I knew it the moment I looked at the goddess photo he took of me. I had found him—the boy who must be punished. The goddess in me came alive at the thought of that. I'll die looking at that photo, knowing he saw me—the real me—the brilliant, beautiful girl I am in my dreams. The girl he should never have pushed away.

CHAPTER FOUR

Sky dries off from a shower and wraps a towel around his waist. Stepping back into the studio, he comes to an abrupt halt. His dad prowls the room, dressed for the office, suit and tie, high polished brogues, carrying Thai-Thai, Sky's baby sister. Clive Hunter, defense attorney, counsel for the Mercedes driving, Armani clad, paper-shuffling thieves of corporate America, Simeon Bosche among them.

"Sorry about this," his dad says. "You know your mother is holding a seminar tonight. I've been called to attend a deposition, and I need you take care of Thai-Thai for a while. It's Essie's day off. Grandma Ellen took Himmie, but she can't manage the baby too."

Clive Hunter gives off a flurry of energy like an eagle coming in for a landing. Sky stands taller than his father by several inches, but he feels like a gangling colt in his presence. The baby stretches her arms out to Sky, smiling and wriggling her little body, wanting him to take her.

"See ... she loves being with you," his dad says. "Here we go." He lifts Thai-Thai toward Sky.

Sky tightens the towel around his waist. "Where's Peru?"

"Your sister is out ... a sleep-over with friends."

His father furrows his brow and twists his mouth, an expression he uses when pinning a witness to an unpleasant fact. Sky takes possession of the baby, and she gurgles and sticks her fingers in his mouth.

"You know her routine," his dad says. "Everything she needs is in here." He dumps a diaper bag on the floor. "No dope, no booze, no sex in front of the baby."

Sky bites back anger. Clive Hunter always does this, treats him like he's a criminal on parole, reminding him of the rules.

"Your mother will be up to get her when the seminar ends." His father slides his hand over his slick dark hair. "She'll call you."

His dad takes off, and Thai-Thai smothers Sky's cheeks with kisses, melting him down. He bounces her like he does when he takes her to the sea and lifts her in and out of the surf. "Waves," he says. She gives off yelps of delight. "W w w." She works her little lips trying to form the word. "Waves," he repeats, bouncing her again. She laughs, all cheeks and eyes and wisps of blonde hair.

He looks around for his phone to cancel his date with Cameron, but he's too late. She appears at the glass doors to the studio, duffle bag and pizza box in hand, the smile on her face fading as she catches sight of the baby.

Sky slides the door open. "I was just about to call you. We'll have to get together another time. I've got to look after my little sister." He shifts Thai-Thai from one arm to the other. "Sorry. I just found out a minute ago."

Cameron looks stunned, as if confronting heart-stopping news. "Oh, wow! Wow!" She rounds her mouth over the sound like someone blowing a smoke ring, then takes a deep breath and comes up with a change of attitude. "So, okay."

She strides in past Sky, and tugs on the towel wrapped around his waist, causing it to fall to the floor. "That's better." She nuzzles her face against his. "I like my boyfriend naked."

Thai-Thai whimpers and buries her head against Sky's shoulder. He pats her on the back, singing the lullaby he wrote for her when she was born. She stops crying, and he places her on the bed. He picks up the towel. "This won't work, Cameron."

"Why not?"

"Thai-Thai is ten months old. I can't fool around with you and look after her."

"She's a baby. She doesn't know what we're doing."

He hauls sweats from a shelf and pulls them on. "I have to follow the rules of the house. When looking after my little sisters they have to come first."

"Okay. I get it, but you're eighteen. You ought to be—"

"Actually, I'm not eighteen, not for another month."

"You're not eighteen!"

She screws her eyes, as if trying to get her mind around that. He scoffs, "So?"

"Okay. No biggie."

She heads to the kitchen, a narrow galley with a microwave, cupboards, and fridge on one side; counter space on the other. He glances at Thai-Thai, who sleeps with her head nestled in his pillow, and then joins Cameron. "Let's just cool it tonight. I'm tied up here—"

"We can watch TV," she says, opening the pizza box.

The smell of pepperoni wafts on the air, and hunger growls. He eyes his laptop sitting on the captain's desk, thinking of time. A Femtosecond is like a second is to thirty-two million years. Imagine what goes on in a minute, and if the big bang theory is correct and everything in the universe exploded in one outward motion, was everything complete at the time of the bang, or might the bang still be banging, creating other universes? He glances back at Cameron. "There's no telling when my mother will come by to collect the baby."

Cameron runs her hands under his sweatshirt and up over his shoulders. "You've got this gorgeous surfer body. It makes me wild. I want you all the time." She grasps his hand and runs his fingers inside her jeans, under the elastic top of her thong. "You want me, I know you do."

Actually, he doesn't. Not in front of Thai-Thai, and not because his father laid down the law, but because he has some recall of being a baby. He remembers looking up at his parents, wondering who they were and how he got to be here with them. "Another time, Cameron."

"We'll be quick ... on the sofa. I love you."

"Come on Cam, you don't know me."

"But I do," she says, taking on a little girl whisper. "You're the boy who never joined any of the cliques in school, yet you stayed friendly with everyone at least on the surface. You're a loner at heart, my loner."

Discomfort shivers on his skin, and he gets that creepy feeling of having been watched by her. He thinks about using Zara's breakup line, *Well, goodbye, it's been fun. Okay?* But he's not a hot-ass guy leaning against a silver Porsche. He's a short-order cook at best, driving Grandpa Max's old truck. "You should go, Cameron."

A slow smile fills her expression. "You see the goddess in me. You love her and you want her. I feel the love building inside you. You can't live without her any more than she can live without you."

Her eyes glow as if in a trance. He should have followed his gut when he paused before sending her that photo. He picks up the duffle bag. "I'll walk you to your car."

She puts up no resistance, and moves easily, guided by his arm at her elbow. He feels strange, like an actor in a movie, drifting off script and into the unknown. Or is it the known—something frighteningly familiar—hammering at the edge of memory, just beyond reach?

Cameron smiles at him from inside her car. "You will never forget me. Never, Sky Blue Hunter, and that makes you mine. F O R E V E R."

TEENS DYING FOR LOVE

SKYCAM: I'm doing it now!

When I went to his place tonight, he had a baby in his arms. OMG! He looked so natural with her that I imagined him with his ex, super-rich-bitch, who I'm pretty sure is pregnant by him. I pictured them living together in a gorgeous house, given to them by her billionaire dad. My knees went weak. I thought I would just keel over and die right there. Then I reminded myself I'm a goddess, a star waiting to be born on TDFL. I must be here until I hurt so much that I can't take another breath.

That moment has come. It's time for me to light the path to death for those dying for love, just like me. I'm sitting on the stairs in my house, gazing at the goddess photo *he* took of me, pills in hand. *Dying for Sky*, my farewell letter to him, lies open beside me. Goodbye, my darling.

CHAPTER FIVE

Sky sits on the bed with his computer on his lap. Thai-Thai rolls onto her side and snuggles up against him, tossing one arm across his waist. He wipes drool from the corner of her mouth with his finger, dries it on the sheet, and opens his laptop.

Since London will be his first stop in Europe, he's already researched the casual job market there. His glance goes to an ad in the upper right corner of a U.K. job site.

Kitchen hand wanted. Penrose Hall, Port Issey, Corn-wall. Temporary. Room and board.

Sky opens Google and types in *Penrose Hall*. A rambling castle-like structure fills his screen, sitting atop cliffs on a rugged coastline. Pillars front the ancient house, weather-stained and green with lichen. Mist hangs over a turreted tower—pink mist. A sense of belonging to something wonderful arises in Sky. He's got to be in this place. He opens Skype and calls the number in the ad.

A woman answers, "This is Lara Penrose." Her voice sounds muffled and mysterious, as if caught in the cob-webs of time.

"I'm calling about the job," Sky says. "Is it still open?"

"Where are you calling from?"

"The U.S. Sorry, I forgot the time change." He calculates quickly. It's five in the morning in England.

"That's all right. If you need a job, it's always the right time."

Her video screen opens. Lara Penrose sits behind a desk cluttered with papers. Shelves of leather-bound books and silver-framed photos fill the wall behind her. She has creamy skin, blonde hair, and pale blue eyes, clear like sea glass. She leans in closer to the screen. "Ah," she says, as if in ah, it's you.

Sky blinks, taken aback, because it feels like he knows her too, or is just that she looks like English women tend to look in the movies?

"I'm Sky Hunter. I'm almost eighteen. I've got kitchen experience, worked in several fast food places. I'll be in England the day after tomorrow, and I'd like the job."

"I need two references. Email them to me."

"I'm sending them now."

"Right. I'll see you in a couple of days."

"Sky! Wake up!"

Sky rolls on his back and rubs sleep from his eyes.

Marco bends over him, his curly black hair framing his face. Alarm whizzes through Sky. "What are you doing here?"

"I gotta show you something."

"It's the crack of dawn. Can't it wait? I just fell asleep."

Marco opens his laptop, turning it to face Sky. The breath goes out of Sky, and his blood runs cold. He stares at Cameron's Facebook page, at photos of him with her, at the party in Venice, and in others taken here.

"It gets worse. There's a letter." Marco scrolls down the page.

DYING FOR SKY

My darling,

I'm taking my life to set you free. I can think of no other way to let you go. I never deserved you in the first place. I'm ordinary in every way and too heavy around the hips, which makes me look ugly in a bikini. But you didn't see that. You saw my inner Goddess. I didn't know she existed until you captured her in that photo. I felt beautiful with you. My Goddess could have become a star. I can't bear it that you don't love her, and I'm afraid my need for you would destroy us both. I end my life, dying for you, Sky.

Cameron

Sky's body goes numb. He runs his hands through his hair. "It's just not possible," he says. "Why would she do this? I hardly know her. Should I call the police?"

"No," Marco says. "Call your dad. He'll know what to do."

Sky rubs his temples, dreading the tirade that's bound to come with that.

"You gotta get help with this, Sky."

His dad answers on the second ring. "It's five a.m. Are you in jail?"

Sky heaves a sigh, wishing that were the case. "A girl I know wrote a suicide letter addressed to me and posted it on Facebook."

A pause, and Clive Hunter changes his tone, taking on his attorney self. "How old is she?"

"Eighteen."

"Are you at the studio?"

"Yes."

"Has anyone contacted you about this ... the girl's parents ... police?"

"No."

"Don't talk to anyone. I'll be there shortly. Meanwhile text me the girl's name, number, whatever you have."

Powerful people need never fail; they need re-orchestrating. — Clive Hunter

Marco leaves, and Sky paces the studio, facing the news alone, waiting for his father. The atmosphere feels thick with traces of Cameron, the smell of Bomb pot and vanilla. He opens the windows, and grabs Leo's watch from the top drawer of the captain's desk. He winds it up, twisting the little knob on the side, running it back and forth between his thumb and forefinger. The Attosecond is an even smaller unit of time than the Femtosecond. The Attosecond equals one quintillionth of a second, which is written as a decimal point followed by eighteen zeroes. How many Attoseconds does it take for the brain to close down and die? He stops pacing. Why doesn't he feel anything about Cameron? Shouldn't she weigh on his conscience like a loss he's accountable for? Why isn't he wishing he hadn't sent her home last night so that none of this would have happened?

Regret hits Sky, but it's over his father, same as when he thought he was dying in the ocean. The bitterness between him and his dad started when Sky was five. Back then, Sky talked freely about the orb, how it came for him at night, pulled him into a body of blue light, and swept him into space. In this light body, Sky had a computer built into his left palm. When he touched a certain icon, ancient civilizations unfolded around him. He gazed at people living in crystal cities, whizzing around on grids of red light. When he woke up, he missed that computer and scratched his left palm, hoping it would appear. This irritated his dad, and he smacked Sky's hand each time he caught him. His mom usually drove Sky to school, and she would listen to his nighttime adventures, never doubting them. Everything changed one day, when his dad had to take him.

Sky bounded into the kitchen, backpack looped over his shoulders, excited to be riding with his dad. "I'm ready, Daddy." He tugged on his father arm, which caused him to drop some papers.

"Don't do that," his dad yelled, picking them up. "You're already making me late for a meeting, driving you to school."

Sky felt his lip pucker, and he began shrinking into a smaller version of himself. Then his mom shouted his dad's name from across the room. "C - l i v e," she barked, hammering it into two syllables. His dad straightened up like a convict to an executioner. "Sorry, son," he said.

His dad's car was immaculate inside and out, washed and polished on a regular basis. The mahogany dashboard shone, and the smell of leather rose off the big bucket seats in the front. Sky buckled up, and reached to turn on the radio.

"Don't do that," his dad said. "Don't touch anything."

Sky consoled himself by thinking about last night's dream when the orb had whisked him into space and shown him the Jeweled Spheres. It made Sky happy to know there was life in other galaxies. So as his dad honked the horn and tried to move from one lane to another, as his face flushed and he rapped his knuckles against the wheel, cursing beneath his breath, Sky told him about how he met the Goddess of Rubies in his dream last night.

Traffic came to a complete standstill, and his dad gazed at him, a pleading look in his eyes. "Can't you just be a normal kid?"

Sky's arms and legs trembled. He needed that magical computer so he could find those people who lived in the crystal city. He had to be one of them. He must have come to Earth by mistake. He dug his fingers hard into his palm, scratching and bending his ear to his hand.

His dad smacked him hard on his knuckles. "Stop that scratching," he yelled, "and stop making things up or I'll take you to see someone who will make you stop."

Hurt and rage tumbled one over the other, and tears thrashed against the back of his eyes, but Sky wouldn't give in to them. He seethed until they reached his school. Then he mustered every ounce of his five-year-old strength and punched his father in the jaw.

They never spoke about what happened that day, and Sky never spoke of the orb again, not to his mother, not to anyone. Normal mattered.

Clive Hunter strides into the studio, dressed in his weekend attire—white shirt, open at the collar, khaki slacks, and suede loafers. He looks around as if noticing the furnishings or lack of them for the first time, and heads for the futon. Having worked his way out of what he calls teeming poverty, Clive Hunter expected his son to seize opportunities handed to him and do better. It was easy to punish him.

His dad pinches his slacks at the knees and lowers his body slowly down onto the futon, wiping his hand over the fabric before sitting. He opens the briefcase, removes two phones and a laptop.

Sky sits on the end of his bed facing him, thinking how different things could have been between them. He could have been the son his father wanted. "Sorry, Dad. I made a mess of things."

"I know I'm hard on you at times, but I'm not here to criticize you, Sky. I'm aware of your qualities as well as your shortcomings. You're a lot like your mother. It's not in your nature to be consciously unkind to anyone, let alone drive someone to suicide."

Sky's jaw falls slack. He'd not expected any favorable comment, not that his dad rides his case all the time. They often have fun as a family, and Sky does love him. "Thanks," he whispers.

Clive Hunter pulls a legal pad from a slot inside the briefcase, lays it on his lap and ticks off a line of writing, probably something to the effect of *make son comfortable.* "I've got investigators on the case," he says. "I'll have answers soon. Meanwhile, tell me about you and Cameron. How long have you known her? Did you tell her you love her? Did she have reason to expect a future with you? Is there a sex tape?"

Sky pulls on focus, forming answers the way his father likes, facts only. "I took the photo of Cameron in the ocean two days ago, and sent it to her. She responded by turning up here that night. We had sex. I told her I was leaving town soon. I never said I loved her. There's no sex tape."

Clive Hunter opens his computer, and browses Cameron's Facebook page, pausing on the photos taken at the party in Venice. Cameron is draped over Sky like a coat on a hanger, and he's staring up at the ceiling, eyes glazed as if locked on an alien spaceship. "That was the next night." Sky cowers at the sight of himself. "I took her home after the party. I was sober by then."

His dad flashes him a querying glance. "She didn't want to come back here for the night?"

Sky hopes to avoid any mention of the encounter with Zara's brother, the reason he'd cut the night short, or anything that would lead back Simeon Bosche, one of his dad's most important clients. "It just didn't work out that way."

His dad scrolls down to the suicide note. "She says here that she never deserved you in the first place." He glances back at Sky. "Did she ever say anything like that to you?"

"No." He sits tight, determined not to run off at the mouth trying to explain the unexplainable, as witnesses tend to do when under his father's scrutiny.

"When was the last time you saw her?"

"Last night. We had a date. She came here a few minutes after you dropped Thai-Thai off."

His dad rubs his chin. "I see," he says, as if realizing he played some part in this. "What happened?"

"I—"

One of his dad's phones rings, a simple ding sound. He answers. "Clive Hunter."

Sky watches him, nodding, jotting notes, and giving orders. It's a long call, interrupted by another call on the other phone, which he answers and puts on hold. He levels his gaze on Sky. "Cameron is alive."

Sky's shoulders collapse, falling down from his ears. "What happened? Where is she?"

"She took about a half a bottle of aspirin. Her mother, a nurse, found her shortly after. She rushed Cameron to the hospital where she works. IV fluids were administered, which stabilized the acids in her system. Cameron was sent home several hours later in her mother's care."

Sky replays the scene is his mind. Cameron knew the hours of her mother's night shift. She'd mentioned them when Sky dropped her off after the party, saying they had time to make out before she got home. "It sounds like she never intended to die. What do you think?"

His father takes another call, grimacing as he listens. "I see. Okay. Good work."

Clive Hunter flips his laptop back to face him, types something in the search bar, then looks at Sky. "Have you heard of a website called *Teens Dying for Love*?"

"What? No." Sky moves over next to his father. "What is it?"

CHAPTER SIX

The orb flashes, and everything Cameron wrote on *Teens Dying for Love* imprints on Sky's memory, even before his father reads her blog. He wishes time would gobble him up, absorb him into its swirling masses of luminosity.

As it is, he stares at Cameron's writing, his blood curdling. The constant reference to the super rich bitch ex-girlfriend screams Zara Bosche, and the celebrity parent with hundreds of thousands of online followers is obviously his mother. Anger torches his soul, and a guttural roar escapes him.

His father taps him on the arm, all the while taking phone calls and scrolling through the website. Bile hits the back of Sky's throat as he looks at girl after girl, their profile photos one step above porn. Stories of heartbreak pour onto the pages, followed by plans for cutting wrists, slitting throats, and inflicting fatal bullet wounds.

Clive Hunter reveals no emotion. The great orchestrator is at work. He's found the guilty party, and he's running on all cylinders. He directs investigations on one phone and consults with a public relations person on the other, laying out plans to keep media attention on *Teens Dying for Love,* and off his family.

Sky forces himself to think back to when he noticed Cameron learning to surf. She'd been in his direct line of vision. Why? Beginners usually take lessons further down the beach in front of the surf school. Had she already picked him out as the guy to use in this suicide scheme? Why would she want to punish him? He's never pushed her away.

His dad packs the phones and computer back in his briefcase. "This is a lot for you to process and I want to help you with that. How are you feeling?"

He'd like to fade away, walk across a sea of light and be with the man with the golden eyes. *Get back in your body. You have a lot to do in this life.* If that's the case, then he'd better get with it. Sky sits on the edge of his bed. "If this goes public, and I don't see how it won't, it'll hurt Mom," he says. "What will her followers think, with me being her son? You always say it's best to get out in front of a scandal and apologize if necessary. I'm willing to do that."

His dad clicks his tongue against the roof of his mouth. "I don't think that's the case here. Cameron wanted to be famous, and you were just a guy she used along the way." He slaps a hand on his briefcase. "I'm hoping the pregnant ex-girlfriend is just more fiction from a delusional a girl. Hum?"

Sky cuts away from his dad's glance. He's got to get in touch with Zara and warn her about *Teens Dying for Love* before she finds out about it from someone else. "I'll postpone my trip, Dad. I've created a lot of work for you. I'll stay and help straighten everything out. You tell me what to do and I'll do it."

His dad settles back on the futon. "I appreciate that, but I've got this covered. It's not my line of work, but I'll collect as much information as possible on *Teens Dying for Love*, and turn it over to the District Attorney's office." He points a finger at Sky. "You're leaving as planned. You've wanted to travel since you were a small boy, and you've worked umpteen jobs and saved every penny to pay for it, refusing any help from your mother and me. I admire that. This is who you are, and you're going in search of the man you can be. That man is not a victim. You can't let this event define your life in any way, and that won't be easy. When you were a little boy and I would scold you for not paying attention in school, you would tell me not to worry about you, that the world would be your teacher. So ... look at this as a world-class, kick-ass first lesson. Learn from it but don't let it make you cynical. Don't shun the next girl you meet because of this one. You're tough. You've got the strongest resolve I've ever seen in anyone, and it comes from a selfless place. Hold on to that. It will lead you to all the best parts of life."

Clive Hunter gets up and leaves the studio, taking slow, measured steps. Sky sits motionless, reeling in the wake of his words. He thinks of when he used to watch his dad in court. Sky always scowled at the defendant, certain he was guilty as accused. Then in his closing argument his dad would sum the guy up, much as he just summed up Sky, which always left Sky wondering if he was too good a man to have committed a crime, any crime.

CHAPTER SEVEN

Zara wends through the olive grove, hair swaying, hiding the sharp contours of her cheekbones. Sky would rather be headed for combat duty than a showdown with her. He ambles outside. "Hey Zara, I was just about to call you."

"What the hell, Sky? I've been trying to reach you for the last hour."

"Sorry. I turned my phone off last night." The sight of her up close tells Sky something's wrong. Her skin is ashen and blotchy, with dark smudges beneath her eyes, and the luscious fullness of her bottom lip is cracked, as if bitten under duress. "Zara, are you okay?"

"Shut up." She strides past him and into the studio. "What have you got to drink?" She rummages through the freezer. "Booze? Like vodka?"

"Just beer." He reaches around her, opens the fridge, and hauls out a six-pack of Bud. "It's seven in the morning," he says, in case she didn't realize.

She pops a can and guzzles the beer down. "Give me another."

He hands it to her. "I'm sorry about all this. I—"

"C a m e r o n?" Zara says, her voice heavy with sarcasm. "Really? You're my ex-boyfriend. How could you?" She gulps down the second beer, burps, wipes her chin with the back of her hand, and gestures for another.

"Let me make you an omelet," Sky says, opening the fridge. "I've got mushrooms and peppers and—"

"No." Zara drags him away from the fridge, lodges her fist in the small of his back, and drives him over to the bed. "Sit." She gives him a shove. He sits. She stands, blinking and heaving breath. "Next Sunday," she says, "one week from today, I will be eighteen years old. Do you know what that means?"

"You can vote and fight for your country."

She clenches a fist to her chest. "On my eighteenth birthday, I should receive the first distribution of my trust. That's ten million dollars, Sky." She glares at him. "I have plans for that money."

He whistles a breath. "Yeah. What?"

She bends and leans closer to him—eyeball to eyeball—hers deep violet like the innermost petals of an exotic flower. "I will only receive that money if my trustee determines I am a stable and sensible young woman. I've been that person, Sky. I've played all those damn stupid games with my family, and brought home the guys I've dated and made them do it too. I did well in school and I'm going to the Sorbonne this fall to study art history." She sits on the edge of the coffee table. "Do you know who my trustee is?"

"Your father?"

"I wish. Daddy would give me the money no matter how I fucked up. No, my trustee is his brother, my Uncle Solomon, who is a religious maniac. Uncle Solomon believes children are God's gift to the world, and it's a woman's duty to bear every child she conceives, no exceptions, not even rape nor certain death. None."

Sky grips the edges of his mattress and swallows hard. "Are you saying you're pregnant?"

She flings herself on the bed and curls up in a fetal position. "Ohmigod!" she wails. "All that stuff on *Teens Dying for Love*. Everyone will know it's me."

"It'll be okay, Zara. My dad's working on this. He'll—"

"I'm not pregnant," Zara whispers, "but no one can find out."

"Okay," Sky says, trying to make sense of that. "And the other good news is Cameron's not dead."

"Fuck her! She started this rumor about me being pregnant."

"Well, you're not, so it'll pass. Your uncle—"

"But everyone will believe it. Ohmigod! Uncle Solomon will never turn my trust over to me."

Zara swings her feet to the floor. "Why didn't you answer my text?"

"I did, the next night. Why? What's going on?"

"I needed you. It was too much to keep to myself."

The gruesome thought of abortion weighs in. They had sex once without a condom, late at night, after a beach party. Everything was hilarious. They had smoked weed and downed a fifth of tequila—Don Julio—five hundred bucks a bottle—swiped from her dad's stash in the back of his limo. Laughing, they ran naked into the sea. Zara stumbled at the shoreline. He tried to catch her, but missed and they fell down together. Zara lay on her back beneath him with her arms stretched above her head. "There's fire in the sky," she said. "It wants us to fuck." That tickled him senseless, but not too senseless to make out.

Sky sinks his head in his hands, trying to find his way into the prospect of the Big Bang going on and on, forming other universes, maybe one he could escape to, anything other than this. "Did you have an abortion?"

She looks at him out of a blank expression, as if disconnected from thought. "Don't."

"Oh, god, Zara. Is there anything I can do?"

"You walked away from me. You got in that rat trap of a truck of yours and drove off."

"Are you talking about when you broke up with me?"

"I said, 'Goodbye, it's been fun. Okay?' That's a question, Sky."

"No. You dumped me, and that hurt my feelings."

She shakes her head, and her hair floats about her like the mane of a pampered racehorse. "When I know I could lose a boy forever, that's when I start to see him for who he really is. That works both ways."

"Like how?"

"When a guy fights for me, says something like, no, Zara it's not okay. I'm too crazy about you to lose you. I ask him why. If he tells me something very specific about me, about how I am ... in here," she says, banging her hand against her heart, "I begin to see what he really means to me. Get it?"

"Why not just talk about those things?"

She sits quietly, rocking back and forth. "You're way out there somewhere, Sky. I don't know where your head is at, but it feels like you're on another wavelength. I think you must be from Saturn or another planet with more than one moon. You're so different. Sometimes, when I looked into your eyes, it was like looking through a mirror into the night sky. I'd see stars, masses of them. I thought that must be the place where you hang out in your head, and if I broke up with you, you'd take me there to win me back. I'd escape all the crap I'm stuck in here."

"I'm into the galaxy, Zara. We could talk about—"

"It's too late." She perches on a stool by the kitchen counter, and slugs down another beer. "When my father calls you, deny I was pregnant. Deny, deny, deny. That's what he does."

"Why would he call me? We broke up."

"My dad likes you. So he'll believe you when you tell him we've become friends, the kind who confide in one another. He thinks you're a genius of sorts, a savant, and he wants you to come and work for him."

"What the hell are you talking about?" Sky grabs a beer, sensing his life is about to come undone. "I'm none of those things, and I'm not interested in business. You know that."

She shrugs. "You should have thought of that before you beat Daddy at every game, including chess, which he's pretty damn good at. You're insanely intelligent, Sky. I like that, and I love it that you don't give a damn about college or figuring out the future. Daddy does too. He was like that at your age. So, just tell him you're going traveling for a while and you'll think about the job, but first have a nice chat with him about me."

"Zara, your dad adores you. He'll do whatever you want."

"Uncle Solomon knows that. They're brothers. Daddy is younger and wildly successful. Uncle Solomon is an ordinary, stuffy old accountant. Sibling rivalry. Daddy has to stay on script with Solomon to win him over. I want to buy a house in Paris. Park my money, as they say. The Russians and the Chinese do that here in L.A. and New York. People will always want to live in Paris. It's a great investment."

Something is very wrong. If Zara wanted to park her money, she'd buy art. She knows and loves it, and she understands how that market works. A house in Paris sounds fishy, like a cover up for something else. He touches her arm. "What's going on, Zara?"

"Real estate is a great investment. Daddy taught me that." She crushes the beer can. "Just repeat this to Daddy. Tell him you think it's a great idea. Then he'll go to bat for me with Uncle Solomon, and he won't get side-tracked by old arguments."

If Simeon Bosche talks to Sky's dad, claiming Sky is so smart he wants him to come to work for him, Clive Hunter will know his son has been deceiving him all these years. Sky rubs his forehead with the heels of his hands. A sharp pain cuts into his heart. "I don't know, Zara. I—"

"I saw you surfing one day," Zara says, lowering her voice to a breathless whisper. "It was in Santa Rosa. It was rough and windy. The waves looked treacherous. A few guys tried to catch a huge wave. It was really massive," she says, stretching her arms way out. "You were the only one who made it. You rode that thing like a wind god, and I said to myself, that guy has balls. Awesome Balls, that's what I called you. That's why I called you to play tennis. I wanted to date you."

He walks to the other side of the counter. What if everything that was meant to happen on Earth happened when the Big Bang exploded? What if we were all just trying to catch up with ourselves? Otherwise, why is he always one step behind what's happening when it's happening?

Zara lays a pleading gaze on him, eyes tilted up, like a holy woman seeking divine guidance. "Can you be awesome for me now, Sky?"

There's something between them, big as a lifetime of memories. What if it dates back to the Big Bang? What if they've already lived through this situation and he messed up and this is his chance to get it right? He rams his fist against the counter, like the gavel of his conscience. "Okay."

She expels a lip blubbering breath, and flops her head on his shoulder. "Thank you. I'm exhausted. Can I crash here for a while?"

He scoops her off the stool, swings her torso over his shoulder, and carries her across the room. She giggles, and grips his butt. "Nice ass."

He unfolds her onto the mattress. "That was a Wind God ride."

"Awesome, Awesome Balls."

Sky lays a blanket over her. "When will I hear from your father?"

"Soon. He wanted to speak to your dad first, you know, clear the air with him, make sure he's not stepping on his plans for you."

"He can't do that, Zara. You've got to stop him."

She puffs the pillow, and turns on her side. "Can't. Daddy just boarded his plane for San Francisco. He'll be in meetings all day. You can talk to him tomorrow."

CHAPTER EIGHT

Sky's phone rings. He closes his computer. Zara is still sleeping on his bed. He walks outside onto the patio. "Hi, Dad."

"Sky." His father's voice booms in Sky's ear, big and blustery, like a gale whipping down from Alaska. "I've got things organized with your case, and I'd like to go over them with you."

No pause for Sky to say anything. Clive Hunter carries on, speaking of the people he's designated to head up *The Case*. Sky ambles outside, listening. He sits on one of the wrought iron chairs on the patio. The wind lies low, and a faint fog clings to the trees. Investigators have discovered *Teens Dying for Love* is run by a couple of guys with a list of sleazy crimes to their credit. The spotlight will soon land on them. His dad's public relations company will make sure of that.

Clive Hunter clears his throat. "I need you to lay low for a few days, Sky. Stay at home."

"Dad, thanks for all you're doing to help me, but I've got a lot planned for the next couple of days. I'm leaving the country on Wednesday."

"This is important, Sky. This is to protect the family. You'll make a statement to the police in the morning. I'll go with you. Cancel everything else."

A scream comes from inside the studio, a stricken, terrified sound. Sky leaps to his feet and runs inside. Zara lies curled up on the floor, her mouth open, caught in agony.

"Zara!" Sky kneels beside her. "What's wrong?" He holds her and rocks her. "Tell me, Zara."

She buries her face against his shoulder, mouth open. Her teeth sink through his t-shirt and onto his skin. He hauls her up off the cold cement floor. His mind runs wild. Is she ill? Should he take her to the ER? "What is it, Zara?" He pries the phone from her hand, uncurling her fingers one by one, and checks the call list. The last one came from her mother. "What happened, Zara?" He hits her mother's number in the call log.

Marilyn Bosche answers, "Zara—"

"Mrs. Bosche, this is Sky Hunter. Zara is at my place. I was outside when you called a while ago. I just found Zara. She's devastated. What's wrong?"

"Oh, Sky. I'm so glad you're there. It's Simi. He had a heart attack on the flight to San Francisco." Her voice trembles. "He's dead."

CHAPTER NINE

Sky leans against the window of the railway car, listening to Kanye West rap *Dark Fantasy*. He taps his foot to the rhythm of the beat, the steady forward motion of the train easing the stress of the last few days.

Simeon Bosche had been one of the richest men in the U.S., and his sudden death put a global spin on the *Teens Dying for Love* scandal. Young, rich, beautiful, and tragic, Zara dominates the tabloids: ZARA PREGNANT. NEWS KILLS HER FATHER. Sky comes in second, with BOY TO DIE FOR, SON OF HAPPINESS GURU, FLEES THE COUNTRY. His mom gets trashed too, in nonsensical headlines like HAPPINESS GURU MISERABLE AT HOME. Cameron's suicide letter, *Dying for Sky,* goes viral, and people quote her blog as if it were the word of God.

With all the publicity, Sky worried that Lara Penrose might not want to hire him. He checked out Plan B, lodgings and jobs available in London. Nothing appealed. Penrose Hall had made an indelible impression on him. He had to be there. Landing at Heathrow, Sky called LP, asking if he still had the job. She said, "Can you still mop floors and peel potatoes?"

The train rounds a curve, and a bridge made of two wrought iron arches comes into view. The River Tamar flows beneath, gray and choppy, coursing into a wide estuary busy with sailing boats and merchant vessels.

The open sea lies beyond—rolling in bands of green and blue, heaving and crashing against a headland, reminding Sky of the rugged coast of northern California.

The orb flashes and tints his vision blue. The train slows down and rolls onto the bridge. Sky clasps the bottom of the seat. Anticipation grips him, like when he's writing music and a tone sounds in his head, a note that belongs in a chord several phrases away but that comes early, pulling the whole composition together.

He gazes through the iron grid of the bridge. A beam of sunlight lands on the river and a girl emerges from its center, her body a glittering maze of silver and gold light. She rises into the air and flies alongside the window beside Sky. Her eyes are aqua, and look too big for her face and too wise for her years. She's got the wildest hair, tangled with daisies and beads and flowing all through the river and up over the banks.

Sky glances at those nearby. The woman across from him continues reading *The Times*. A family on the other side of the aisle plays cards. Others doze or tap screens on their phones. No one notices the luminous girl, although her light reflects on everyone, falling like sparkles from a glitter ball.

He looks inward to the orb. *What's going on?*
River Spirit has come for you.

The dazzling girl opens her arms. "Come to me, Sky Blue."

Her voice sounds familiar, haunting, like notes on an oboe. He dissolves into his body of astral light, just like he does when the orb comes for him in his dreams, but this this is different. It's broad daylight and he sails through the window of the railway car, leaving his physical body on the seat. The river girl grips his hands. He treads water in the air, his mood at once buoyant and happy.

"Who are you?" he asks.

"I am Tamara, Spirit of the River Tamar. I am your soul guide, and you've known me for a very long time."

"How do I know you?" Sky asks.

"I came from the Sun Kingdom with my father, Sun Lord Luca, many ages ago. We knew one another in a land called Ruberah, home of the first civilization to inhabit Earth."

Ruberah! That's the place he's visited in his dreams—a land with crystal cities and people who travel on lines of red light. Images from that time crowd Sky's mind: Volcanic fire rages and the beautiful buildings crash to the ground. Crowds rush toward a harbor. Their screams thunder in Sky's ears. "Stop!" he yells.

Tamara touches his forehead, and the horror subsides.

"You lived in Ruberah as a young man called E'am," Tamara says. "Do you remember anything about that?"

"E ... who?"

"E'am ... said like Ian but with an m."

Sky racks his brain. "Um ... I don't know."

"Well ... when Ruberah suffered a disaster, its sacred jeweled mountain—Mt. Rube—sank to the bottom of the ocean. E'am witnessed that, and he wrote a sacred future. Does that feel familiar?"

"What is it? A sacred future?"

"A promise to right a wrongdoing, or a vow to help mankind evolve into a greater state of awareness."

Sky shakes his head, his thoughts scrambling, uncollectable. The man with the golden eyes comes to mind. *Get back in your body. You have a lot to do in this life.* That directive lives with him, like a command he cannot refuse. "What do I have to do?"

"E'am promised to return in a future life and raise the sacred mountain and restart the Age of Jeweled Intelligence on Earth. That vow has come due, and the job falls to you."

"I have to raise a mountain?" Sky says, his voice going squeaky high. "You must be kidding."

The river girl laughs. "I said 'learn how to do that.' You will return to Ruberah and become E'am again. He has the knowledge you need. I will be your guide. You can do this, Sky Blue."

Sky's mind wobbles on overload, close to freaking out. "You know," he says, "I don't use the Blue part of my name. It's Sky, just Sky."

Tamara touches a sparking finger to his forehead. "Fore'tune to travel well, Sky."

TIME OF RUBERAH

CHAPTER TEN

E'am cuts across the water gardens, ducking spray from a grotto of fountains. Pathways of crystals crunch beneath his feet. Some slip inside his sandals. He stops and kicks his foot against a sundial. Sol'aria's call notes chime on his astral disk, three chords, two rising, and one falling. He taps ANSWER, and her face fills a screen floating above his hand. He meets her eyes, green like ancient jade, still heavy with sleep.

"I awoke alone," she says. "I want you. Come back."

"I'm headed for my morning meeting with your father."

She lays a lazy hand against her throat. "Daddy, dear, darling Daddy. Don't let him die, E. Promise you'll stop him."

E'am walks on slowly, weaving through white marble pillars, wondering why people assume he could influence Luca about anything. "But that I had that power, my love."

"You won my heart. You could persuade the stars to fall and live among us, if you wanted to." She blows him a kiss. "Talk to Time. *Please.*"

E'am closes the screen, and approaches the royal wing of the palace. Glass doors sweep open as he draws near, and the smell of pine rises from incense nestled among plants and sculptures. He paces beneath the corridor of carved golden arches leading to Master's apartments. People swish by, dressed in simple white robes, their bodies adorned with ruby bangles and necklaces, earrings, and elaborate headdresses. E'am nods to them in passing, raising his left hand, palm forward in the common expression of goodwill. Many work for him, either in Rube Operations, a force of two thousand based in the Crystal Temple of Science downtown, or at Rube Enterprises, located here in the west wing of the palace.

He swings into the entrance gallery of the royal suite, a large square hall with black marble floors. People circle around a big oak table, filing into various conference rooms. E'am spots Nett, Luca's executive assistant—short of stature, hair parted in the middle, sleeked to his ears.

"Good morning, E'am." Nett drops his head in a perfunctory bow. "Did you send the visuals for Rube?"

"I did." E'am feels a touch of guilt, as he always does around Nett. As children, he and Sol'aria had played practical jokes on Nett, like placing containers of water on the top of a door that fell as he entered the room. "How is Master today?"

Nett grimaces. "If the governors' conference is still in progress when you leave him, please join us. People are worried."

"Post questions on RubeScreen," E'am says. "I'll respond by the end of day."

E'am heads down the corridor leading to the royal suite, and pauses at the door to Master's bedroom. Luca, Spirit Master for Earth, King of Ruberah, and E'am's beloved teacher, lies in bed with his back propped against pillows, diminished of his usual vigor. Earth's crown glows upon his head—twelve golden suns, radiant with the light of the Lords for Earth.

The gravity of losing Master lies heavy on E'am's soul, but he must not dwell upon personal sorrow. He must act fast and enlist Luca's help with the dangers threatening Ruberah. E'am squares his shoulders and enters the room.

Queen Leah sits at Master's bedside in a mauve silk chair, her brow creased with concern. Quick of mind and sensible in ways that endear her to all, Leah lives under the rays of the amethyst kingdom. Her aura shimmers in shades of violet, lavender, and lilac. Gems line the ledges of three wide windows facing the water gardens, some raw, and others tumbled and polished. The minerals emit lines of light and sounds, barely audible to the ear—healing forces directed by Leah to her husband.

The queen smiles upon sight of E'am, and his heart warms to her. He was seven when he first came to the palace to study the cosmic forces of jewels with Luca. His father brought him every day after school. Leah treated E'am with loving care, just as she did her daughters, the princesses Sol'aria and Li'ram. E'am adored her from the start, and the sight of her face always brings back memories of the warm grasp of her hand, pressing sweetmeats into his.

Leah rises from her chair and hugs him. "Luca is not improving," she says. "I visited your father at the Healing Center yesterday and watched him put a woman with a fatal lung disease into the Cube. Rube regenerated her damaged cells. She was healed. Rube could repair Luca's heart."

"Luca knows these things, Leah. We have to trust his judgment."

She wipes a tear from her cheek. "When I first met him he told me he would live for another thirty-two years. He was eighteen. I thought little of it. After our children were born, I pictured us always being with them, or at least until they married. I never thought he'd leave before then." Her eyes scour E'am's. "Could you persuade him to stay?"

There it is again, the same request. "Luca wrote a contract with Time, Leah. I can do little—"

"But you understand Time. You can communicate with that intelligence. Can't you…" Leah bites her lip. "I'm sorry. I shouldn't trouble you with these things. That you will soon wed Sol'aria eases my sorrow."

Leah sweeps from the room, and E'am sits in the chair vacated by her. Luca's prearranged life span is well known to him. Master is a Lord of the Sun Kingdom, the universe beyond this one. He comes to Earth as requested by Time, materializing a physical body as needed, and always arriving as a young man of eighteen. Luca has done this four times in the five hundred years since Earth spun into existence—preparing the land for the civilization that exists today.

E'am leans in close to Master. "Luca … it's me." He touches his arm lightly, thoughts of life without him lumping in his throat. Master has imparted a wealth of knowledge to E'am about the laws of Time, which made it possible for him to gain custody of Time Blade last year.

Master's eyelids flicker open. "Ah," he says, his voice thin and raspy. "What brings my Witness to my side?"

"I come every day at this time." Luca's failing memory upsets E'am, and he mentions the healing powers of the Cube again, but Master raises his hand and stops him.

"You saw the death cloud shadow my presence last week in the Council of the Lords. Do not question what you observe as my Witness."

Until seven days ago, Luca lived as a strapping man in his early fifties. Then his death cloud appeared and he took on ill health. He chose heart disease as if selecting a meal from a menu, and drew its weaknesses to him. The Master must die as an ordinary man, Luca said. The people need to witness his death.

"We need you here," E'am says. "Dark Master is gaining power in the Emerald Kingdom."

Luca waves a dismissive hand. "Using his jeweled intelligence, the least evolved among us is more powerful than Dark Master."

True, but with failing health, Master has become forgetful of how challenging it is for the everyday person to remember his jeweled wisdom. It requires stepping back from lust, jealousy, or any desire of the lower nature, seeking its guidance. E'am has lived in the uplift of Master's presence for the last ten years, and he still falls victim to his weaknesses.

"Dark Master has created a campaign to incite the people of the Emerald Kingdom," E'am says. "It's called EMFIRE, YOUR DREAM LIFE NOW. Citizens of the EK want the riches it promises, and they're demanding Prince Da'krah raise the astral fire of emeralds."

"Ah, greed." Luca rolls his head from side to side. "The ruler always does well with greed."

E'am sits forward on the chair. "Da'krah is used to being adored by his people and he's weakening to their demands. This is not the right time for man to use the fire of emeralds. You said so yourself. We must do something to stop this."

Luca props himself up, rearranging pillows to support his back. "If the Prince of the Emerald Kingdom seeks my opinion, I will give it to him."

"Luca! Your daughter Li'ram confers with the prince about helping him kindle the forces of emeralds—using her sacred powers as High Priestess of Rube."

Luca chuckles. "Li'ram considers herself deeply, wonderfully, and heroically in love with Da'krah. What can I do about that?"

E'am bites back annoyance. Li'ram and her romantic illusions will be the end of them all. "If EmFire is brought to life on Earth now, it will be a force beyond our control. It could destroy our entire civilization. We cannot let this happen. Let me deal with Da'krah."

"I have taught you nothing, E'am, if I have not ingrained it upon you not to impose your opinion on others. Wait to be asked."

E'am shifts uncomfortably in his chair. His quest to win the Sun Heart and transcend to the Sun Kingdom reigns foremost on his mind, a carryover from his previous life on planet Miron. He'd been close to transcendence back then, living as Rae Blue, but he made a stupid mistake. Anger overtook Rae Blue when he realized Master allowed millions to perish in the fires of a supernova because no one remembered to ask him to use the SunShield to save them. That anger stalks E'am today—fire in his solar plexus, ever ready to break loose. He speaks, choosing his words carefully.

"I'm asking you, Luca, please use the light of the Sun Kingdom to save Ruberah from destruction by EmFire."

"Is EmFire happening now?" Luca asks.

"You know what I mean, Master."

"Ah ... my beloved E'am. You are not here to save the world. It is every man's task to save himself. Man comes to Earth to free himself from the shadows on his soul. He must use his jeweled intelligence and conquer his lower nature. I must not take this power from him."

E'am wriggles in his chair, balking at this truth. "But," he says, "Da'krah is one of the most powerful men on the planet and he cannot use his jeweled intelligence. Dark Master blocked it from him at birth. Surely, under these circumstances, we can intercede."

"No. We cannot." Luca withdraws a large, white hand-kerchief from his sleeve and blows his nose. "We must allow Da'krah the chance to awaken to the spell Dark Master cast over him. A lot would have to go wrong ..." His voice trails off as he gazes into the distance.

E'am's heart thuds in his chest. "What is it? What do you see, Master?"

"Enter your Sapphire Mind, E'am. Let us travel beyond the chaos of this life."

Master sweeps his glance upward, and the suns in Earth's Crown radiate and flood the room. E'am bows mentally to the orb inside his head. *I come to serve.* The visionary planes open, and he transcends into his astral form.

The Council of the Lords appears: pillars of light—tall and never-ending. The twelve Lords assigned to Earth form an inner circle within the pillars. They look like columns of light too, but with smiling faces and flowing hair. E'am kneels beside Luca in their center, and looks back to Earth. Pale pink light pours down from the Ruby Sphere, doming the land of Ruberah, creating an atmosphere conducive for human life.

One of the Lords taps EARTH IMAGING on a panel of instruments, and a large screen drops down. The Emerald Kingdom comes into view, a small island lying alongside the west coast of Ruberah, separated from the mainland by the River Az. The Lord leans in close, studying the picture. A blue-black haze clings to the towers of Da'krah's palace, influences rising up from the Black Heart, Dark Master's seat of power beneath the ocean.

The Lord speaks. "This is a critical time for the Prince of the Emerald Kingdom. We must hope he awakens to the shadow Dark Master laid upon him at birth. Consider the magnificence of his star body."

The light of the Council dims, the session ends, and E'am returns to waking consciousness, sitting in the chair beside Luca's bed.

Master rubs his eyes. "There you have it," he says, "just as I said."

E'am sighs inwardly. The Lords work in an even more abstract field of possibilities than Luca. "Have what, Luca? What did we learn?"

"These meetings with the Lords bring the awareness of the Council into the world. You carry that with you, E'am, and since they discussed Da'krah today, the prince could be affected by that grace, as it passes through you. Meet him with a pure heart and kindness on your mind."

E'am doubts anything as subtle as grace could rise above the passions of Da'krah's mind. The prince is a self-indulgent man with an appetite for fine wine, fashionable attire, and women. "Time Blade would be more effective," E'am says. "I could offer the prince an Honor Killing."

Luca raises his eyebrows. "I wondered when you would get to that."

"It fits the situation, doesn't it?"

"The Lords said to consider the magnificence of Da'krah's star body. Compassion first."

E'am squirms, resistance on the rise. Luca can dive into compassion for anyone on a moment's notice, drawing E'am in with him. It's like being pulled by an unstoppable force—into the glories of that person's soul. "You've taken me to Da'krah's star body any number of times, Luca."

"And yet it seems you are not eager to go again?"

"I appreciate Da'krah came to Earth to help the human race, and it's tragic that Dark Master came between him and that purpose, but that doesn't alter the fact that he presents a grave danger to mankind."

"That he does," Luca says, "but if you desire to kill the prince, you will not be effective with Time Blade."

"I will work on myself."

"Sleep with the Blade tonight. Review the rules. We will consider an Honor Killing tomorrow."

CHAPTER ELEVEN

E'am opens Ruby Transit RT on his astral disk, and a map appears. He taps on a red line close to the palace. It pulses to life beneath his feet. He selects Mt. Rube as his destination and leans forward as the light path moves over the land. He swerves through the streets of Az'Rayelle, and slows down as he enters the Crystal District, home to the towering Crystal Temple of Science. Moonlight glows on the great golden pyramid atop the building. People hop on and off light paths, gathering in the plaza of the Temple for the evening chant to Zan'drah, Goddess of Rubies.

E'am used to attend these nightly meditations with Sol'aria before he took leadership of Rube Enterprises and work laid claim to so many of his evenings. Not that he would give up the challenge of running RE, but chanting to the Goddess with his fellow man had reinforced gratitude for his place among them. He leaves the Crystal District, the sounds of the chant filling his ears.

He glides alongside the River Az, where people mill in and out of restaurants, dance clubs, and places to play Virtual Universe, a game of life in other galaxies. Some recognize E'am. "It's the Killer E," one boy says.

In his early teens E'am fell into one fight after another. He studied with the Masters of the fighting arts and trained hard to gain custody of Time Blade, and couldn't resist a challenge. Gossip journalists—known as the razz—set him up one night, drawing him into a fight in a back alley. They filmed the duel. E'am won, inflicting a few bruises on his opponent, then slapped hands, as is the custom. The razz edited the video, showing E'am striding away from a brutally beaten boy, and dubbing him the Killer E. The name stuck.

As the light path leaves the city, E'am ups his speed and veers onto the wide-open plains. Wind whips in off the Sea of Ruberah, blustering his clothes and hair. He passes the space terminal, where triple-decked airships nose up to departure halls. Some are designed for day trips, carrying a thousand people at a time. Others are equipped for world exploration—offering living quarters, dining rooms, and ruby-powered vehicles for land travel.

Mt. Rube rises in the distance, glowing red in the light of the moon. Vapors puff from its base, layering the plains with drifts of pink mists. E'am cuts his speed as he approaches a set of golden gates leading to the mountain. A sunburst of diamonds sprawls to the heights and widths of the towering edifice. He swerves left, heading to the rear of Mt. Rube.

The Ruby Hot Pools—hundreds of individual spas— spread all the way down to the Sea of Ruberah. Leafy trees and lush shrubbery meander around each pool, giving privacy. E'am lays his left palm against a screen in the arched entrance. A sound like wind whooshing through a tunnel stirs the air, and a shield of light rises. He treks over pathways lined with towering bamboo. The scents of wood and flowery fragrances ripple the atmosphere. At the entrance to his spa, he leans his left eye to a sapphire embedded in the wall. The gate swings open.

Ruby mists rise from a square-shaped pool big enough for six people, although he seldom uses it with anyone but Sol'aria. A fire pit casts a warm glow on a white structure. Stepping inside, he taps his astral disk, and the roof slides open. Stars scatter the skies, sparkling beneath the pale pink dome that covers the land of Ruberah. He strips, tosses his clothes and sandals on a bench, and swipes a robe from a hook by the bathroom.

"Hello, Witness Boy."

Sol'aria stands in the doorframe, tall and statuesque, one hand on her hip, eyes glowing like polished jade. She sweeps the fall of her flaming red hair over one shoulder. His heart does a flip-flop. In six days they will stand in the Rings of Ruby Fire and be mated for life. "Come here."

"You dare to command me, Witness Boy? Do you not fear my powers? I could melt you with one spark of the Sun Flame."

"Then who would satisfy your wanton desires?"

"You think I would be short of suitors?" She tilts her chin, holding herself aloof, eyebrows raised.

"I do."

"What insolence. You will have to earn your way back into my favor."

"And how shall I do that?"

She regards him with a sideways glance. "You will arouse and satisfy me five times, and then I shall exact my pleasure with you, performing whatever reward you have due, if any. Then you will make love to me, which must result in ecstasy, such as I have not experienced before. Do you accept?"

He files her haughty expression to memory, a joy to savor again in conquest. "I do."

She raises her arms above her head. He loosens the strap of her robe. She turns slowly, like a figurine in a music box. He unravels chains of rubies around her waist. Her robe drops to the ground. She stands naked—her breasts small, high, and firm, the red triangle of her pubic hair trimmed to a narrow V. He kneels, unties the jeweled straps of her sandals, and slides them from her feet.

He drops his robe, scoops her into his arms, and carries her outside. Lowering her into the bubbling hot waters, he taps EROGENOUS ZONES on his astral disk, and selects HERS. The gentle vibrations of Rube run down his arms and tingle his fingertips.

He touches the sensuous areas around her nipples, kissing her neck and her cheeks. She moans and grips his head in her hands, her breath coming faster. He kisses her breasts, moving his hands over her back. She tenses her body.

"Yes."

Lifting her from the water, he sits her on the edge of the pool and parts her legs. She leans back, resting her torso on her elbows, tilting her head to the sky. He slides his fingers inside her. Her muscles tighten. She stretches her body taut, crying out to the sky. Moving his head between her thighs, he slips his tongue inside her, keeping his other hand pressed lightly against her pelvis. She lies flat on her back, her body writhing as he brings her to one orgasm after another: five.

She lolls her head against his shoulder, kissing him tenderly. He strokes her hair. "I need to be inside you."

"Not yet," she says. "It's my turn to delight you."

"I'll collect that another time."

"That's not what we agreed to."

She taps on her astral disk, bringing up his Reward Program, things she's convinced him he wants her to do to him. "Oh, MIRROR MY HEART," she says, licking her lips. "I adore doing that with you."

MIRROR MY HEART is a visualization practice for couples deeply committed to one another. He sometimes thinks Soli wrote the program, as it's her intuition that tells her what he wants. E'am would rather bring her to the orgasm that must surpass all others, but MMH is a mental orgasm for Soli—control she will not surrender. "What do you have in mind?" he asks.

She lays a finger on the sapphire inked over his abdomen, tracing a ray of light into his pubic hair. "Take me to the records of planet Miron. I want to meet you as Rae Blue. Daddy said you were very handsome." She giggles. "Not that you aren't now, but—"

"No. It's dangerous, Soli. Time does not always bend to the will of the traveler." E'am has firsthand knowledge of this. In the past, he's programed to visit an exact event in his life as Rae Blue and ended up exactly where he didn't want to be: losing his temper with Master.

"Um, but I like danger."

"No." E'am lifts her up, carries her into the spa, and lays her on the bed. She rolls from under him and straddles his body. It's wet between her legs. He aches to be inside her, but she's sliding through options on her astral disk. A smile creeps across her face, growing wider by the second.

"If not back to Miron, then forward to our wedding day?"

E'am nods. "Proceed."

"Look into my heart through your Sapphire Vision."

He does as told, for hers is a beautiful heart to behold, lit by the light of the Pearl and Ruby Kingdoms. Mates are usually attracted to partners from a different jewel kingdom than their own. Soli's father entered life through the Ruby Sphere and her mother the Pearl. Both of E'am's parents came through the Sapphire, hence he is a double sapphire.

Soli consults her astral disk, and then places her left hand on her heart and her right on E'am's. He enters the visionary plane with her, and they walk together over the twelve petals of her heart. The Sun Flame burns in their center, a spark from Earth's sun star, which Soli uses to energize the astral forces of rubies as they flow into Mt. Rube.

The days preceding their wedding speed by, but stop abruptly before the actual date. Soli taps rapidly on her astral disk. "That's strange. MMH has vanished from my screen."

E'am rejoices, silently, pulling her beneath him. "Then it must be time for that orgasm that must supersede all others."

CHAPTER TWELVE

The night air falls cool and misty over the palace grounds, and the swish of the Atalan River runs by, whispering a murky story. The Atalan begins in a range of snow-clad mountains bordering the land of Ruberah, and then courses over the plains, picking up silt and shale, and the ruddy hue of Rube. The sparkling, pink-tinted waters of the River Az, home to River Spirit, flow on the southern side of the city, fed by the cosmic waters of the Great River of Life.

E'am treads over crystal pathways leading to the Hall of Time, an imposing glass-domed structure surrounded by lawns that roll down to the Atalan. A wide marble staircase leads to the gilded doors of the main entrance to the Hall of Time. Thousands climb them, students and families alike, as they come to attend Luca's weekly lectures on the Nature of Time.

Skirting the base of the Hall, E'am arrives at a black-painted door with gold lettering: THE WITNESS. He leans his eye to the lens beneath the sign. The door swings open. His breath catches in his throat, and his heartbeat quickens. A simulated version of the Cycles of Time hangs inside the massive crystal dome. Soft pink light illumines the loops of the past and the future. His boyish laughter echoes in the lofty hall.

Can we work with Time Blade today, Master?

Yes, we can.

E'am always knew he would study with Luca. Master visited his parents before he was born and told them their son was destined to be his Witness. "I will need him to question me well," Luca had told them. "Encourage his curiosity." E'am's parents lived gracefully with Luca's instructions, instilling in E'am a sense of honor and gratitude for the place he would take beside Master. His curiosity needed no fostering. He often dreamed in the silver-blue light of planet Miron and perceived himself living as Rae Blue, as a young boy like himself.

When E'am turned seven, his father brought him to his first lesson with Luca, lifting him at the Witness Door for security to read his eye. "Remember to respect Master," his father said. "Ask questions but don't answer him back."

E'am entered the great hall alone but excited. Luca stood tall, broad-shouldered and erect beneath the Cycles of Time. Earth's crown blazed on his head, and his golden hair hung heavy with sun crystals. Time Blade glistened in his hand, the jewels of the seven kingdoms sparkling in the crossguard. E'am's heart caught fire, and he ran up to Luca. "That's mine," he said in an accusatory tone, as if Luca had stolen the knife from him.

"Not yet," Master said. "You have to win it. Are you ready to study the laws of the Blade?"

"I am."

Master's eyebrows shot up. "Excellent! 'I am' is always the correct answer for you."

"Why?"

"Because E'am means 'I am,' which is why you are here with me."

A silvery glow wafted off Luca and fell over E'am, familiar and rich with knowledge. Studying with Master is like listening to music or looking at art. Understanding comes as a reactionary response, appearing in visions and feelings, which Luca says arise from E'am's own inner knowing—his eternal truth. E'am had adored Master as a small boy, but when he turned twelve he dreamed of being Rae Blue on planet Miron. The death of their sun star had killed millions of people, and Rae Blue realized Master had not saved them because no one asked him to. When E'am awoke, Rae Blue's anger cut into his heart—sharp, like shards of glass. It's stayed there, and it pains E'am. He loves no one as he loves Master. He would die in his place without qualm or quarrel.

E'am pauses beneath the simulated version of the Cycles of Time, and steps onto a replica of the Passing Stone. The real stone is a golden tablet laid into the ground at Peacewater Bend, by the River Az. The dead rest on the Passing Stone before floating upriver on a bed of flames.

Life is now. Death is now. Eternity is now. Time Blade begins every journey in the Now.

"How, Master?"

To stop, cut, or reverse Time, you will stand on the Passing Stone at Peacewater Bend and ask Time for permission. If granted, the skies will part above you and the Cycles of Time will appear. Cast your eye down the ridge of the Blade and aim the tip into the dot of the Now.

"Then what?"

Time will advise you.

"Time speaks?"

You surrender and Time acts upon you.

"How?"

Time is a law—a post of consciousness—composed of multi-billions of particles of perfect impersonal intelligence—the soul of the world. We all live under the law of Time. Events come upon us as needed, although that is often not understood, except in retrospect.

"Why do we need the Cycles of Time?"

So we can be conscious of our life on Earth. Without the Cycles, Time is no time or all time all the time.

"Like 'I am' but organized to suit mankind."

Luca's gaze bored into E'am, long and silent, and then his face broke into a smile that stretched across his cheeks and up into his eyes. *Excellent.*

Having just pleased Master, E'am asked the question he'd long wanted to ask. "Can I kill someone with Time Blade?"

If a person poses a threat to the future of mankind, you may approach him and offer him an Honor Killing.

"What will I say?"

You will know when the time comes. Time Blade offers a quick, karma-free death, and the intended recipient will understand the magnificence of that in his own terms. You, as guardian of the Blade, will have trained in the fighting arts and be capable of causing death with one thrust of the Blade.

"Will I cut his throat?"

No. You will learn a move known as the Glorious Thrust. The Thrust requires great skill. You must stab the Blade below the ribcage, push up through the diaphragm and the lungs, and enter the heart, killing swiftly.

E'am had salivated, thinking of the *Glorious Thrust.* Violence was shunned in Ruberah. Fighting was an art.

Young people trained and fought in competition. Most used light blades—lasers powered by Rube. Taking someone's life was forbidden, but killer instinct had a mind of its own. E'am felt it rising in him as he prepared for a fight, and he could smell it on his opponent. He trained in all the disciplines and competed with lasers, fists, wrestling, and spirit fire, the art of using the opponent's energy against him.

Stepping from the Passing Stone, E'am strides through the great hall toward the north end. He enters a darkened sanctuary and approaches an altar welded to the floor. Time Blade lies inside the steel oblong. E'am kneels and lays his left hand on the cold surface. A seam splits open in the altar. Time Blade rests on a bed of black silk. The jewels of the seven kingdoms sparkle in the crossguard. Elation swells in his chest. He grips the steel-rimmed handle of Time Blade, and the fiery forces of the jewel kingdoms ripple through his body.

He carries the weapon into a small, whitewashed room with a bunk bed. He's slept here frequently over the past ten years, always before taking the tests he had to pass to win guardianship of the Blade. He undresses, climbs under the blankets, and slips the Blade beneath the pillow.

I give you my mind, my body, my heart, and soul. Teach me what you would have me know.

CHAPTER THIRTEEN

E'am skirts the southern boundary of the palace nearing the end of his morning run. Sweat drips into his eyes, blurring his view of Na'ma, the old river house where he and Sol'aria had played as children. Currently under restoration, Na'ma will be his first home with Soli. He's not been inside for six months. She's taken control of the project and wants to surprise him with the results on their wedding night.

Cutting sharply to the right, he passes the Hall of Time and enters the East Wing of the Palace. He resides on the second floor, directly above the executive offices of Rube Enterprises. Inside his apartment, he towels sweat from his hands and grabs a fifty-pound rod wrapped with rope. He squeezes his fingers around the rough twine and lifts the weight, pulling the rod to his shoulder. He does a hundred repetitions, then changes hands— building strength and balance.

He showers and dries off under warm air pouring down from vents in the ceiling. His weekly meeting with Da'krah is scheduled for this afternoon. The prince will be at ease, ready to discuss the energy needs of the EK. This could be an advantage for E'am, if he obtains permission to offer him an Honor Killing.

He centers his sapphires on his head and slips on wide gold wrist guards and special sandals, their soles inlaid with gold—metal to ground him to the Earth's heart. In the kitchen he finds breakfast—grilled fish, a large bowl of fresh greens, and an assortment of fruits and nuts. His trainers order his meals, passing directions to the palace chefs.

A staircase leads down from his apartment and into the offices of Rube Enterprises. He enters the operations center, a large, lofty space ablaze with floor-to-ceiling monitors. Hundreds of people study the screens, tracking Rube as it flows into the city of AzRayelle and the Emerald Kingdom. He chats with the managers of the three main divisions—industrial, domestic, and public—and reviews graphs from Rube Distribution, located downtown in the Crystal Temple of Science. All appears normal. He moves to the Elite team—the best and the brightest—five women and five men, sitting at a long desk in the center of the room. He greets each person, glancing at screens tracking the astral energies of rubies as they leave the cosmos and filter into Mt. Rube.

Several graduates from his class at the Institute of Astral Sciences work for *Elite*. One, Ka'rine, darts him a flirty smile, running the tip of her tongue over her lip. He had a close encounter with her once. He'd lusted after Ka'rine in school—dark sleek hair, sultry brown eyes, big bouncing breasts, rumored to go all the way. Ka'rine had been sixteen at the time, a year older than E'am. One day after school, she ran up to him, shiny black hair flying in the wind, mouth parted, pink and wet. She lowered her astral disk to her abdomen and flashed the screen at him. "It's a safe time for me. Do you want to?"

Yes, he did. He kissed her, slipped his hands under her clothes, and felt her breasts. She pulled down his undershorts and gripped his throbbing erection. He was close to being inside her when Time Blade flashed upon his conscience, and his head cleared as if he were standing under a fall of icy water.

The man who carries Time Blade is not reckless in his dealings with others. He is well thought out, law-abiding, and careful in all measures of his life - The Pure Heart rule.

He stepped back from Ka'rine, desperate, trying to think of what to say. "You deserve more than a quick fuck with me or anyone else," he managed.

"Are you asking me to be your girlfriend?" she said, eyes flashing.

"Um ... I wish I could," he said, stumbling over the words. "But I'm fifteen, not yet allowed to download EZ."

She fled. Who would want a boyfriend who couldn't pleasure her with EROGENOUS ZONES? He feared Ka'rine would tell his classmates that he'd turned her down. He'd be mocked forever after. Who would obey the rule of not engaging in sexual intercourse until age sixteen, given a chance with Ka'rine? She did not spill the story, probably because she could have been expelled for approaching a fifteen-year-old.

He knew she'd turn up on the Elite team one day. She had the brains. He couldn't refuse her the job. He avoids the flirty smile seemingly glued to her lips. The palace frowns on conspicuous displays of affection between co-workers, a frown that appears to go unnoticed. As head of RE, he's expected to set a good example, but he treads on rocky ground. Sol'aria works for Rube, although directly for the Goddess, and he is formally engaged to her. Still, he'd be uncomfortable exerting authority over an employee distracted by an office love affair. He's had days like that himself.

E'am retreats to his private office, and doesn't notice Ka'rine as she sneaks in behind him. She runs her hands over his shoulder. He pushes her away. "Don't do this."

"You want me." She slides her hand inside the slit of her skirt, cut to her thigh. "And I want you, and that's a force that won't go away."

E'am plunges into his chair. "If can't you be professional about your work here, you will have to leave."

"Ha!" Ka'rine leans over the desk, squeezing her breasts together. "You can't dismiss me. I'm smarter than anyone else on Elite."

"You're replaceable."

A glazed expression crosses her eyes. "One of these days, I'm going to give you the fuck of your life." She licks her lips. "Think of that first touch between us. Nothing will ever be as exciting as that. Mmmm." She sweeps from the room.

Against the love he feels for Sol'aria and all that he knows will keep him faithful to her, Ka'rine ignites the boyish lust he'd felt for her. Had it not been for the Pure Heart rule, they would have had sex that day after school, and he'd be forgotten along with all her other conquests.

E'am glances at RubeScreen glowing on his desk, and responds to questions from the governors' meeting. A report from Security captures his attention. A number of young women entering the EK have been

sexually assaulted, reportedly by a gang of youths hanging around the Az Bridge. A warning has been issued
on RubeVision suggesting women do not enter the EK
without a male escort.

His father's ring tone sounds. E'am transfers his call
to RubeScreen, and a visual floats in front of him. His
parents greet him, and then his young twin brothers leap
into the picture.

"When are you going to take us camping?" they ask.

"Soon."

"You said that last week," Mu'ri, the more aggressive
twin, says. "You work too much."

Ka'rum chimes in. "Where's Soli? I want to speak to her."

His father escorts the boys off to another room, leaving his mother alone in the kitchen. "Come for dinner
tomorrow night, darling. We miss you."

"I'll try to be there. 'Bye."

Both his parents are healers. His father specializes in
cellular regeneration and his mother in fertility and BHS,
Broken Heart Syndrome, an emotional disorder that affects
girls. Pregnancy is easily avoided by checking Rube Fertility on the astral disk, but casual intercourse is discouraged.
The male sperm carries the astral consciousness of the man,
which can linger inside a woman for months after sex. A girl
could feel love for a boy who has left her, and long for him to
be hers again. This can cause Broken Heart Syndrome.

Luca sits in a wheelchair, running his fingers over the
minerals on the windowsills. Sunlight catches mist rising
off the water gardens outside, casting rainbows in the
fountains. Master directs E'am to the mauve silk chair.

He's barely seated when the light of Earth's crown brightens the room, lifting E'am into the visionary plane. He sails into the Council of the Lords with Luca and kneels beside him. Master asks if E'am should offer an Honor Killing to Da'krah, Prince of the Emerald Kingdom. The Lords confer with one another and decide that Time Blade might light up the prince's memory of his Diamond Intelligence. In other words, yes.

The Council vanishes. E'am slips back into his waking mind. His heart pounds in his chest. He's competed in fights against Da'krah dozens of times, losing to him more often than winning. Master reminds him of that, saying if Da'krah declines the Honor Killing, which he deems likely, E'am will have to fight for his life.

"There will be no referee to bar the prince from killing you."

E'am reigns as champion with light blades. He has for five years, but Da'krah cannot use spirit fire, as that requires jeweled intelligence. Da'krah employs brute strength, fighting with his fists, doubly empowered by his attachment to Dark Master. E'am can alter the course of Da'krah's punches using spirit fire, but it's a sacred force. He must be well balanced to use it.

"I've been fighting against the masters, practicing patience," E'am says. "I've improved. I can handle Da'krah."

"If you fall short, even for a second, Dark Master will seize you."

E'am's throat goes dry. He'd rather die than be captured by the ruler and imprisoned in the Black Heart, which fate he would surely meet. "I know," he whispers.

Luca stares out the window. "This is not your time to die."

"All the better."

"That doesn't mean you can't be killed. It's up to you to guard your life, to make sensible choices."

"The Lords said Da'krah should be offered an Honor Killing."

"Are you disciplined to the Blade?"

"I am."

"Do you claim a pure heart? Can you honor the Blade above all personal causes?"

"You know I can."

"What proof do you offer?"

E'am gulps a breath. "I passed that test two years ago. You said so yourself."

"Remind me."

E'am crosses and uncrosses his legs. He told Luca about Ka'rine offering him sex when he was fifteen, because embarrassing as it was, it proved he wanted Time Blade more than sex, which was monumental at the time. Luca had not made light of it. He had congratulated him, saying he had won the pure heart status. E'am repeats the story.

"Ah, yes, Ka'rine. I'm told she works for you now."

"She qualified for Elite."

"Pretty girl. Promiscuous too, so I hear. Is she an ongoing challenge?"

"Of course not. I'm about to marry your daughter."

Luca drops his head and falls into one of his sudden silences. E'am fights back annoyance with Master. He taps his fingers on the arm of the chair, hoping his absence will be brief. It isn't. Minutes pass, and then Luca yawns as if waking from a deep sleep.

E'am raises an eyebrow. "Am I to offer Da'krah an Honor Killing today?"

Master speaks softly, his voice low and lyrical. "Do you remember when you first committed to serve Time?"

"When I lived as Rae Blue?"

"Yes. You bowed into Earth's brand new Cycles of Time, offering your sapphire intelligence to be called upon, as needed."

E'am thinks back. "Yes. I recall that."

"What did I say to you, to Rae Blue, when I pulled you up from the Cycles of Time?"

E'am strokes his temples, trying to remember. "I would have to travel back and become Rae Blue again to retrieve that memory."

Luca leans forward in his chair. "In the interest of time would you like me to remind you?"

E'am nods, selecting the right words. "I would like you to remind me of what you said to Rae Blue at that time."

Master says, "I warned you to think carefully about the Blade. I told you Time would be your master and Time blends souls and intelligence to suit evolution. It does not recognize the feelings of the human heart—the Earth heart—such as yours."

E'am ruminates on the warning. "And does this affect my offering Da'krah an Honor Killing?"

"It doesn't. You may proceed with that."

Master's expression falls blank and unreadable, a sign he is withholding information, knowledge he will not offer without specific questioning. The heart is a large and complicated field of emotions. E'am would have to concentrate long and hard in his jeweled wisdom to comprehend what Luca has in mind, and that could take more time than he can spare.

"I stand in good stead with Time Blade?" he asks.

"You do."

E'am pulls on courage. He's waited for this day since he first held the Blade in his hand, but reality strikes a bitter chord. He might kill a man today, or be taken prisoner by Dark Master. He stands. "Thank you, Master, for your kindness and patience with me. Thank you for all that you have taught me."

Luca nods. "Fore'tune to travel well."

CHAPTER FOURTEEN

The light path swerves through the busy streets around the Crystal Temple of Science. Time Blade hangs in a sheath behind E'am's right hip, hidden beneath the official white silk tunic of Rube Enterprises. He passes a group gathered on the riverbank waiting to seek guidance from River Spirit. Her aqua gaze falls on E'am, seeming to call him to her. He'd like nothing better than to spend time with the beloved guide, but he's already running late for his appointment with Da'krah.

He swings onto the Az Bridge. Someone leaps onto his light path.

He glances over his shoulder. Luca's eldest daughter, Princess Li'ram, grins at E'am from behind a hooded cloak. He draws the path to a halt and pushes his hand out to keep her from leaning against him. If she detects the Blade, that will be the end of his mission with Da'krah. "I can't take you with me, Li. Get off."

Li'ram bats her sea-green eyes. "Just escort me over the bridge, E. That's all I ask, then I'll jump onto the royal dock and make my way into the secret tunnel."

The secret tunnel that's not so secret. High on wine, Da'krah likes to boast of how his ancestors escaped death through that passage, using a door in his bedroom hidden behind a portrait of his great grandfather. If Li'ram enters the palace through that door, she'll think nothing of bursting into Da'krah's study, where E'am usually meets with him. "Not today, Li. The escort rule just went into effect. Get off my light path. I'll ask Da'krah to send someone for you."

"Then it won't be a surprise, will it?"

It occurs to E'am he's caught in a no-win situation with Li. If Da'krah accepts an Honor Killing, she will be heartbroken at the loss of her lover, and Sol'aria will never forgive him for that. The princesses are celestial sisters in service to Earth. Li'ram filters the astral sounds of rubies into Rube, and Sol'aria works with the Sun Flame. They usually stick together as a formidable team on just about everything, but E'am has his own priorities. He lays a hand on the Blade under his tunic. *I give you my mind, my body, my heart, and my soul.*

Li'ram purses her lips, no doubt pondering some means of persuasion to win a ride over the bridge. "I'll take your side the next time you upset Soli."

"I don't need you to defend me with Sol'aria."

"You will. Ka'rine has designs on you. Soli knows it, and she doesn't like her working so closely with you." Li laughs. "I could easily ratchet that up a notch or two."

"You cannot come into the EK with me today, and that's that."

"Tut ...tut. You're about to be my brother-in-law. You should be winning my alliance."

"I'll have to chance getting along without it."

Li'ram tucks a strand of honey-colored hair inside her hood, acting coy, like a woman used to getting her way with men, which she is. E'am watched her dazzle Da'krah a few years ago. He'd been sitting next to Li at a lecture at CTS when the prince arrived. Li gasped upon sight of Da'krah. "I love him," she whispered, and then directed a stream of ruby light from her heart to his, a definite misuse of her jeweled forces.

"You would also risk Da'krah's goodwill?" Li'ram asks, her voice trilling high.

"Call one of your own guards to come and—"

"I can't." Li'ram opens her cape. She's clad in tiny black panties and a tight-fitting bodice that swells her breasts to overflowing. "I think Daks would rather you escort me."

"I doubt that. Get off my light path."

"Oh!" She releases another trill of laughter. "That's the third time you've asked, but I'm still here."

E'am pushes her, shoving her off the path. "Not anymore," he says, watching her land in the midst of the crowds waiting for River Spirit.

People fawn over their princess, thrilled by their chance meeting with her. Li'ram glowers back at E'am, gathering the cape close to her body. E'am speeds over the bridge.

The difference in the atmosphere of the EK hits him the instant the light path crosses the River Az. It's been a week since his last visit, and Dark Master's influence has increased a hundredfold, hanging over the city like smog.

E'am taps EARTH IMAGING, and visuals pop up all over the city, the glamorous life style the people could expect in a world powered by EmFire. There have long been citizens of the EK who resent adhering to the policies of the Ruby Kingdom. Rube is free for everyone's personal use. Industries pay a percentage of profits to maintain Mt. Rube, the Crystal Temple of Science, educational institutes, healing centers, safety patrol, and public cleaning services.

E'am glances at Da'krah's palace, sprawling atop a hill above Na'paz, a metropolis similar in size and design to Az'Rayelle. He taps RT on his astral disk, looking for a light path, but people throng the streets, gazing at the *Dream Life* images, too many to ride through them.

He strides into the crowds, and a *Dream Life* image swoops down in front him. He faces a life-sized girl whose eyes glow deep green. "Pleasure me as I will pleasure you," she says, her voice resonating in a playful tone almost identical to Sol'aria's. She wears nothing but a string of emeralds winding between her legs and around her hips. She caresses her breasts, and lust zips through E'am. He reaches out to touch her, but his sapphire orb spins, shooting blue fire through his brain, bringing him to his senses.

A man nudges his shoulder. "If you don't want her, I'll take her."

Anger flares up, as surely as if the girl were actually Sol'aria. E'am tightens his muscles and pushes the man away. "Leave her alone."

"Hey." The man raises his fist and shakes it in E'am's face. "She's asking to be fucked. Get out of my way."

E'am whacks the man in the jaw, then swipes his hand through the screen, smashing it into a pile of shimmering pieces. Regret comes quickly. Anger has alerted Dark Master to his presence in the EK. People crowd around the man lying on the street, urging him to get up and fight. "Fight! Fight! Fight!"

"Not likely," the man says, wagging his finger at E'am. "He's the Killer E."

The crowds fall back, and E'am surrenders to his sapphire orb, asking to be realigned with his purpose. The orb spins and shoots light in all directions through his aura. E'am offers his hand to the man he knocked down. "I'm sorry," he says. "I had no right to strike you."

The crowds boo E'am, and urge the man to fight. "You watch yourself," the man says to E'am. "When we have EmFire we won't need you anymore."

The man storms off, the crowds disburse, and E'am strides on. He keeps his eyes down, trying to avoid other *Dream Life* images, but they pop up everywhere: villas by the sea, sprawling homes in the Atalan Mountains, emerald lasers erasing age lines.

People tug on his arm, their voices urgent with concern. "Don't cross Da'krah's decision to raise the Emerald Force." E'am shakes them off and walks faster. Last week people inquired about Luca's welfare. As spiritual leader for Earth, Luca was revered. Now it appears Dark Master's promises reign supreme.

E'am keeps his thoughts on his mission. If Da'krah accepts the Honor Killing, humanity will survive. If he refuses, all could be lost. An Honor Killing can only happen if Time Blade clears Da'krah's Diamond Intelligence long enough for him to receive a sweeping recognition of Time, and his place in it. The prince must remember his true purpose on Earth. Then Dark Master's treachery will be apparent, and Da'krah will realize he cannot escape the ruler on Earth. Death by Time Blade comes as a friend.

Leaving the city, E'am pulls up a light path, and rides the steep incline to the Emerald Palace, a citadel of grandeur at every glance. Four towers climb into the sky, connected by long arched buildings inlaid with mosaics of gold and carnelian. Gardens run down the hillside, ablaze with flowers laid out in geometric patterns and crisscrossed with pathways of crushed emeralds. RT ends a short distance from the palace. Guards parade along the top of a tall stone wall, daggers flashing, clubs swinging. Crowds riot at the palace gates, the young, the old, and the infirm, shouting *EmFire Now! EmFire Now! EmFire Now!*

At the walled entrance to the palace, E'am passes the scrutiny of two guards, and enters the front courtyard of the palace. Four men fall in behind him, suited in armor.

"The prince expects me," E'am says, annoyed, as he has never been followed by guards before.

The men ignore him, their eyes fixed on something above his head. E'am balls his fists, then relaxes them. *Focus. Time Blade. Honor Killing.* He skirts a bank of fountains ablaze with emerald light. People stream in and out of the palace, guards in tow. Wind ripples the edges of the silk tunic hiding Time Blade. Some think the Blade is a myth—a tale told to inspire people to value their time on Earth. Few know E'am won guardianship of the Blade last year. Luca thought it best not to announce the transfer of custody due the razz's constant referral to him as the Killer E.

Entering the receiving gallery, E'am glances at murals painted on the vaulted ceiling, mostly of naked women frolicking in woods and meadows. The main staircase stretches before him—an extravaganza of marble inlaid with emeralds and gold. He mounts the stairs slowly, and the guards follow on his heels, their disgruntled breath falling hot on his neck.

At the second floor, E'am turns right and stops outside the wood-carved doors leading to Da'krah's study. "Advise the prince the Master's Witness awaits him."

CHAPTER FIFTEEN

Da'krah lounges behind his desk, a gleaming slab of lapis lazuli perched on blocks of gold. He wears a lavish crown of emeralds and diamonds—gems darkened by the long shadows of Dark Master's cape. The ruler's presence is more intense than usual today. He lurks behind Da'krah like a giant bird of prey, and his influence gives rise to E'am's ego. *I am the mightiest man on the planet. The prince will tremble and fall before me. I am unbeatable.* E'am glances inward to the orb. *Cleanse me of these ravings, please.*

The prince shuffles documents, keeping E'am waiting, as he always does. E'am endures his attitude, as he always does. Rivalry festers between him and the prince in and out of the sporting arena. They clash like opposing forces of nature, as if needing to diminish the other in order to survive.

"Ah ... E'am!" Da'krah looks up, acting surprised to find him in the room. "I trust you are well."

E'am nods. "Never better."

"Good ... good. Sit ... please. Give me another moment."

The prince wears robes encrusted with jewels and knee-high boots cut from animal skins, embroidered with ferocious, cat-like creatures leaping through fire. One such breed bounds across the tunic he wears today, covering his chest. E'am takes note of the design, mapping the route of the Glorious Plunge against the animal's body.

E'am has not visited Da'krah under circumstances that could result in physical violence before. He notes the slant of the wood-planked floors, the placement of hand-woven rugs, chairs and sofas, and a long marble conference table. A wall of floor-to-ceiling windows offers sweeping views of the Sea of Ruberah. Wooden rafters span the ceiling, supporting iron-winged chandeliers.

Da'krah rises from his chair, his sharp-boned features twisted in question. "You're still standing."

"I am." At the mention of those sacred words, Time strikes the folds of Dark Master's cape, rendering him motionless. E'am feels his consciousness rising. Like a silver cloud, it sails free from the causes of his worldly life, and settles in his atom of brilliance—his place among the multi-billions of others. The light of Time shines through his eyes and onto the prince.

Da'krah's body jerks as if having a seizure of sorts, then little by little, his shoulders drop and he relaxes his stance. The prince's own jeweled intelligence shines clear and bright above his head, and the revelation of his true purpose on Earth unfolds in his memory.

E'am speaks, his voice coming softly as if reading a bedtime story to a beloved child. "Da'krah, I visit you on behalf of Time." He withdraws Time Blade from its sheath, touches the tip of the blade to Da'krah's chin and tilts the handle so the jewels of the seven kingdoms reflect in the prince's eyes. "Through no fault of your own, you have been possessed by Dark Master, and your plan to ignite EmFire poses grave danger to humanity.

You cannot escape the Ruler of the Underworld, except by death. You are hereby offered an Honor Killing—death by Time Blade—swift, erased of karma, and with safe return to your star body. Da'krah, do you surrender your life for the benefit of mankind?"

The prince's eyes remain glazed, captured in the reflection of the gems on Time Blade. The warmth of his life force grazes E'am's hand.

The Glorious Thrust can only be executed with compassion.

E'am feared that would be a feeling beyond his reach, but it is not. It arose with the offer of death—love for the one he must kill.

Entranced by his celestial origins, Da'krah looks posed to accept the Honor Killing. E'am lowers Time Blade, as the prince must be free to respond from his worldly mind. Before he can utter a word, Dark Master's cape swings back into action and falls over Da'krah, blinding him to his jeweled intelligence. The ruler's tinny voice echoes in E'am's ear. *Kill the Master's Witness!*

Da'krah clenches his jaw. Outrage burns in his eyes. He points a trembling finger at E'am. "You dare to make me this offer ... you who are not even of royal blood?"

E'am lays Time Blade on Da'krah's desk, as it cannot be used in conflict with mankind. The prince will seek his death as commanded by Dark Master. It's written in the stiffening of his body and the grimace on his face.

Da'krah crouches, fists up, a sly grin creasing his face. "Show me the Killer E now?"

E'am laughs, a goading sound. "Are you sure you want to fight, Dakky Boy, in those pretty clothes?"

The prince lunges forward and barrels his fists into E'am's chest. E'am leaps right, then left, taming his temper, enough to pull on his sapphire forces and soften the blow of Dak'rah's punches.

Da'krah grins, baring clenched teeth. "Sol'aria will help me raise EmFire. You didn't know that, did you?"

His words stir E'am's doubts about Sol'aria and EmFire, but he cannot afford that distraction. The prince draws upon the brute strength of Dark Master. Spirit fire is E'am strength, but he must stay centered to use it. Mentally, he bows to the orb, evokes the power of sapphires into his hands, then smashes his knuckles into Da'krah's jaw, once, then twice. "You will never raise EmFire!" he yells.

Da'krah pummels his fists into E'am's ribs, driving him backward. E'am makes brief eye contact with him. The prince smirks. "Sol'aria likes me."

E'am jumps sideways, avoiding the prince's attack. "You'll have to do better than that, Dakky Boy. The ruler has already played the Sol'aria card today." E'am directs the forces of sapphires into his feet, and leaps into a backward somersault. No sooner does he land, than Da'krah charges him, driving his head into E'am's neck. E'am kicks him in the shins, knocking him off balance.

"You're nothing but common filth," Da'krah yells, coming at E'am again, ramming his fists into E'am like a machine stuck in high gear.

"At least I'm not Dark Master's puppet, the scum of the world." E'am knees Da'krah in the groin. He winces. E'am breaks free. "That's you, Dakky Boy." He floods his hands with the fire of sapphires, and drives his fists into Da'krah's temples. The prince's skin splits. Blood oozes.

Da'krah's eyes bulge like those of the wild animal on his tunic. He swats the air between them as if losing direction, but he hasn't. He grabs E'am by the waist, drives him against the wall of windows, and bangs his skull against the panes. The glass cracks. Blood trickles down E'am's neck. The prince gains a chokehold on his throat.

"How do you like that, Killer E? Give me the codes to siphon Rube into my kingdom, or your life is over."

A thousand red-hot pokers dig into E'am's head. He closes his eyes, blocking Da'krah's face from sight.

The prince tightens his grip. "The codes, or death?"

Dark Master's shadow closes around E'am. Fear mounts—visions of living forever in the prison of the Black Heart. *No.* E'am glances inward to the orb, and looks back at the prince through his jeweled sight. The radiance of Da'krah's diamond intelligence glows at the top of his head, beneath the shadows of the ruler's cape. E'am lifts a panel of the diamond light from the prince and slides it down in front of his body. Da'krah's hand falls away from E'am's throat. *How about that, Dakky boy?*

Confusion contorts the prince's features, but he keeps pounding his fists against the panel—the energy of his very own jeweled power. With a momentary advantage, E'am drives the prince back to the middle of the room, but Da'krah is far from defeated. He withdraws a dagger from inside his boot and lunges at E'am.

E'am jumps onto the conference table, then leaps, reaching for a wooden beam. He misses. The prince is on the table, coming at him with the knife. E'am quicksteps backward, then leaps again. This time he grabs the arms of a chandelier and swings his feet, kicking at Da'krah's head. The prince whacks at E'am with the dagger wildly as if making his way through a jungle. The blade slices into E'am's right calf. Blood plops onto the table. E'am feels dizzy, as if losing consciousness. *No. Not here. Not now.* He keeps swinging on the chandelier until he gains enough momentum to latch onto a wooden beam above. He hauls himself up and lies on the wood, his breath coming short and fast.

Da'krah scoops a chair onto the table, coming after him. E'am steadies his mind and gazes back into the glow above the prince's head. Using his spirit fire, E'am lifts another three panels from Da'krah's diamond power. The prince climbs onto the beam, eyes blazing, dagger pointed at E'am.

"Ready to die by my blade, Killer E?"

"With that little knife, Dakky Boy?" E'am pants under the effort of aligning the diamond shields to cover his body.

"Your blood looks good on my table," Da'krah says, "and you're losing it fast. I'll nick your jugular and let you bleed out. Watch you die."

The prince thrusts the dagger at E'am's throat, but it falls blunt against the light panels. Da'krah stabs again and again, his eyes growing wide with fear.

"What's wrong, Dakky Boy? Can't bring yourself to kill me?"

The prince leaps onto the floor and heads toward the door, shouting for his guards. E'am drops the four light panels over Da'krah, boxing him in, and stopping him dead in his tracks. The prince bangs his fist against the panels, yelling for help. His pleas echo around and around, bouncing off the light of his own diamond intelligence.

E'am limps up to him. "How do you like that, Dakky Boy? Aced by the Killer E."

CHAPTER SIXTEEN

He lies on a table in a consulting room in the palace clinic, his breathing weakened from the loss of blood. Verez, the medical director, lifts instruments from a tray and pries glass from E'am's skull. He hasn't seen Verez since his early teenage years when he wore her patience thin, always turning up with broken bones and bloodied noses.

"Those are knife wounds, E'am. I'll have to file a report."

"I was on an assignment for Luca. He would not want you to do that."

"When will I hear that from Luca?"

"Come on, Verez. You can trust me."

"I have three sons, remember?"

The Vertical, a long cylinder of ruby light, bubbles beside E'am. Verez selects metal arms from the tube, arranges them over his head, and unwraps blood-soaked linens on his arm and leg.

"This is a sheet embroidered with the emblem of the Prince of the Emerald Kingdom," Verez says, examining the item up close. Her eyebrows shoot up. "You fought with Da'krah?"

"It was nothing."

Verez shakes her head. "I hope Sol'aria can handle you." She swabs his cuts and adjusts the arms of the Vertical over his wounds. E'am lets out a breath of relief as the pink mists of rubies sink into his body, easing his pain.

"You know the procedure," Verez says, leaving the room. "Work with Rube. I'll be back in ten minutes."

Healing is a joint venture between patient, practitioner, and Rube. E'am looks into the rosy mist emanating from the Vertical, holding gratitude in his heart for his life, his place beside Master, for being entrusted with Time Blade, and the love he shares with Sol'aria. As the mists seep into his skin, he visualizes the healing essence of rubies filtering over the planet, helping all in need of care. Ruby rays zap his body, closing the cuts on his skull and the gashes in his arms and legs.

Sol'aria greets E'am in a flurry of distress, touching his cheeks. "You're flushed. You've been under the laser. What happened? Were you badly hurt?"

"No."

"Oh!" She gushes, "Really, E, I don't understand why you go to the public clinic instead of my father's doctors. Verez is such a bossy bitch."

"Maybe I'm used to that."

She frowns. "Are you implying—?"

"I am. Come here." He wraps an arm around her waist and nuzzles her neck, but she pulls away.

"Not yet. What happened? LiLi said you tried to kill Daks."

"Does that sound like me?"

"No ... but ... did you?"

"Did you tell Da'krah you'd help him raise EmFire?"

"I don't report to you, E'am. I work for the Goddess."

"And it's all right with her if you help Da'krah—"

"E." Soli levels a purposeful gaze on him. "We agreed not to question each other about our work."

E'am backs down because he has a great deal he cannot tell her. She cannot know he offered Da'krah an Honor Killing. His work with the Blade is sacred, between him and Master.

Soli swishes her hair over one shoulder, a sensuous move with the promise of sex. "Why did you fight with Daks?" she asks.

"You know how we are," he says in a casual manner. "We goaded each other and things got out of hand."

"What did Daks say to raise the beast in you?"

"That you agreed to help him ignite EmFire."

"I listened to what he has to say about EmFire. I have to, out of respect for LiLi. Don't fight with me over this, darling."

"I don't want to, but you must know I am opposed to EmFire. We're a long way from being ready to use the power of emeralds. I've searched the astral forces—"

"Don't." She wags a finger at him.

"Don't what?"

"Give me a lesson in cosmic science."

"Come on, Soli. You know that wasn't my intention."

"Good. I want to talk about us."

She leads him to a small sofa in a bay window overlooking the water gardens. He hopes she's not thinking of changing the menu or the flowers for the wedding banquet. She's done that three times already, drawing E'am into decisions that cause chaos for palace staff. He sits beside her. Plants rise from bright colored pots and trees fill the bay, branching over the loveseat.

"About my darling sister LiLi." She darts him a steely glance—a warning not to interrupt her. A change in wedding festivities seems suddenly less daunting. "We're going to be family, E, and I can no longer bear it that you don't see LiLi for who she truly is. I'm going to share something sacred about her."

"If it's sacred between the two of you, you probably shouldn't."

Soli wrings her hands, and sets a pleading gaze on him.

"Right. I'm listening."

"I just want us all to be happy together," she says in a wistful voice.

"I do too, my love. I'll try to be more thoughtful."

She nuzzles his cheek and cups his face in her hands. "LiLi first met Daks in the primordial," she says.

"Didn't we all meet there?"

"Honestly, E'am! My father says you're good at listening. Could you just apply that talent to me for a few minutes?"

"Yes. What happened?"

She tells him the story he already knows about Da'krah, but he keeps quiet and listens.

"Li'ram left her star in the Ruby Sphere at the exact time as Da'krah left his in the Diamond Galaxy, in response to Gold's call for star beings to come into life on Earth and help rebuild the human family. LiLi and Daks collided while riding the golden highway into the primordial. Literally," she says, eyes glowing, "they fell into each other's arms and into love."

Her skin glows, as if radiated by the Sun Flame in her heart. He thinks of last night at the ruby hot pools, of looking into her heart. How loving she is on the inside, how luscious on the outside.

"LiLi loves *that* man… the star being who volunteered to become Prince of the Emerald Kingdom, to guide and cherish the emerald mountain and its great force. That's who LiLi sees when she looks at Daks. Isn't that divine?"

E'am manages a smile. Many people know the cosmic origins of their love, but it's typical of Li'ram to claim that hers with Da'krah eclipses all others. "Yes. Wonderful."

"There's more, darling. Daks had his little star daughter with him when LiLi met him on the way to Earth." Soli grips E'am's arms as if clinging to edge of life. "LiLi fell in love with the child too, and that little girl is in the golden sands of the primordial waiting to be born to her and Daks." She presses his hand against her heart. The iridescence of the pearl kingdom shimmers in her eyes. "LiLi is already pregnant with her!"

"Why?" he asks, surprised, as it's considered an advantage for the child if it's conceived after the Goddess blends souls in the Rings of Ruby Fire. It helps bring the abundance of rubies into the child's life—a talent for creativity and happiness.

Soli glowers at him. "I just told you the most wonderful news, and you ask me why. What is the matter with you?"

"We've always been careful not to get pregnant, following the advice of the Goddess. I don't understand why Li'ram would ignore that."

"Lots of people don't wait for the ceremony of the ruby rings, and they have beautiful children. Why aren't you happy for LiLi?"

"If she's happy, I'm happy for her."

"You're just saying that. You're not exuding happiness."

"You're being offhand about an issue you previously held sacrosanct."

She heaves a heavy sigh and looks at him as if at her wits' end. "When a child is already on the way, it changes everything."

He backs off. The subject has crawled under her skin, and he senses nothing but trouble should he argue further. "Did you get my message about having dinner with my parents tonight?"

"I can't, E. I can't leave LiLi. She's in my bedroom sobbing. She can't even talk to Daks, as he is anesthetized and under the care of his doctors."

"Da'krah is pretending, Soli. He's playing for sympathy. He was in better shape than I when I left him."

"But he can't heal himself with Rube, can he? If you had escorted LiLi into the EK as she asked you to do, this would never have happened."

He shifts his glance away from hers. Da'krah might claim E'am tried to kill him but he will not mention the offer of an Honor Killing. That would imply a wrongdoing on his part, a concept foreign to Da'krah.

His astral disk dings, reminding him of his meeting with Luca. "I—"

"You have to leave," she says. "Are you going to see Daddy?"

"Uh-hum."

She smiles, a sweet parting of her lips. "Darling." She edges closer to him. "You know, the only reason LiLi and

Daks aren't married is because Daddy hasn't given them his blessing."

"Maybe it's not the right time. You know how your father is. He looks at everyone from his Sun Heart. He sees all that we could be and he likes to allow that to unfold."

"Yes, but LiLi feels she would be quicker to realize all that if she was married to Daks. She would be of great help to him. You could tell that to Daddy. He loves and respects you. You're the son he never had. You can ask him for anything, and it would make him happy to know you cared about LiLi, especially since you just had a fight with Daks."

There it is again, the assumption that he could influence Luca. "I'm your father's student and Witness. It would be inappropriate for me to question his decisions about Li'ram."

"Hail, Zan'drah!" She flings her arms over head, wailing the Goddess's name. "Don't be so damned high-minded. Get down here with the rest of us and help LiLi."

CHAPTER SEVENTEEN

Luca lounges in his wheelchair, talking to Nett. An attendant lays a shawl over Master's knees and another on his shoulders. E'am enters, grief pinching his heart. "How are you?" he asks, striding up to Luca.

"Better than you, by the looks of you."

Master dismisses Nett, and he leaves the room, glancing at E'am and shaking his head, his mouth in solemn repose.

E'am knows nothing of Nett's background, where he comes from or how he met Luca. Nett keeps to himself, as tightly as he carries his arms to his sides, but he's more than just an executive assistant. Luca retreats into the Atalan Mountains for the last three days of every month. No one knows where he goes or how to reach him, except Nett. During these absences, Nett handles Luca's affairs with the ease of someone in full command of the Master's world.

Luca coughs and sputters. E'am draws close to him. "Can I get you some water?"

"No."

Luca dismisses his nursing staff, and E'am draws up the mauve silk chair.

"I understand from Verez you took quite a beating," Luca says.

"I won the fight."

"How would you rate your performance with the Blade?"

"Excellent."

"Did you use the exact words given by Time when you offered the Honor Killing?"

"I did."

Luca rolls his hand, inviting more information. E'am describes Da'krah's reaction, the moments when he appeared ready to accept an Honor Killing, and then E'am's own experience of being in Time.

"Ah." Luca beams. "You went into timeless time: *I am.*"

"I think so. It felt like I became a part of Time, one of those multi-billions of perfect consciousness."

"You are. Everyone is. Why would we live under something we had neither knowledge nor control of?"

"Control?" E'am asks.

Master pulls on the shawl covering his legs, tugging it up to his waist. "When it comes to Time, surrender is control. You experienced that firsthand today." Luca rolls the chair toward his bed. "It's a gift to meet *I am.* Did you thank Da'krah before you left him?"

E'am glances down—ashamed he forgot to honor his opponent. "I'll do better next time."

Luca scoots the wheelchair up to the windows. "Sleep with the Blade tonight. Review the laws."

Another night away from Sol'aria. He considers asking Master about blessing Li'ram's marriage to Da'krah, as she requested. More important issues come to mind. "May I ask you something about Sol'aria?"

What is it?"

"Da'krah told me Sol'aria had agreed to help him raise EmFire. At the time, I thought he was just goading me, but Sol'aria is so committed to her sister. She wants Li'ram to be with Da'krah... I don't know. Would she help Da'krah? Could she?"

"I hope not, but you carry Time Blade, E'am. You know the rules."

"I must not inflict my will upon her?"

Luca chuckles. "You'd have better luck trying that with me than my daughter. Loving a woman is a precarious journey at best, and even more so for a man with commitments to Time, Earth, and mankind. It's hard to juggle devotion."

"You do it."

"The Sun Heart is not ruled by emotion." Luca wheels the chair around to face E'am. "One person might be so traumatized by an event that it knocks them free from their ego and awakens them to their place in the wonder of creation. Another might become lost in a field of great suffering and commit unimaginable offenses against others, and an infinitesimal gap divides the two."

"But Sol'aria carries the Sun Flame. She must consider that above all other causes."

"And you bear guardianship of Time Blade, yet you did not bow to Da'krah in gratitude for presenting him death by the Blade." Luca holds his hand up to prevent E'am from speaking. "Don't berate yourself. E'am. Forgive yourself. You're loved in a magnitude beyond the understanding of your Earth heart. Trust in that."

The filmy elixir of bliss floats over Master's eyes. E'am feels it shading his vision too—a soft golden glow. It's perfect sight, open only to the magnitude—the love that keeps on giving.

CHAPTER EIGHTEEN

Nett messages E'am, "Where are you?"

"Leaving my parents' home. Why?"

"Go to the Hall of Time."

E'am's heart lurches. The land sways. "What's happening?"

"Hall of Time. Hurry!"

He runs through the palace gardens, and enters the Hall. It's cool and strangely silent inside. Blood pounds in his temples. His heart hammers in his chest. An eerie luminosity hangs over the Cycles of Time.

"E'am!"

He looks about him. Brilliance floods the hall, coming at him from all directions. "Luca, is that you?"

"It is."

"Where are you? I can't see you."

"I'm in my death process."

"No!" E'am yells. "No ... please don't die, Luca." Tears stream from his eyes.

"Control your mind, E'am. Do not fall into your emotions. I will pass this plane within minutes. Absorb the light of my death. You will need it."

"I'm coming to see you."

"I ask you not to. Those gathered at my bed weep. You are of greater use to mankind where you are. Remember the magnitude, E'am. Trust in that."

"Please ..." His voice breaks, and tears choke his throat.

"I have instructions for you, E'am. Tell me you stand ready to receive them."

"I ..." He musters his will. "I'm ready."

"My funeral will take place tomorrow. You know the plans. After my body is burned, the palace scribe will read my Will for the People. Slip away then, unnoticed. Travel to my retreat in the mountains. Tell no one of your whereabouts. My spirit will be in the Council of the Lord Gods. We will meet there."

"I will see you again?" E'am asks.

"Indeed. You are my Witness. You will attest to my life review in the Council of the Lords."

"Luca ... please ... you can't leave. Not now."

"It is my time."

The brilliance vanishes. E'am doubles over, gasping as the loss of his teacher unravels and swells in his heart. Aloneness eats at the core of his being, ravishing him like a beast claiming its due. Chimes ring on his astral disk. He glances at his messages: twelve from Sol'aria, alone.

He checks RubeVision. FAREWELL BELOVED MASTER. The funeral route is displayed. Tomorrow will be a holiday—a national day of mourning. Pictures of Luca flow across the screen.

E'am messages his parents, assuring them he is coping with the loss of Luca. He feels divided, shredded into a thousand pieces—caught in a death of his own—which he is—the death of his dependence on Luca.

He approaches Sol'aria's apartment via a rear staircase, avoiding those teeming through the main hallways. He messages her. "I'm outside your bedroom door."

Sol'aria swings the door open. "Where have you been?"

Her grief hits E'am like a blast of humidity. Her eyes are red and puffy and her hair disheveled. "I'm sorry," E'am says.

"Sorry?" Soli tugs him inside. "Why didn't you come when I needed you?" She slumps on her bed, and slaps her hand against her heart. "The doctors predicted he would die tonight. Where have you been all evening?"

"Having dinner with my family. You know that."

She looks up, sniffles, and wipes her nose with the back of her hand. "He loved you … more than anyone."

"That's not true. He loved you—"

"Don't. He left me. He chose death over me." She sobs.

He hugs her. "Soli, he had to honor—"

"Don't!" She gasps a breath. "It's not just the loss of Daddy. It's everything. LiLi is devastated. Can you imagine? Daddy … dear, darling Daddy who never spoke against anyone's deepest longing, died without blessing her marriage to Da'krah."

E'am expects her to ask him if he'd mentioned that to Master last night, but she doesn't. She's probably too upset to remember.

"How could he leave me?" Soli asks, her eyes searching his.

"He didn't, Soli. He kept his contract with Time."

"Don't!" she yells. "I don't want to hear about Time and its bloody hold on us."

She crumbles into tears again. "And now Mummy won't allow Da'krah to come to the palace tonight to comfort LiLi."

"That's a matter of protocol. Da'krah has to arrive tomorrow as the Prince of the Emerald Kingdom." E'am wonders how he will he get through tomorrow. He has to walk in the funeral procession beside Da'krah.

"Darling." She heaves a hefty breath and runs her palm over her stomach. The corners of her mouth twitch in a tiny smile. She eases her arms around his neck. "Let's create something beautiful from our sorrow. I just checked my cycle. The time is right for me to conceive. Give me a child."

He should have expected it. Li'ram is pregnant, and so she wants to be too. "I think we should wait for the Goddess to blend our souls in the ruby rings. We've always said we would."

"I need to be carrying life. My father left me. I need a part of you alive in me."

"In a few days the Goddess will harmonize our souls in the Ruby Rings. That's a definite advantage for the child."

"We are in harmony."

"Let's not take a chance on that."

"What?" Her jaw drops open and shock freezes her expression.

He swallows hard, the crucial issue of EmFire pounding on his conscience. "I'm not sure where you stand on EmFire."

She furrows her brow. "How could you bring that up at a time like this?" She pummels her fists into his chest. "You uncaring, beastly man."

"Come on." He strokes her cheek. "I'm the man who loves you."

She sniffles. "I never thought you would deny me a child."

P. Christina Greenaway   137

"I'm not. I believe in the wisdom of the Goddess, and we have a lifetime to build a family."

Her eyes flood with more tears. "I thought Daddy would at least stay alive until we were married."

"I doubt he had control over that."

"Come to bed. Hold me the whole night through."

He feels ripped down the middle. He must walk away from the girl he loves on the night her father died, and tomorrow he will vanish from her father's funeral without telling her why or where he's going. "Your father left instructions—work I must do on his behalf. I have to start on that tonight."

"You're leaving me, now?"

"It's not a choice, Soli."

She pulls away from him. Hurt darkens her eyes, and the silence between them shatters his hearing. Nothing should be more important than helping her through this time of loss, and yet it is.

"Soli," he whispers, "your father worked for the people. He held their cause above all others and he asked me to complete certain tasks for him. You work for the people too. When the Goddess requires your services you respond, regardless of all other plans."

She draws her arms around herself, her bottom lip quivering. "But I need you tonight."

"I'm sorry." He backs slowly away from her. "I have to meet your father's dying requests."

Nett waits for E'am outside the Hall of Time, arms close to his body, tucking grief behind duty.

"Master asked me to offer my services to you," Nett says.

"In what way?" E'am asks.

"He informed me that you will leave for his mountain retreat during the funeral ceremonies tomorrow. He thought you might like me to tell Sol'aria after you have gone."

"What will you tell her?"

"The truth—just carefully worded."

"I thought no one was to know."

"Not prior to your departure. It will be easier that way."

"Where is Luca's retreat?"

Nett places his hands together in front of his face, tapping his fingers. "You will travel there via SunTransit. Ride a light path to the eastern end of the Atalan Mountains, and then contact Astral Command. The Goddess will link you to SunVision."

E'am runs a hand through his hair, his mind racing. "Where is Master's retreat?"

Nett shakes his head. "I cannot tell you."

"Why not?"

"It's a high and sacred place unknown to anyone in Ruberah." Nett bows. "Fore'tune to travel well."

CHAPTER NINETEEN

Wrapped in white silk, Luca's body lies atop a pyre made of tree limbs, assembled by the palace gardeners—the men who shoulder him on his final journey. A sash of sun crystals glitters on his chest.

The funeral procession departs the palace. Queen Leah, Li'ram, and Sol'aria walk behind the body, dressed in the silks of their native jewel kingdoms: amethyst for the Queen, pearl for Sol'aria, and ruby for Li'ram. E'am follows the royal women, walking abreast with Da'krah, Prince of the Emerald Kingdom. Da'krah rode into the palace ten minutes ago astride a white steed—a fanfare of wind instruments announcing his arrival—an unseemly extravagance considering the occasion. Anger rages in E'am, a sorry bedmate for grief.

The cortege heads west into the peach and gold skies of the setting sun, and E'am catches a close-up view of Da'krah. His skin is pasty, thick with make-up, and his hair has been combed forward in an attempt to cover the wounds he sustained in yesterday's fight. They have not acknowledged one another. Violence lurks between them.

Queen Leah holds her head high, looking regal and resolute. The funeral was planned weeks ago, but several key people could not work at Rube Operations today. E'am spent hours at CTS filling in for them. Duties as princess of the realm have kept Sol'aria busy. They have not spoken since E'am left her last night, but she messaged him a few minutes ago.

Our house is ready. Meet me there after the funeral.

Another change of heart. Soli had cherished the idea of them being there for the first time as man and wife.

The voices of the Deva Chorus rise from Mt. Rube and float over the river. People line the streets and the riverbanks, chanting with the Devas. The cortege moves slowly. Governors and other dignitaries walk behind E'am and Da'krah. The palace staff, headed by Nett, takes up the rear. The procession arrives at Peacewater Bend, a grassy curve on the banks of the pink, sparkling waters of the River Az. The gardeners lower the pyre onto the Passing Stone, a golden square mined from the Earth's heart and laid into the ground by the first inhabitants of Earth.

The Now is always above the Passing Stone.

A fire blazes in a cauldron to the right of Luca's body. To the left is a small platform where the palace scribe will read Luca's Will for the People. E'am read that earlier today, as he will slip away at that time. *Slip away.* He's slipping away from Sol'aria—away from his family—slipping into the unknown. A chilling sensation creeps over him—as if deep inside he knows exactly where he is going, and yet he does not.

River Spirit swims up to the Passing Stone, her soft aqua gaze resting on Luca's body on the pyre. Oohs and aahs pass among the crowds. River Spirit beckons to Queen Leah, and Leah approaches the river and kneels. River Spirit touches Leah on the forehead, and they spend a few minutes together. Li'ram visits River Spirit after her mother, and then Sol'aria. E'am catches

Sol'aria's glance as she walks back to the Passing Stone, her eyes flooded with tears.

River Spirit beckons E'am to come forward. He kneels before her. Luca, her beloved father from the Sun Kingdom, has left the planet, and yet she radiates peace and joy, as she always does.

"Beloved, E'am, is there anything I can do for you?"

"Grant me a little of the grace that flows through you," he says. "I am lost and fearful."

"My love is ever with you."

For a moment he feels mercifully distanced from the grief tearing at his heart. There must be a hundred things he should ask the beloved guide, but Sol'aria tops his concerns. "I'm worried about Sol'aria. I think her sister, influenced by her love for Da'krah, sways Sol'aria's thinking about EmFire. I'm afraid Dark Master will prey upon her."

River Spirit touches her fingers to E'am's forehead. "We are all tied to the Black Heart through weaknesses unique to our own nature. Love, if it blinds you to your true self, becomes a weakness. Both Li'ram and Sol'aria suffer from this condition. Great gifts from the soul are hard to manage in the material world. Have compassion for them."

He bends closer to River Spirit. "I must fulfill Luca's last wishes, which require that I leave Ruberah today. I am forbidden to tell anyone where I am going, not even Sol'aria. She will be hurt and probably angry with me. Please look after her."

River Spirit brushes a glittering hand over his brow. "My darling child, Sol'aria has but to remember me and I will be with her." She holds E'am in her soft aqua gaze.

"The student burns the Master's body," she whispers. "Do that now."

E'am rises, and stands beside Luca's body. Faces blur into the glitter of jewels. He lifts the sun crystals from Luca's body and lays them over Leah's shoulders. Leah clings to his hand. "Don't go," she whispers.

Her eyes plead, as if warning him of some terrible danger lying in wait for him. "I will always be here for you," E'am says, slowly withdrawing from her.

He picks up a long-handled flare, dips it in the flames, and bows to Luca's body. He stifles sobs rising in his chest and plunges the fire into the wooden raft. The gardeners push the pyre from the Passing Stone into the river. Luca floats upstream, an island of flames.

The people chant with the Deva Chorus and hold their hands to the sky, emitting rays of pink light—love to guide Luca's spirit home. The Palace Scribe steps onto the wooden platform and unfurls the scroll of Luca's Will for the People. Silence falls. The royal women gaze steadily at the scribe. E'am steps backwards into the crowds, slipping away. Looking over his shoulder, he scours the scene. All eyes rest on the scribe as he reads Luca's Will for them—a tribute filled with gratitude for the time Luca had spent among them, his beloved friends.

E'am quickens his pace, keeping his gaze down, avoiding eye contact with others. He darts through backstreets and side alleys and climbs a hill near the outer limits of the city. He pauses and looks back to Peacewater Bend.

The scribe descends the platform and people disperse. Sol'aria glances around, looking for him, no doubt.

Da'krah slips an arm around Li'ram's waist and then around Sol'aria's. E'am feels sick and retches as if to vomit. Leah attempts to draw Sol'aria away with her, but Sol'aria remains with Li'ram and Da'krah. A sense of foreboding creeps through E'am.

He spots Nett shouldering his way toward Sol'aria. The little man draws her aside. What carefully chosen truth does he tell to explain E'am's absence? Whatever, it leaves Sol'aria aghast. Li'ram rushes to her side. Sol'aria buries her head in her sister's chest, sobbing.

E'am aches to run back and comfort her, but Da'krah assumes that role.

Time Blade chose you. It trusts you.

Dusk falls. Smoke drifts into the afterglow of sunset. People continue to stream into the city, surging toward the river, following Luca's body upstream. E'am catches a light path and crosses the plains. He travels at top speed, zipping past Mt. Rube, and then further out past the air terminal. The light path comes to an abrupt end. Az'Rubia, the jewel of the Atalan Mountains, towers 27,000 feet above him, its snow-clad peak shrouded in mist.

He taps ASTRAL COMMAND, and lowers his eye to the sapphire orb glowing on his astral disk.

"This is Zan'drah."

Reaching the Goddess directly knocks E'am off guard, as the fire of her presence makes him nervous. He usually talks to at least two or three people before connecting with her, giving him time to gear up for the speed-of-light responses she expects. He clears his throat. "This is E'am."

Ding ... beep ... ding.

"Your disk is now programmed for SunVision. Do you have any questions?"

Pressure pounds in his head, and his screen glows with umpteen icons, all unknown to him. "Where is the Sun Transit symbol?"

"First screen, second to last icon on the right. Anything else?"

He pictures Zan'drah in Astral Command, scanning instruments that track the lights and sounds of rubies as they interact with other galaxies and planets. He perceives her assessing multiple situations, of which his is one. "No. Thank you."

"Fore'tune to travel well."

Ding ... beep...ding.

E'am wipes sweat from his forehead, feeling a nudge of anger at Luca. Why didn't he tell him about all this? His finger hovers over the Silver Sun emblem. The loss of his teacher settles like a hollow in his soul, sloshing grief over his every thought. He taps Sun Transit.

A voice responds. "I am Ami, programmed intelligence. Speak your destination."

"Luca's retreat."

"That destination does not exist. Do you refer to Ataleah?"

The name means nothing to E'am but since he doesn't know where he's going anyway, he says, "Yes."

"Ataleah is a preset destination. Do not attempt to alter your speed or direction while traveling. To ascend, place your heels firmly against the base of the mountain, lean back, and press your spine to the rock."

E'am follows the instructions, the hard surface of AzRubia digging into his back. A luminous white glow spreads beneath him, and his feet leave the ground, holding him in a cloud of silver light.

Ami speaks. "Focus on your orb. The jewels in your headband and your sandals will seal you to SunVision. Do not move your feet while traveling. Keep your arms close to your body. Do not look down. Ascent will begin in ten seconds."

Fright seizes E'am. What if he moves his feet? What if ... *No!* He focuses on a simple breathing exercise to prevent thought. He closes his eyes, looks inward to the orb, and inhales. *One ... two ... three ... four... exhale, one ... two ...three ... four.* His body begins to ascend. His heart leaps to his throat. He continues the count, keeping his feet and arms frozen in place and his eyes glued shut. Inhale ... exhale, over and over, breathing in and out until his breath locks into the rhythm of four. The orb glows brighter and brighter, exuding multiple streams of light that spin over and around each other, moving faster and faster until they blur into one blaze of white light. He zones out. Nothingness.

"This is Ami. You have arrived at the Ataleah Ledge."

E'am coughs, gasping for air in the thin atmosphere, and blinks, adjusting his eyes to the glare of sunlight on snow. A silver glow floats over his face and his breathing becomes normal. The wind howls as if caught in an echo chamber, and the frigid air holds him captive. He fights to remain conscious, but the freeze tempts him to let go ... to become one with it. He senses that would be spectacular—cold, colder than death. What secrets lie there?

Another layer of silver light settles over his body, clinging to his bones like a second skin, radiating warmth.

"This is Ami. Your SunShield is affixed. Are you comfortable?"

"I am."

"You are now disconnected from Sun Transit. The Atal will come for you."

CHAPTER TWENTY

He stands on a plateau at the base of the peak of Az'Rubia, rising some five hundred feet above him. The sun breaks through clouds and burns mist off the land. A green valley comes into view, streaming with vines, orchards, and vegetation. As if in a mirage, a girl walks toward him, holding a small iron pot in her hands. Her head is shaved, except for a band of short, dark gold hair in the middle. Inked drawings cover her scalp, abstract symbols unrecognizable to E'am. Hundreds follow her, snaking back through the valley—men, women, and children, their skin a darker shade of bronze than the average Ruberian, and even the most aged among them bears the supple carriage of youth. Four young men flank the girl, two on either side, their features similar to hers in a familial way. She spreads her arms, holding the men back, and steps forward, approaching E'am.

"I am Asari," the girl says, "the leader of the Atal."

Flecks of gold sparkle in her eyes, evoking familiarity, but E'am cannot fathom why. He introduces himself to her, and she chuckles as if she already knows him. "I am not informed about your tribe," E'am says, raising a brow, waiting to hear of their origin and purpose.

"Master's soul." Asari holds the iron pot out to him.

"For me?" He taps his finger against his chest, feeling inadequate and unprepared.

She nods. "Not the all of it, just the pattern for his last life."

She tilts her head and studies him from a different angle, as if assessing him from a fresh viewpoint. She's slight, with narrow hips and shoulders. A saffron-colored skirt falls from her hips to her ankles and a band of the same material covers her breasts, barely. Inked drawings decorate her midriff—geometric symbols similar to those on her scalp.

He lifts the iron vessel from her hands. "What am I to do with this?"

"I will show you."

Five small children run up to him, and he crouches to meet them. They finger the sapphires on his head. "Why do you wear these?" a little girl asks.

"They make me smarter than I am."

"You won't need jewels up here," Asari says. "We live under the light of the Sun Kingdom. If you gaze long enough into the sky you will see traces of silver-gold— the SunShield made from Master's Sun Heart."

"It's easier to see at night," a small boy says.

Asari caresses the child's head. "These are my nieces and nephews." She introduces them to E'am, and then beckons for the young men who had walked beside her to come forward. "Please meet my brothers, Amah, Manne, Erose, and Zata." The men welcome E'am, bowing with hands clasped to their faces. He returns the gesture, and the brothers leave, taking their children with them.

"Children like you," Asari says, her voice lyrical with merriment.

"I have young brothers."

"Yes. Twins, is that right?"

He nods, feeling uncomfortable, as Luca has obviously told her about him and he had not known she existed. Asari turns and waves at the tribe, holding her arms above her head and bending her waist deeply from side to side. The people do the same in return, and then shuffle back through the valley.

"I will take you to the retreat house, yes?" she asks.

"Thank you."

She opens her hand and taps the screen of her astral disk. "I would like to document your visit to Ataleah. May I capture you on SunVision?"

Capture? That's exactly how he feels, a stranger caught in a land 27,000 feet above sea level, wearing a skin of light from the Sun Kingdom, in the hands of this girl, slight of build but obviously strong. "All right," he says.

"Thank you. That's lovely." She taps the screen again, selecting settings. "There," she says. "You won't be disturbed by a camera. SunVision follows thought."

A warning gongs in his head. "I'm not sure I understand. How does that work?"

She darts him a quizzical look, as if dealing with a backward child. "SunVision detects my thoughts. When I want a picture of you, filming begins."

"I ... er..." He scratches his head, thinking of the downfalls of such a system. "Why don't you just let me know when you—"

"Yes, of course." She grins, fluttering her thick black lashes, which appear too heavy for her eyelids. "There's the element of trust. You have my word I will only film you when I am with you. Shall we go to the house now?"

She doesn't wait for his answer. Holding her body erect, she takes off in long, purposeful strides. He catches up to her, letting go of the filming issue, as he has no idea how to deal with her. The hems of her skirt swish, revealing an anklet of sun crystals and golden rings on her toes.

"My mother has prepared foods for you—my father's favorite dishes."

"I hope I get a chance to thank her."

She laughs as if knowing something he doesn't, which no doubt she does. "How did Master's soul pattern get inside the pot?" he asks.

"When he first came to Earth from planet Miron he brought five segments of his soul with him and left them in five different vessels. The one you are carrying is the fourth, which means he will return to Earth once more to complete his contract with Time. Didn't he tell you this?"

"He mentioned it once, a long time ago. When I questioned him, he said I would know more about that if and when I needed to."

Asari laughs. "He was all too fond of that answer, wasn't he?"

E'am laughs too, bonding with her over Luca, which brings an element of comfort. He gives up wondering what he is supposed to do next, rolls his shoulders, and relaxes.

"I am seventeen," Asari says. "Like you, yes?"

He nods, and she tells him about her family. "We grow grapes and make wine," she says. "My brothers work for the vineyard and all of them have chosen life partners. I have not. I have something I must do first."

He waits, expecting to hear what that is, but she falls silent. He feels baited, as if she wants him to pursue the matter. The ancient knot in his chest trembles under a storm of gathering emotions. He changes the subject. "Do you work?"

"Among other things, I copy the classes given in your schools and reprogram them for SunVision. The Ataleah Valley wraps around the entire mountain and many children live in isolated areas. They study at home."

"You copy the courses?"

"Perhaps steal would be more correct."

"I'm sure we would give them to you if you asked."

"Our tribe is secret upon Earth."

"Why?"

"I will explain a little later. Here we are, the Master's retreat."

The house is a long stone building wedged between the peak of Az'Rubia and the rim of the Ataleah Ledge. Asari twists a crystal knob and opens the door. They enter a lofty hall with a large, wood-framed window at the other end. Endless sky fills the view. Sandalwood and amber scent the air—incenses Luca had often burned. The ache of his passing digs deeper in. E'am will miss him forever.

"The kitchen is down here," Asari says, swishing down a corridor.

She turns left and points to rooms along the way, a reading room and Master's study. The kitchen forms a perfect square with a table in the middle, laden with bread, fruits, nuts, and a dish of baked vegetables. Asari pauses, and flashes her left palm in his face. "Filming now."

He ducks, feeling self-conscious. "As long as you only film me when we're together—I'd rather not know when that happens."

She giggles and taps a jug. "Mountain water." She caresses a smaller pitcher. "This is Oooh." She purses her lips, whooshing the word on her breath. "Oooh is Master's divine nectar. He blended the grapes and made it himself. No one knows the ingredients. It's potent." She widens her eyes. "Very potent." She waves a warning finger. "One small glass."

"Or what?" he asks.

"Or Oooh to you."

"What does that mean?"

"You will fall into a sleep such as none other."

"And why wouldn't I want to do that?"

"Master said you were an astute student."

"That's different from doing as I am told."

She laughs a trill of musical notes. "I expect it is. Come ... I will show you the other rooms."

He follows her down another hallway. "Master's bedroom suite." She strides inside like a warrior to battle. The room rims the edge of the mountain with floor-to-ceiling windows. An oversize bed sits on an angle facing the peak of AzRubia. Bright colored rugs soften the stone floors.

She points to a doorway. "That's the bathroom and there's a hot spa outside, if you like to bathe under the stars."

He tightens his grip on the pot bearing Luca's soul, fighting off thoughts of bathing with her under the stars.

She opens the doors to a wardrobe. "You will find an assortment of clothing in your size."

He glances at togas, long pants and shirts—styles he wears at home. "For how long have you expected me?"

"Always."

"Always?" He grips the iron pot, fighting another bout of annoyance with Luca. How could he land him in a situation like this?

"Come." Asari pats her side as if calling a pet to heel. "I will show you where to place Master's soul."

She zips down another hallway, her skirts swishing, her bare shoulders brushing against his. The thrill of her rides over him, a girl like no other girl. The knot in his chest throbs. They pass under one of many arches leading into an enormous circular room, perhaps twice the size of the Hall of Time, with a silver domed ceiling. She taps her astral disk and the dome rolls open, revealing the peak of AzRubia, cutting into the sky, glacial and serene. E'am presses the iron pot against his heart, filing the image to memory.

"This is the Hall of Harmonies," Asari says. "Our tribe will meet you here tomorrow for Master's life review."

A low, soft humming tone fills his ears. "What is that sound?"

"It is the sound of you. It is your note in the universe."

"How do you know?"

"I answered it a long time ago."

"What does that mean?"

She fingers the iron pot carrying Luca's soul, and a cast of sadness crosses her expression, dimming the gold of her eyes. The long wave of his own grief thrashes against his heart. She touches his arm.

"You are a beautiful man. I hope you like me too."

He might be taken aback, but he's not. She looks at him with such sincerity, as if her life depends on his answer. "I like you very much," he says, sensing something grand and expansive running between them, long and fluid—the waters of Time.

"Until later, then." She departs, passing through a stone archway, leaving him in need of a glass of Oooh.

CHAPTER TWENTY-ONE

E'am finishes dinner, and carries the carafe of Oooh to the bedroom to savor a second glass. The nectar tastes both sweet and sour with a rich nutty undernote. The flavors blend in and out of each other, causing the need for another sip and then another to determine which is which. He soaks in a bath of bubbling hot water sunk into the edge of the mountain. The glow of the SunShield shimmers like a spider's web, undulating high and low behind the stars of the Ataleah Valley. He looks down over the long descent to Ruberah, over rock, glaciers, and valleys filled with clouds, mist, rain, and snow. Swallowing a fourth glass of the liquor, he relaxes, leaning back in the bath.

The night sky blurs into a haze of silver-blue mist, and he finds himself slipping in and out of memories from his life as Rae Blue. A girl bounds backward through the black hole, coming from the Sun Kingdom. She bows into Earth's Cycles of Time, offering her Sun Intelligence to serve mankind. Rae Blue's heart jolts in his chest, as a knot of feelings settles in—indecipherable in nature.

E'am sits up bolt straight in the bath, gripping the stone-rimmed edge. Had Asari been that girl? He squeezes his eyes open and closed, trying to clear his mind.

Think carefully about the Blade, Rae Blue. Time will be your master. Time blends souls and intelligence to suit evolution. It does not recognize the feelings of the human heart.

E'am grabs the carafe of Oooh, swigs the dregs of the liquor, and wanders into a fuzzy, funny world. "Oooh!" He pokes bubbles in the water and snorts and giggles. "Oooh!" Another bubble drifts toward him, huge and bright like a spacecraft powered by moonglow. He jabs it with his finger and laughs, a great bellowing roar of amusement, coming louder and louder, causing an ache in his ribs.

"Oooh, no! No. No. No. Oooh, I can't laugh anymore!" *One glass.*

He heaves himself from the bath, grabs a towel, and plunges onto the bed.

You are a beautiful man. I hope you like me too.

Heady feelings rush over him—delightful, delirious. Her laughter rings in his ears. She fills his sleep.

"Asari means happiness. You are happy with me, yes?"

"I am."

He caresses her head, running his fingers over the symbols on her scalp. "What do they mean?"

"They are the cosmic shapes of music."

He kisses her shoulders and her neck. She smells like clean air and sunshine.

"You are my first lover," she says.

"Are you sure I should be?"

"I am."

They kiss, and he feels like a man ripped from the pages of destiny—he has no past and no responsibilities but that of being her lover.

"Do everything to me," she whispers.

Being with her is like being a flame thrown into kindling. He's in a new place, unmarked by custom and unattached to consequence—free. He kisses her breasts and the symbols on her midriff. She tastes like morning dew. He enters her, she flinches briefly, and they move into the long, fluid strides of passion, traveling through that clear, crystal filament running between them—the waters of Time.

"Ascend with me into your astral body," she whispers. "Love me among the stars."

She leaves her human form and takes on her astral body—a blaze of suns patterned after her mortal self. He rises with her, melting into his body of sapphire light, all the while staying inside her in his physical form, feeling all the sensations of human passion. They twist and turn among the stars, coupled, like lovers from ages past and future, sweeping from one galaxy to another.

The radiance of The Curve comes into view, and the roar of z27 fills his ears. She guides them onto the arc and lays her back against its glow. She throws her arms over her head and arches her body. He thrusts into her, deeper and deeper. The sound of their ecstasy blends with the roar of the black hole. Celestial music drifts around them, forming shapes like those inked on her skin. He watches them float through the universe, linking the stars and planets.

Streams of silver-gold light pour from the black hole on the other side of The Curve and form an island in the golden sands of Earth's primordial plane. Two little children appear, a boy and girl, chasing each other around, playing tag.

"Twins," Asari says. "They're coming to us from the Sun Kingdom. Beautiful, aren't they?"

CHAPTER TWENTY-TWO

E'am awakens with a start, his head hurting as if filled with sand, his mouth tasting dry and bitter. He peers through half closed eyes, identifying his surroundings. Light streams in the windows, bouncing off the fresh snow blanketing the peak of AzRubia. He trudges to the bathroom, sloshes his face with cold water, and rinses his teeth with mint extract. Through the window he spots the tub at the edge of the mountain. Memory comes creeping back.

You will be my first lover.

Asari? Had he made love to her? Surely not. He must have dreamt he did.

You will fall into a sleep such as none other.

Her dewy scent laces the air as if she'd just left the room. Had she come to his bed last night? Had he, in an instant of passion, forgotten he was betrothed to Sol'aria? He clutches his stomach, nausea threatening.

He pads down the corridor to the kitchen and finds a fresh array of foods on the table. He drinks a jug of mountain water, and hunger strikes. He feasts on berries, creamy cooked grains, and green leaves tossed in oil, thinking about Asari, wondering why she had needed him to like her. Why wouldn't he? Anyone would. He carries the dishes to the sink, treading carefully over the worn floors, thinking of the many times Luca must have trodden them before him.

He returns to the Master's suite, still pondering Asari. She tempted him with the liquor—just one glass, or else—but he took her bait, and oh, so willingly. *You are a beautiful man.*

That had knocked him out of his senses and stranded him on uncertain turf, and he's still there, treading quicksand, and all the worse for drink. He showers, selects a shirt and a pair of pants designed for long hours of meditation, and climbs into them. The bed catches his attention.

You will be my first lover.

He grips the rumpled blankets and hauls them off, his glance landing on the fluids of passion and blood staining the sheets. With a quick rap on the door, Asari sails into the room, but then stops in her tracks at the sight of the bed.

"Why?" he asks.

She pulls on his arm. "Come outside with me."

They sit at the edge of the mountain, legs dangling, he uneasy, like a man awaiting judgment. She folds her hands together and looks to the sky.

"The Atal insures the future of the human family," she says. "Master brought them with him when he first left Miron—two hundred souls—those who died while saving others. The cream of the human family, he called them. No matter what befalls Ruberah, the tribe will survive."

Personal angst, hungry as it is, retreats for the moment. He works for Time, and the evolution of the human family must precede all other causes. "Luca never mentioned the Atal to me."

"Then it must be one of those things you would know when you needed to know." She glances at him sideways. "It's always fun when one of those arrives, yes?"

"I would have preferred to know about your tribe before I met you. Are you saying that if EmFire happens, Ataleah will not be destroyed?"

"That's right. The entire Atalan range will fall, but the SunShield will hold the Ataleah Valley and the tribe intact."

He swallows, digesting all that, his old anger at Luca but a heartbeat away. "And last night," he says, "what was that about?"

"Time called us to fulfill a destiny we agreed to eons ago, a way to ensure the evolution of humanity."

He stares at her, his jaw hanging open. "What destiny?"

"E'am." She touches his hand. "On the day Earth was born, we gave ourselves to Time, but what happened between us last night does not have to affect your relationship with Sol'aria. What is done in Ataleah is done for Earth and bears no karma in Ruberah. I am empowered to take the memory of us from you, and you will be just as you were before we met."

I am empowered? His heart skips a series of beats. He's never heard anyone but Luca use that expression. He studies her gold-flecked eyes, tall angular body, and the power and the steadiness of her purpose. "Are you Luca's daughter?"

"I am, and my brothers are his sons."

He blows out a long breath, trying to stabilize his mind. How could Luca lead a double life without so much of a hint of it to him? How could he send him here without a word of warning? Most fathers would kill a man who slept with both of his daughters, and yet it feels like Luca arranged it for him. "What ... what? Those children in the primordial?"

She speaks in whisper-soft tones. "I conceived two souls with you last night. Luca fathered five children with my mother. Those, plus our twins, are the seven destined to lead our people into the seven continents of the world. That's why Time brought us together."

"Don't you think you should have told me this before we—"

"You knew. Time paired us when we bowed into it, devoting ourselves to the evolution of the human family. I'm sure Time prompted your memory of that before we made love last might."

Made love!

Drunk as he had been, he recalls drifting into the silver-blue mists of Miron last night. He had seen himself as Rae Blue bowing into the Cycles of Time. "You're from the Sun Kingdom, aren't you?"

"I am. Time called me back to have these children with you. They will have my heart—the steady, intuitive Sun Heart—and your ability to focus and use your sapphire intelligence."

He gazes into the sky, her words crushing in on him. How will he manage his life from here on? "Did Luca know?"

"I am his only child from the Sun Kingdom. He knew I had a specific destiny, but we trod around it like skilled dancers. You know how he was, careful not to seek information about others unless invited to. I hope he didn't know. It would have been hard, even for him, to watch you and Sol'aria falling in love, knowing you had yet to meet me."

"How long have you known that I would—?"

"Father my children?" She chuckles, just like Luca used to when bemused by the world around him.

"Yes, that."

"From the first time I saw you on SunVision. Luca documented your classes on the Laws of Time Blade, and he sometimes let me watch them. I was seven when I first saw you."

"Seven! You knew about this ... about last night ... when you were seven?"

She expels a rise of laughter. "Not literally. I knew you were in my destiny." She takes his hand in hers. "You live in Ruberah. Let me take this memory from you."

"I can't. If Time called me to create these children with you, I will be their father and take care of them for as long as I live."

"Time does not require that of you."

He thinks of how his father had cautioned him to be careful with girls. Being a parent was a sacred calling. If he made a girl pregnant, then he had answered that call. "I require it of myself."

"What about Sol'aria?" Asari asks. "What will you tell her?"

"The truth. She'll be upset, of course, but Sol'aria carries the Sun Flame. She can center in her Pearl Intelligence and know what is right for mankind."

Asari looks over the edge of the mountain, twirling her feet and swinging her legs. "Yes, but in telling her

about us, you are likely to knock her into such an emotional turmoil that she might not even remember her
jeweled intelligence."

"I doubt that. Solaria works for the Goddess. She can't
afford to lose contact with part of herself."

Asari gazes at him through the tangle of her lashes,
steady and intent. "I will offer to take this memory from
you again before you leave. Think about it, please."

CHAPTER TWENTY-THREE

The tribe sits cross-legged on the floor, hundreds of them filling the Hall of Harmonies. E'am sits likewise in their midst. Everyone chants OM, producing layers upon layers of notes, rising and falling. The iron pot containing Luca's soul pattern rests beside E'am. He closes his eyes to surrender to the orb, fighting his way past thoughts of Sol'aria. He's here for Luca, his beloved teacher. The spaces between the chant get longer and longer, and regret fades into oblivion.

He picks up the iron pot with Master's soul pattern, and holds it against his heart. A silver-gold brilliance wafts in through the open roof, and Luca walks toward E'am, handsome and strong, the man of his youth. Love rules—strong and steady—the love above all others.

"Come with me, E'am."

He grips Master's hand, and they walk into the Council of the Lords, as they have done so many times before. The twelve lords for Earth gather around them. Everyone bows to everyone, and Luca directs E'am to place the iron pot inside the light of Earth's crown, which lies on the floor in their midst. He does as asked, clutching Master's hand as if holding himself from death's door.

Luca whispers, "You're ready, E'am. You can do whatever is asked of you."

"I don't know about that."

"I do."

Luca pats him on the head in his manner of saying all is well, you will understand. "Free my soul," he whispers.

E'am removes the lid from the iron pot, and the silver-gold light of the Sun Kingdom showers the atmosphere. Luca's life review speeds by, a flood of images streaked with a single line of white light. Everything Master did, he did for the benefit of mankind. He created no causes in need of correction. He would return to Earth by choice or invitation.

The Lords confer with Luca, and then Master returns to E'am, beaming and exuding good humor. The floodgates of regret open for E'am. How could he ever have been angry with this man? "I'm so sorry," he says, "for all the times I was ungrateful toward you. Can you forgive me?"

"There's nothing to forgive. In fact, quite the opposite." Luca rests his arm on E'am's shoulder. "You wrote a destiny with the anger you held against me as Rae Blue— one that pleases me greatly."

"What?" E'am tightens his fists. Surely Asari is more than enough destiny to inherit from Rae Blue. He glances down, avoiding Luca's eyes, hoping he does not know what passed between him and Asari last night.

"My beloved E'am, what have you done that I have not done?"

He looks into Master's gaze, wondering how he will he live without his understanding. "What shall I tell Sol'aria?"

"There is no right or wrong way to handle that. It's a matter of what you can live with."

E'am rubs his eyes. "I should have heeded you when you warned me Time would be a hard master."

Luca chuckles. "Every now and then someone has to leap boldly into Time as you did when you lived as Rae Blue. It is a noble act, and the human family evolves by the grace of those who do it." Master lays an arm on E'am's shoulder. "The Sun Heart is not easily won. To love mankind above your own desires requires great sacrifice. You have come so far on that journey, don't falter now."

"What destiny did I bring upon myself by being angry with you for not saving the people of Miron?"

Master gives his shoulder a big squeeze. "It is one thing to understand the law intellectually and another to uphold it, especially in the face of disaster. When you questioned why I did not save the millions who died on planet Miron, you opened the door to know the answer firsthand. Now, you must go forth and take my place as Master for Earth."

"No!" E'am shouts, but the forces of Luca's Sun Heart rush around him, a blaze of white fire, whirling like winds at hurricane force—making mush of his will. He holds his hands up, trying to avoid the onslaught, but it's hopeless. He's inside the white fire with his mind stretched to the far corners of the cosmos, his body bouncing on a sea of silver-gold suns.

CHAPTER TWENTY-FOUR

E'am speeds through the hallways of the palace, wearing a hooded sweater to conceal his face. He ducks in the back door to his private office. Nett waits for him, sitting on the far side of his desk.

"Thank you for being here." E'am flops in his chair. Earth's crown sits on his head, a mass of luminosity—feather light—heavy with responsibility.

Nett peers over the tops of his glasses, eyes up. "It suits you," he says. "Congratulations, young Master."

"Please ... I'm not comfortable with that title." E'am glances at RubeScreen on his desk. Messages drift by—hundreds of them—at least a dozen from Sol'aria and one from Queen Leah marked MOST URGENT. Nett's memo, the one that had called E'am back to Ruberah, still glows on the screen: EMFIRE GAINING APPROVAL IN RUBERAH. "Fill me in on EmFire," he says.

Nett taps his fingers in front of his face. "While you were gone, Princess Li'ram attempted to enter the EK disguised as a man, her way of getting around the escort rule. She was so convincing that a couple of teenage girls locked arms with her and asked her to take them into the kingdom. Li'ram tried to shake them off but the girls didn't give up. A fight broke out. Security hauled the three of them off to prison. Li'ram's true identity was discovered, and the royal counsel was called. Palace Relations created a story and released it to the public."

"What story?"

"That Li'ram had been willing to risk her own safety to be able to tell the people firsthand how dangerous it was, or was not, to enter the EK. Prince Da'krah embellished the tale, saying he had guards waiting on the other side of the bridge ... three men who would follow Li'ram to the palace. The couple appeared on RubeVision the next day, speaking of how much they loved one another and how they hoped their marriage would ensure the happiness of the people of both kingdoms. There was lots of snuggling, handholding, and talk of how EmFire would enrich everyone. The people adored them, and the merits of EmFire have gained wide appeal here in Ruberah."

E'am rubs his temples, raging inwardly at Li'ram. He'll have to act quickly, address the nation and outline the perils of the project. It would help to find out what Sol'aria knows about Da'krah's plans first, a daunting quest considering he must also tell her about Asari.

"The people know Luca made you Master," Nett says. "Unbeknownst to me or anyone else, Luca produced a video wherein he made the announcement. He programmed it to appear on the great screen in CTS Plaza the night of his funeral, after you had arrived on Ataleah."

"What did he say?"

"He told the people you had won guardianship of Time Blade, that you had studied hard for years and passed all the tests, and that he believed absolutely in your ability to guide the nation."

"Would you be comfortable working with me, Nett?" E'am holds up a hand. "Before you answer, let me first apologize for all the practical jokes I played on you as a child. I hope I didn't hurt your feelings."

"Nonsense, I was secretly every bit as amused as you."

"You hid that very well."

"That's one of my talents."

"Hiding things?"

"I am hiding a crime I committed a long time ago."

"Did Luca know about it?"

"He did."

"That's good enough for me."

"It's not a small crime. You should know I intended to kill a man."

E'am leans back, surprised, although after Luca placed Earth's crown on his head he thought nothing could ever shock him again. "You don't have to tell me about it. But for Luca, I would have killed Da'krah by now."

Nett pushes his bottom lip out, appearing lost in thought. "A man broke into my home when I was away and murdered my wife and child," he says, a pained look crossing his face. "Two years passed and the police did not find him. I hunted him down. Revenge ruled me." He looks E'am in the eye. "I had a knife to the man's throat when detectives burst upon the scene. I had been their prime suspect and they had shadowed me."

E'am rests his elbows on his desk, leaning forward. "I'm so sorry. I had no idea you suffered such a terrible loss."

"I was tried and found guilty of intent to murder and sentenced to life in prison. It didn't matter. I had nothing to live for, but then ..." He glances down, clasping his hands in his lap. "One day Luca visited the jail. I caught his glance as he walked by my cell and I felt myself lifted out of my misery. Luca asked the guard if he could speak with me privately." Nett pauses, his breath catching in his throat. "Master told me told me he was looking for a man he could trust, a clever man who would keep his secrets." Nett sighs. "Three days later I moved into the palace as his executive assistant. Of course grief returned, but I knew it didn't have to swallow me whole. I could find peace giving my all to Master, and I did."

Moved by the story, E'am feels doubly shamed for all the times he made fun of Nett. "Master often said, but for you his world would fall apart. I would greatly appreciate your help, Nett. Would you be willing to work with me?"

Nett drops his head in a bow. "I would be honored."

E'am leans across the desk and slaps palms with Nett. "I'll need thirty minutes on RubeVision, early evening, when families are gathered together. Can you arrange that?"

The queen stares out the window of her sitting room. Her shoulders slump forward and her hair falls unkempt, as if she just arose from her bed.

"Leah." E'am walks to her side. "You needed to see me?"

"Imagine," she says, gazing into the fountains outside, "I lived with him for years before I knew he had another family in Ataleah. I kept hoping to give him a son, when he already had three of them."

E'am closes his eyes to the sight of her pained expression. "Is there something I can do for you?"

Leah faces him. "I'm worried about Sol'aria. Will you also marry an Atal woman and have children for Earth?"

The directness of her question surprises him. "Sol'aria will be my only wife."

"Earth is a mistress more terrible than any woman, E'am. We can't live without her. She wins every hand every time." She releases a long sigh. "It happened in a glance, you know. I suddenly knew about his other family."

"I'm sorry, Leah."

She looks back to the window. "Every month when he returned from his retreat, I asked him about his time in the mountains. He always smiled in response, you know, gazing at me through those golden eyes, so mystical, so beautiful. Then one day when I said how was your retreat, his glance traveled past me, taking on a look of wonder—wonder that I knew had nothing to do with me. I confronted him. He told me. Asari had been born—his child from the Sun Kingdom."

He lays a hand on Leah's shoulder. "Luca loved you, Leah. You can't doubt that?"

She relaxes her back. "I was never unhappy in his company. The light of his Sun Heart washed jealousy from my own. I understood the Atal had a mission on Earth, and in some better part of myself I was grateful for them. It's just that now Luca is no longer here, it's hard to find that better part of myself, and I'm worried about you and Sol'aria. I see a change in you, E'am, and I sense the cause. What will you tell Sol'aria?"

E'am thinks of the children he glimpsed in the primordial, his with Asari. "I'll tell her the truth."

"And you think she'll understand?"

"You did."

Leah makes a throaty scoffing sound, then presses her lips together, holding her silence.

CHAPTER TWENTY-FIVE

Sol'aria struts the length of her drawing room gripping her head. "Where have you been? My father died and you disappeared!"

"I'm so sorry, Soli. I had to leave for the Master's retreat. I couldn't tell a soul about it. Only Nett knew. Didn't he explain to you?"

"This is us, E'am." She comes to a halt in front of him. "You and me," she shouts, banging a fist against his chest. "We promised each other we would never let anything come between us."

Fury fires off her, and the scales of justice swing in her favor. He'd better level the ground a little before she throws him out. "Our work comes first for both of us," he says. "We answer to a cause greater than ourselves. This is the path to the Sun Heart, Soli, and you know it's littered with sacrifice. Your father left instructions for me. I had to—"

"Secret instructions," she yells, eyes flashing, pacing back a few steps, then forward. "Secret from me, the woman who loves you, who gives herself to you, body and soul."

"Soli." He reaches to grasp her hands, but she dodges him.

"Don't. Stay where you are."

"Look," he says, "I don't intrude upon your work with the Goddess."

"But you know it takes me to the Sun Sanctuary at CTS. You could find me if you had to. Don't become my father, E. You can't vanish into the mountains for days, unreachable and unwilling to speak of where you are or what you're doing."

He wraps his arms around her before she can stop him. She wrestles with him, digging her elbows into his ribs, damming and cursing him. He keeps tightening his hold on her until she relents. "I'm sorry I hurt you," he says. "I had no idea Luca would make me Master. I'm having a hard time adjusting to it. I need you to understand, Soli."

Her voice quavers, and tears stream down her cheeks. "I can't believe Daddy did that, not that I doubt you can do the job, but how could he do this to me ... to us?"

"He did what was best for everyone," E'am says, stroking hair off her face. "He always did."

She sniffles. "You feel different, like you're not entirely mine anymore."

He feels wretched, like a traitor realizing the measure of his wrongdoing. "Soli," he whispers, "we share a bond, in that we both work for the people. If you do what is right as Sun Master, and I do what is right as Master for Earth, and if we accept one another in these causes— nothing can come between us."

She frowns, pulling away from him. "What is this leading up to?"

He guides her to the sofa in the bay window, thinking of how to tell her about Asari, a prearranged destiny called in by Time, the need for two souls from the Sun Kingdom to be born on Earth.

"Something has changed between us," Soli says. "What is it?"

He's not ready to tell her yet. He needs to soften the mood between them. "You've just suffered the loss of your father, and I wasn't here for you. You feel like I let you down."

"You did, but that's not it." She wrings her hands and sighs. "LiLi and Daks are so happy together. Everyone admires the love they share."

She flips her hair to one side and leans close to him, resting her head on his shoulder. Her fragrance permeates the air, amber, rich and sultry. His history with her marches across his mind's eye—the cheeky, smart little girl who always had her hand up in class, ready with answers. The years of fun and friendship, their first kiss, right here on this sofa. Catching the fire between them. It's all just a breath away, but is it a breath too far?

She brushes her lips against his ear. "I want you back."

"I'm here."

"Are you? Why aren't we in bed?"

His thoughts scatter, recalling the many times he's visited her here, scooping her up and whisking her into the bedroom. "I'm worried about EmFire," he says, saddened by how their lives have changed. "What have you decided about that?"

She jerks her head from his shoulder. "Everyone wants it. Daddy didn't question the project."

"Oh, he questioned it. He just didn't voice his opinion, as he didn't about anything, unless he was specifically asked to do so."

"You're lecturing me."

"Did you ever ask him what he thought about EmFire?"

She stiffens her back, distancing herself from him. "I asked you not to fight with me about this."

"I don't want to fight. I just want to know where you stand."

"Oh!" She flops back against him, lifting his hand and placing it against her heart. "You know, LiLi couldn't live without Daks."

Her breasts feel warm and inviting against his palm. "Dark Master shadows Da'krah," E'am says, pushing on. "He's a danger to mankind."

"LiLi is very powerful. She can resist Dark Master as well as you or I can. Eventually, she will knock him out of Da'krah's life."

"No one can do that for anyone else. You know that."

"Blending souls in the Ruby Rings brings rites, you know." She lowers her hand and caresses his thigh. "If you didn't have your head stuck in Time, you might discover these things."

He lifts her hand from his leg, holding it gently in his own. He cannot make love to her without first telling her what happened with Asari, and EmFire precedes all else at the moment. "Dark Master has gained a lot of power over the people," he says. "They believe EmFire will afford them riches, like villas by the sea and private spacecraft. Things they don't need."

"Who says they don't need them? We have these things. Why shouldn't everyone?"

"I don't have them, and I don't care about them."

"You do have them, through me," she says, snatching her hand from his.

"I don't need things to be happy and I don't know anyone who does. Rube gives us all we need. It heals us, brings love and happiness and opportunities to create new inventions, new industries. Isn't that enough?"

"You've never wanted for anything, E'am," she says, implying he could have no idea what that feels like, as if she did.

"No one wants for anything. Rube is equal among us."

"Well, then that can't be enough, because everyone wants EmFire."

His breath tremors in his throat. "Are you telling me you will assist Da'krah with the launch?"

"As you said, I work for the people."

He looks into her aura through his sapphire vision and detects a series of tiny black dots drifting close to her forehead—influences from Dark Master. Everyone carries them to some degree, but hers are clustering together, gaining power over her thinking process. The muscles in his chest tighten as the light of Earth's crown shines upon his mind's eye, reminding him he must not inflict his knowledge upon Sol'aria. How she uses the Sun Flame creates the path she must walk to find the Sun God within.

"Not everyone wants EmFire," he says. "I'm sure if I ask my friends and colleagues—"

"The majority wants it," she snaps.

He sits up straight. "We'll see. I'm going to put EmFire to a public vote."

"That vote is in. EmFire will happen on Sunday at midnight in the sky sanctuary at CTS. There." She falls back into her loving self, caressing his cheek. "I've confided in you. Please, my darling." She nuzzles his ear. "Don't resist this. I miss you. I love you. No more talk of work." She grins, assuming her playful manner. "Now you may begin your efforts to win my forgiveness for leaving me when I needed you."

Part of him longs to stay with her, to try to bring back the girl he loves, but another part of him counts the time ticking between now and EmFire.

"I can't stay. I have work to do."

She jumps to her feet and blocks his passage. "You're always working. Stop it. I need you. We need to heal this rift between us. Stay. Make love to me and we'll find our way back to each other."

"I cannot."

Her gaze bores into his, hard and accusing. "Is there someone else?"

His world shifts, and his carefully rehearsed story lays frozen in his mind.

"There's another woman, isn't there? That's what's wrong between us." She rams her fists against his chest. "Is it Ka'rine?"

"Of course not."

"Who then? Tell me?"

Loss settles over him, cold, empty and inevitable. He takes her hands in his. "It wasn't like that. It—"

"Don't touch me." She shakes herself free of his grip. "How could you?"

"It was ..." He stumbles, blood pounding in his temples. "It was predestined and based purely on genetics."

She blinks as if trying to bring him into focus. "Genetics? Are you telling me you made another woman pregnant after you refused to give me a child?"

"I did what Time asked of me. I did it for the future of the human family."

She slaps her hand against his cheek, stinging him with the full force of her fury. "Never come near me again," she shouts, her body shaking with rage.

CHAPTER TWENTY-SIX

E'am enters his private office, the sting of Sol'aria's hand still burning on his face. His body feels empty, as if life has been sucked out of him. He expected her to be hurt and angry, but he's not only lost her, he's lost her to EmFire.

Nett appears in the doorway, looking tentative, as if happening upon something he shouldn't see.

"Does anything need my immediate attention?" E'am asks.

"You must be tired. We could go over things in the morning."

"I'm fine. Sit, please." He gestures to a chair, and swivels a multi-screened monitor so they both can see it. "Anything unusual with Rube?"

Nett taps a keyboard and the RubeVision logo appears. He selects SUNDAY PROGRAMMING. Documentaries about EmFire fill the day, beginning at ten in the morning and running until *Blast Off* at midnight. *EmFire: Your Dream Life Now, Designing Your Beach Villa, Beautiful You, Your Family Airship, Your Genius Child,* and on and on.

"I've watched them all," Nett says, "and I've written a synopsis of each program and sent them to you."

"How did you manage that?"

"I have my ways."

"Who conducted the vote for EmFire?"

"Vote?" Nett frowns. "There's been no vote. A poll was taken shortly after Da'krah and Li'ram appeared on RubeVision. Seventy-four percent in favor of EmFire."

"Who took it? Who was surveyed?"

"I can get that information for you."

"No need. I want a public vote, and I'll set it up." He faces Nett. "You should know, I visited Sol'aria. She has agreed to help Da'krah raise EmFire."

"Ah!" Nett draws in a deep breath. "Sometimes the strongest of us are also the most fragile. Before I lost my family I was an architect, the lead designer of a new city to be built on the other side of Mt. Rube. I was among the happiest and the most grateful of men for the blessings in my life." He pauses, rubbing his eyes. "When I lost my family, I lost consciousness of my jeweled intelligence. It happened in a blink. I ... fell into darkness and I didn't care. I—"

"Don't go back there, Nett. It's not worth it."

"I think it is. Dark Master threatens us all. When I lost my family, I welcomed the swirling black masses of his cape. I lived for revenge, and I forgot all about my jeweled awareness and never thought of the city I had been commissioned to build."

Nett peers over the top of his glasses. "Do you feel compassion for me?"

"Of course."

"Then feel that for Sol'aria too."

Master's words come to mind. *One person might be so traumatized by an event that it knocks them free from their ego and awakens them to their place in the wonder of creation. Another might become lost in a field of great suffering and commit unimaginable offenses against others, and an infinitesimal gap divides the two.*

Nett fell through that gap and climbed out by the grace of Luca. Is there hope for Sol'aria? Might the Goddess offer her a helping hand?

CHAPTER TWENTY-SEVEN

Earth's crown lights up, and the Lords for Earth shimmer before E'am. "How may we help you, beloved E'am?"

"EmFire is scheduled for Sunday night. I must speak out against it, although as Master I know that is not wise. I am not able to sit by and let it happen. I will surrender the crown, should you ask me."

One Lord steps forward. "You were chosen for the man you are. The crown will remain under your care."

"I fear I might use these powers for personal reasons. If EmFire happens, I cannot leave my young brothers to certain death. I ask that I be allowed to take them to Ataleah. I'd like to take my parents, too, and as many children as I can gather."

The Lord responds, "You may escort your brothers to Ataleah, but if you mention your concerns over EmFire to your parents, you will make it harder for them to part with the twins. Your parents are healers. They would not leave the people in the face of disaster."

"And the other children?"

"You have no custody over them."

"Why not?"

"In supporting EmFire, their parents speak for them."

"I can't accept that. They are young and innocent. I cannot decide who should live and who should die. It's just too awful."

"You do not decide. The people do."

CHAPTER TWENTY-EIGHT

The white marble house where E'am grew up comes into view, situated on a creek near the Crystal Temple of Science. Shrubbery and flowering plants surround the gardens, and a typical collection of gems and crystals lines the front porch. E'am lays his left hand against a panel, and the front door eases open. "Hello, it's me!"

Mu'ri and Kar'um bound toward him, excited by the adventure finally coming their way. He hugs them both and kisses his parents. His mother tells the boys to go and collect their camping equipment, and immediately asks E'am about Solaria.

"You left her at her father's funeral without telling her where you were going," she says. "She came to see us. She was devastated. I wanted to balance her chakras, but she wouldn't let me. That's not like Sol'aria. She loves having me do that for her."

"We will talk about that." His father appears, and whisks E'am to his study.

The *Scrolls of Healing*—his father's writings—stack one upon another, covering the walls from floor to ceiling. "We had no foreknowledge that Luca would make you Master, E'am, but since he told me he would never ask you to do anything you were not prepared to do, I congratulate you. How are you managing?"

"As best I can."

"About Sol'aria." His father lowers himself onto the couch, indicating E'am should sit beside him.

"Dad, I—"

"Let me speak. Sol'aria ran from our house, sobbing. I tried to catch her and bring her back, but she caught a light path and escaped. Your mother and I came to the same conclusion: Sol'aria exhibits all the symptoms of Broken Heart Syndrome."

"No. That's not possible. Not Sol'aria. She's the strongest-willed person I know. Her father died. I had to go out of town. She's emotional. She'll come out of this."

"She's lost control. Young women in this state do reckless things. Obviously, something has come between you. Repair it, E'am. Spend time with her. Reassure her of your love for her."

"How far up are we going?" Mu'ri asks, gazing up the mountain.

E'am steers his brothers toward the place where he caught SunVision on his last visit. "We're going to the Ataleah Ledge, about five hundred feet below the mountain peak. It is a very special place known only by a very few, because it is home to a tribe whose mission is secret on Earth."

The boys bubble with questions. He silences them, telling them they will spend time with the tribe and learn about them firsthand. "But," he says, looking from one to the other, "I want your solemn promise this trip will remain a secret between the three of us. That you will never speak of Ataleah or the Atal to anyone—not even to Mum and Dad."

The boys promise and cheer and slap hands. He locates Sun Transit on his astral disk and explains to the boys how it will carry them to the Ataleah Ledge.

"When we arrive, a glow of light will cover your body, providing oxygen and protection against the cold. After a few moments, you won't notice it anymore. Are you ready to go?"

"Ready!" they shout.

He gathers the boys in his arms, stands with his back pressed against the mountain, and connects to Programmed Intelligence. Ami responds, asking for his destination.

"Ataleah."

"Ataleah is a preset destination. Do not attempt to alter your speed or direction while traveling."

The lustrous shining of the Sun Kingdom spreads beneath E'am's feet. Seconds later, he and his brothers ascend the mountain. The journey is not as harrowing the second time around. Caring for his brothers occupies his mind.

Asari greets them at Ataleah, introducing herself to the twins, telling them her name means happiness.

"I'm Mu'ri and this is Ka'rum," Mu'ri says boldly, "but we don't know the meaning of our names."

"Then that's something we will find out." Asari beckons to her brothers' children—three boys and two girls—to come and join her. Mu'ri and Ka'rum run into the valley with them, never looking back.

E'am starts after them. "I must tell them I'm not staying the night."

Asari tugs on his arm. "Give them a chance to bond with our children first. Come, let's walk together."

He follows her onto a trail at the base of the mountain peak. She wears white pants today, falling from her hips to her ankles, and an orange bandana around her breasts. Being with her feels like stepping into an alternate universe, a place far from the heartache of Sol'aria.

"EmFire is scheduled for Sunday night," E'am says. "Sol'aria has agreed to help Da'krah with the launch."

"Today is Saturday. She could change her mind by tomorrow."

"I did a terrible job of telling her about us."

"There was no good way to do that, E'am, but Sol'aria had probably decided about EmFire before you told her."

"Yes. She suddenly sees herself as a girl born with privileges that others should have too. In her new altruistic world, she believes EmFire is the answer. Dark Master has influenced her. I picked up on his presence in her aura."

Asari links her arm through his. "I think she's driven by love for her sister, wanting her to be happy with Da'krah, more than she has consciously chosen to support EmFire."

"But she carries the Sun Flame, and she must not use it except with full awareness. If in doubt, she should consult the Goddess."

Asari slows her pace. "I could still take the memory of us from you. I am Sol'aria's half sister. The helix of our ancestry is very strong. We feel inexplicitly connected to those in our bloodline. Sol'aria could sense my presence through your thoughts. If I am gone from your memory it could lessen her pain."

E'am draws them to a halt. "I've tried to reach Sol'aria again and again, but she doesn't answer my calls. I can't pursue her anymore. I have to give my all to stopping EmFire, and I can't have any gaps in my consciousness."

She tilts her head, reappraising him like she did when they first met, and then walks on. "I must not fall in love with you."

His foot freezes mid-stride. "Is there any danger of that?"

"If I become emotionally entangled with you, I will create causes that will draw me back to Earth. I will not be able to return to the Sun Kingdom at the end of this life."

"Having children together is a big entanglement, isn't it?"

"Yes, more than I bargained for."

He'd not thought about falling in love with Asari, but now that he knows he must not, that knot in his chest unravels and the idea takes on a life of its own. The path becomes steeper and rockier. Love comes forward, all of a sudden, as if out of a secret hiding place—flooding the corridors of his heart. They tread over vines, twisted and sprawling along the path. Asari hangs on his arm, hugging close to his body. His hand falls on her bare skin, over the inked drawings of the music of the cosmos.

"Do you know where Luca is now?" he asks, needing a change of subject.

"Yes."

"Where?"

They round a corner and arrive on the far side of the mountain. Asari sits on a grassy ledge, and he joins her. He senses her blending with her Sun awareness, a familiarity gained from all his years with Luca. Looking into the orb, he drifts into a plane of silver-gold light with her. Clouds fill the vista—some puffy and white, some thin and streaked with gray, mauve, and gold.

Asari speaks as if reading a story drifting across the sky. "On planet Miron, Luca wore the Sun Crown—ten thousand suns, each a universe unto itself. After *The Ending* of Miron, he tossed that crown into the Cycles of Time. Luca is in all those suns. He's here too." She pats the earth beside her. "His fifth soul pattern is buried here, the life he has yet to lead on Earth." She trails her fingers over the grass. "Lovely isn't it? He warms the ground upon which we sit. Can you feel it?"

E'am does, but whether by fact or by suggestion, he cannot tell. "What is it like in the Sun Kingdom?"

She draws her knees to her chest and rests her elbows on them. "It is like when you are one with the happiness of Rube."

"What do you do?"

"What did you do the last time you felt the happiness of Rube?"

He recalls being in the palace clinic. Rube had healed the wounds Da'krah inflicted on his body. He felt the happiness then. "I shared it," he says. "I sent the light of Rube over the planet, asking it to help those in need."

She smiles. "That's what we do in the Sun Kingdom."

"Tell me more."

"When you share the blessings of Rube, the twelve petals of your heart chakra ascend to the top of your head and blend with your crown chakra. You are one with your true nature, and there will come a time when those petals will remain there. You will not drop back into the emotions of your Earth Heart, and then you will find the Sun Heart."

"Thinking and living in the highest realms of my soul?"

"That and more. Universes are being born all the time. Some need our help. Others are highly developed and help us to grow. The Sun Kingdom is but a link in a chain of ever-expanding consciousness. We are destined to ascend the Sun Kingdom, just as you are destined to enter it. Nothing stays as it is. Wonderful, yes?"

Maybe, if you never fall from the high realms of your soul, such as he did in his life as Rae Blue. "Where is Luca in this grand scheme of things?"

"Everywhere. He always said he's just unfolded a greater understanding of creation than most of us."

"Did you go to the Sun Kingdom from Miron, or were you born there?"

She stretches her legs out and twirls her feet in circles. "I lived hundreds of lives on planet Miron, sometimes as a powerful leader of industry and sometimes a sad person bereft of love. My last life, according to Luca, was my crowning glory. My mother was a servant in Luca's palace, a cleaning lady assigned to his private suite. She trained me to work with her. You know how Luca was with his staff. He treated them as extended family. My mother revered him and considered herself the luckiest woman in the world to be of any significance in his life. She passed that reverence on to me. I cleaned his rooms for all the days of my life, made complete and joyful by the touch of his presence. When I died, he appeared to me and asked me if I would like to live in the Sun Kingdom."

That couldn't be more different than E'am had imagined. He had assumed it would take some heroic measure of courage to pass through z27. "What was it like, going through the black hole?"

"You're in your astral body, of course—the pattern body for the human form. The darkness inside z27 is actually the inside out of light. Once you enter the hole, it becomes sheer brilliance—brighter than ten thousand Sun Crowns stacked together. As you leave z27, your astral body dissolves and the patterns for the organs and glands in your human body burst into stars and planets. You birth your own universe, and your Sun Heart shines at its center, giving life."

He peers at her from the corners of his eyes, wondering if she's playing with him. She faces him full on. He searches her gaze—the light of truth.

Wind sweeps snow off the mountain and whirls it around them, dusting her lashes with flakes. He'd like to hold her and kiss her, but EmFire weighs him down. "I'm addressing the people tonight on RubeVision. I'll spell out the dangers of EmFire. Then a screen will pop up on everyone's astral disk and they can vote for or against EmFire, right then and there. If half the population votes NO, the government can stop the launch. It's not a permanent solution, but it will give me time. I can devise

ways to help people remain more alert to the tempta-
tions of Dark Master."

She smiles, a dazzling beam that defies her narrow
features, then looks back to the sky. Silence falls between
them—the soft silence of precious time. "I filmed us the
night I conceived our children," she says. "Not all of it,
just when we looked into the golden sands of the primordial. Would you like to see that?"

"Yes," he whispers.

She taps her astral disk and a visual pops up, showing the golden sands of Earth's primordial plane. His
face appears at the edge, leaning in, gazing at his children, a girl and a boy chasing each other around, playing tag. They catch his glance and wave back at him.
"Daddy."

His voice chokes with feelings. "They're beautiful."

"My mother filmed Luca's expression when he first
gazed at me. Love poured from his eyes, just as it did
from yours at the sight of our children. I feel my father's
love every time I watch that video. It is ever alive, and it
keeps me on track with my purpose."

"Can you copy this video to me?"

"Are you sure? SunVision will remain in your astral
disk for as long as you live on Earth."

"I'm sure."

"Remember, the love we shared to bring these children to Earth came from the Sun Kingdom. It is not ours
to keep."

"No one controls my heart but me, Asari. No rule, no
kingdom beyond this one."

She taps her astral disk. "The visual is with you."

A feather-soft energy whisks over him, light as air but laden with the graces of happiness, peace, and a sense of harmony with all creation. He's lost the girl he's always loved, and loves a girl he must not love with a love that it is not even his—but this airy happiness, this gift of fathering two beautiful little souls will live on.

Nett's call notes chime, and E'am glances at his astral disk.

EMFIRE RE-SCHEDULED FOR TONIGHT!

CHAPTER TWENTY-NINE

Nett ushers E'am to the Elite monitor, and highlights the AUXILIARY, a secondary force designed for emergency use. Excessive amounts of Rube rush through passages burrowed deep beneath the ocean, headed for the emerald mountain—enough to launch EmFire within the hour.

"Someone deliberately blocked the AUXULIARY from view," Nett says. "I discovered it in a random search using SunVision. Da'krah must have an accomplice at CTS."

E'am steels his mind against doom and disaster, keeping space for the Lords to advise him. Obviously, Da'krah reasoned E'am would speak out against EmFire, and so moved the launch forward. The Elite team gathers around him, pitching solutions. Ka'rine pushes up close, breasts bulging, robe skin-tight. "I'm sorry to hear about you and Sol'aria," she whispers.

Despite imminent disaster, E'am recalls the feel of Ka'rine's hand inside his shorts that day after school. Hunger glows in her eyes, wild and unnatural. E'am cuts away from her glance, connects with Earth's crown, and asks the Lords for guidance on EmFire.

Light illumines his thoughts. He opens SunVision on his astral disk, and cuts Rube at its source. The room goes dark, as does the whole of Ruberah and the EK. Sirens wail all over the city and emergency evacuation procedures go into effect. People leave homes, offices, and schools and gather in shelters designed to withstand extreme weather conditions, mostly hurricanes and tidal waves—nothing that will protect them against EmFire.

He activates RUBE II, an emergency generator dedicated to RE. The screens blaze back to life. Moving to the front of the group, E'am addresses his co-workers. "Disaster is by no means certain," he says. "I will work with Time Blade and do everything possible to avert EmFire. Go home. Be with your families."

No one moves. All stand still, as if in a group sculpture. He's touched by their loyalty. "You can do nothing here," he says, "but you can be of comfort to those who love you. That will be of the greatest help to me."

People file out, bidding him farewell. Ka'rine clings to his arm, insisting she stay. He steers her to the door. "I can only work alone."

"Be mine. Come into the next life with me. We'll spin the world a little faster and draw all things wonderful to us."

"You have to go."

"I want you, E'am, and I always get what I want."

The cold glint of determination darkens her eyes. E'am grips her by the shoulders and shoves her through the doorway. "Go home."

She glances back at him from the hall, curling her lips in a crooked smile. "You shouldn't have pushed me like that. You'll regret it, and you should have fucked me when you could. Now you'll die wanting me, and that makes you mine.

F O R E V E R."

E'am tries to blot out her words, but they echo on and on in his head. He curses his foolishness. He's indebted himself to unfinished business with Ka'rine, but he can't think about that now. He beckons to Nett. "You must leave too," he says, holding the door open.

Nett shakes his head. "This is my home. I will look after things in the palace." He pushes his glasses up his nose. "Luca would be proud of you."

E'am runs through the Hall of Time and enters the north sanctuary. Moonlight pours through the massive blue and gold stained glass window, glistening on the steel altar. He lays his left palm against the cold, hard metal. The lid rolls open. Time Blade rests on its bed of black silk. Despite EmFire, excitement prickles his senses. He lifts the knife, and the astral fires of the seven jewel kingdoms run through his body. He rolls his shoulders, taking on their power, then holds the Blade against his heart. *Whatever you ask of me, I am.*

Using EARTH IMAGINING, E'am scans the coastline of the EK. Torches of fire light up the land, and people swarm the beaches and the cliffs, linking arms and chanting, *EmFire Now.* Waves lap against the emerald mountain a short distance off shore, still half submerged beneath the sea. Da'krah's palace towers high on the cliffs, but the prince will not be at home. He'll be in the Sun Sanctuary in the golden pyramid atop CTS, the place where Sol'aria and Li'ram command the cosmic forces of sound and sunlight.

E'am tilts the EI lens down and scours the ocean bed. Ruby fire swirls at the base of the emerald mountain, mounding and gaining momentum. He has about ten minutes to reach the Passing Stone, cut Time, stop the launch, and expel the leaders of EmFire from the planet.

E'am dashes from the palace, heading for Peacewater Bend, lengthening his stride with every step, willing his body to go faster and faster. People crowd the streets, chanting, *EmFire now!* Their faces skew with worry at the sight of him flying past them waving Time Blade.

A man shouts, "The Killer E has Time Blade! We're all going to die!"

He keeps flashing the Blade, all the while veering left toward Peacewater Bend. Hundreds gather by the Passing Stone, where Luca's body had lain just two days ago.

"Move," he shouts. "Get off the Stone."

Most flee. A few remain, shouting for EmFire. E'am points the Blade at them. They cower away, moving backwards, their eyes glazed with fear. His heart thunders in his chest and blood drums in his temples. At last the Killer E nickname is working in his favor.

Aim the Blade at the pyramid atop the Crystal Temple of Science. Cast your eye along the top edge of the rim. Once aligned, tilt the blade straight up. The Cycles of Time will appear and the tip of Time Blade will be on the black dot in the center—the Now.

Easing his eye to the ridge of the Blade, E'am follows the protocol. The skies part, and the Cycles of Time shine through. The great loops of the past and future glow with the pink light of rubies. Time hums, low, immense, and eternal. E'am lodges the tip of Time Blade into the black dot where the past and the future cross over—the Now.

Permission to cut Time and prevent EmFire.
Granted.

Using EARTH IMAGING, E'am scours the inside of the emerald mountain. A column of ruby fire spirals from the base to the peak. His blade arm trembles. EmFire is already in action! He has but a few seconds to cut Time. He steadies the Blade on the black dot, then axes it straight down through the Now. The knotty cords of the past split open but a millisecond too late. EmFire explodes, ripping the emerald mountain from the ocean and tossing its massive jeweled body into the air. Rivers of green fire blaze over the land of Ruberah.

Cliffs crack and crumble. Red-hot lava plunders the hills and rolls into the streets. Buildings collapse. Crowds surge toward the quay, stumbling over the dead as they attempt to leap onto ships and sail away. The Crystal Temple of Science splinters, then shatters to the ground. Gale-force winds lift large plates of glass from the streets, blowing them this way and that, slicing limbs from those caught in the crossfire.

Failure daunts E'am, and Dark Master swoops in, waving his cape. "Get away from me," E'am yells.

You belong to me. Everyone belongs to me. Give up your foolish fight, and I will give you a seat of power beside me.

E'am's body shakes, and his breath tremors with fury.
You will never take me.

Fire burns E'am's feet, but he steels himself against pain. He draws a breath, gathers energy from the orb, and blasts Dark Master with the flames of sapphires. The ruler whips his cape from side to side, dodging them.

EmFire is mine. I have all of eternity to claim it. You will perish soon, but your weaknesses will live on, and I'll be waiting for you in your next life.

The ruler flees, and E'am thinks back to his lessons with Master.

If you miss the mark, you may ask to rewind Time.

The land rumbles and cracks beneath E'am, and the gold in the Passing Stone splinters apart. E'am widens his stance. He must keep both feet firmly planted on the mineral, connected to Gold, the Earth's Heart. He holds the Blade against his heart.

Permission to rewind Time and prevent EmFire.

Your request is in review.

Luca warned E'am this could take a while. Time must search eternity and evaluate what is best for the evolution of mankind. E'am prepares for the wait, breathing in and out to the count of four, keeping his mind open to the Lords.

A tunnel of white light opens in space, and an object sails down through it, fluttering like layers of silk on a summer breeze. E'am adjusts EI and magnifies the scene. A design is printed on the square of light—a circle with twelve triangles inside. It lands at the base of Mt. Rube, and the land separates in twelve sections. Mt. Rube sinks through the opening, dropping all the way down to the ocean bed, settling without so much as a splinter to the massive jewel.

E'am bows his head, and words pass his lips without thought. "I will raise Mt. Rube back to Earth."

The Lords for Earth speak: *Remember the twelve diagonals. Imprint that pattern on your jeweled intelligence.*

E'am speaks: *It is done. May I reverse Time now?*

That request is still in review.

The Reverse must be completed within two minutes of the disaster or the effects will become permanent. The seconds drag by like hours. E'am peers through soot and dust, looking in the direction of the Atalan Mountains. Nothing remains of the range, but the SunShield—the light that had lain like a spider's web behind the stars above Ataleah—waves over a strip of land by the Sea of Ruberah. E'am trains EI on that area, but he can't see anything. The debris of EmFire clouds his view.

All around him lie dead, their bodies burnt beyond recognition, but if he can reverse Time, life will be restored, and everything will be as it was before EmFire. Patience escapes him. *Permission to Rewind Time. Answer me!*

Dark Master shoots up through the roiling seas, his massive shoulders filling the skies. He soars over E'am, swirling his cape and lowering his head so close that E'am can almost see through his mask. Lore has it that to see his face is to die, because his face is none other than your own and the horror of that will stop your heart. E'am grips Time Blade with both hands. *Get away from me.*

Step into my cloak and I will return Sol'aria to you, just as she was before I took her over.

E'am tightens his grip on the Blade, and slashes the ruler's cape, slitting into its deepest folds. The ruler retreats, flying through skies like a bat-winged demon, torn and tattered.

Permission to Reverse Time granted.

E'am realigns the Blade with the Cycles of Time, easing the tip into the dot in the center. Heaving and twisting, he turns the Blade anti-clockwise, his body shuddering under the effort. The seconds inch by, unlocking and replaying the disaster that happened one minute and ten seconds ago. The suffering of the dying becomes E'am's to bear.

Don't fight the pain of human suffering. It's the price of missing the mark. Take it on, or it will shatter your soul.

E'am caves to the feel of water flooding into his lungs, of lava scalding his skin, and the trudge of the masses stomping over his back. Pain overloads his senses, and he falls numb to suffering. The Reverse ends, the Blade falls slack in his grip, and all is just as it was before EmFire.

People talk excitedly about the riches that will soon be theirs. The shimmering city of Az-Rayelle stands solid, glistening under the pale pink glow of the ruby dome. EARTH IMAGING calculates forty seconds until the blast-off that will destroy the world.

E'am swivels EI, searching for Da'krah, Li'ram, and Sol'aria. They had not been in the golden pyramid above CTS as Sol'aria said they would be, and that had cost E'am the precious seconds he needed to cut Time. Seething, he searches the EK, aiming the lens on an opening in the cliffs beneath Da'krah's palace. His heart falls to his feet. Da'krah, Li'ram, and Sol'aria gather inside a cave. Da'krah stares at a stopwatch, counting the seconds to blastoff.

E'am prepares to cut Time and expel Da'krah, Li'ram, and Sol'aria from Earth. He grounds his feet to the Passing Stone, banishing thoughts of Sol'aria perishing in space, and raises the Blade to the peak of the golden pyramid atop CTS. Earth's Cycles of Time appear. He aims the tip of the blade into the dot of the Now. The world goes blank. *Come home, Beloved.*

TWENTY-FIRST CENTURY EARTH

CHAPTER THIRTY

The ruby bullet smashes through rocks and thrusts Sky into a narrow, musty tunnel. His head hurts, as if wedged under an iron helmet.

"Welcome home, Sky."

He squints, adjusting his eyes to the darkness. A girl in a body of glittering light rounds a curve in the tunnel. She feels familiar—something about her eyes—aqua, clear, and sparkling. "River Spirit!"

"That's right, but I'm called Tamara now. I am your guide in Twenty-First Century Earth, remember?"

Sky flexes his hand open and closed. "Where's Time Blade?"

"You've been in the astral record of your life as E'am, but you're back now. You're Sky Hunter again."

His head swims. Sparks of green fire flash before him. "What happened?" He rubs his eyes. "Where's the Blade?"

"It has returned to Time. You will win it back one day. I will help you with that."

Sky stares at the girl. "You're Luca's daughter from the Sun Kingdom. Where's Master?"

"You're home now, Sky. You returned on the Ruby Ley Line. We're in an old tin mine beneath the cliffs of Penrose Hall."

Sky digs his toes into a steel track burrowed into the ground, and rubs his temples. "It's a muddle in my head."

"Let me help." Tamara strokes his forehead, and a sparkling essence pours from her fingers. His life as Sky comes back to him. Sky Hunter, going where chance takes him. "What time is it?"

"You left at five o'clock yesterday afternoon. It's now one minute past."

"But I was gone for ages." Sky rubs the back of his neck. "I was in a terrible disaster ... EmFire. I had things under control. I had Time Blade in my hand. I could have saved everyone, but then ... I don't know."

"Your visit to the astral record ended. You traveled back to Ruberah to become E'am, your ancient self. E'am had the knowledge you need today to raise Mt. Rube back to Earth. Do you recall that information?"

"Someone said, 'Come home, Beloved.' Did I die?"

Tamara moves closer to Sky. "E'am died," she says, "but you are very much alive."

His left palm itches, and that old, infernal ache returns. "Where's my astral disk?"

"It has fallen asleep. Rube is not in use on the planet."

His body jerks, hurting as if someone ripped out his backbone. "I've got to have it."

"Good, because you'll need it. E'am watched Mt. Rube sink into the ocean. Do you remember what he saw?"

Sky clutches his head, pressure banging in his ears. "There's green fire everywhere ... I can't."

"That's all right. It will stop." Tamara steers him down the tunnel. "Lara Penrose is waiting to meet you. I think she will be a calming presence for you, Sky." T points to a ladder going up the mineshaft. "Take the cliff path at the top. You'll see the hall in the field ahead of you."

Lara Penrose rises from her desk, stretching her hands toward Sky, welcoming him like a long-lost relative. And that's just how he feels. Lara could be no one other than the reincarnation of Queen Leah. She resembles Leah in stature, but it's more about the way she is— warm and welcoming, just like she was to E'am.

"I'm so happy to meet you, Sky."

He blinks rapidly, fighting emotion. It's surreal, like being in a dream. "You look so much the same," he says.

Lara laughs. "I wish I still had that beautiful bronze skin. You're so suntanned you could pass for E'am, and you have the same eyes."

She gestures to a couple of chairs in front of French windows leading onto a patio. Sky recognizes the room from when he talked to her on Skype. Books and silver-framed photos line the shelves behind her desk.

"I wasn't surprised when you called about the job in the kitchen," Lara says, sitting in one of the chairs. "Tamara told me your sacred future had come due. Once that happens the Goddess of Rubies takes over and you're on your way." She smiles, wrinkling her nose. "Ruberah." She bites her lip, and slumps her shoulders, like Queen Leah did when bearing the loss of Luca. "Did you ... well, no, I shouldn't ask."

"I was with him." Sky looks out through the French doors. The sea stretches into the horizon. Time lies hidden, floating in the recesses of dark matter. How and where does it hold Time Blade? "I was studying with him," Sky says. He wipes his brow, and looks back at Lara. "How lucky was I?"

Her pale blue eyes mist over. "He loved you so much. We all did. When you first arrived at the palace, you were the most adorable little boy." She swallows hard. "Oh, my goodness. I must stop before I fall apart."

Sky shakes his head. "You won't. Luca always said you were the one who held everything together." He touches a hand to hers, "So, am I working in the kitchen?"

"That's up to Tamara, T as we call her among ourselves. Right now, sleep is the best thing for you. When your mind is rested it will be easier to recall the information you need. We put your backpack in the loft above the stable. If you're not comfortable with horses—"

"I love horses." Sky mentions the summers he spent at a dude ranch. "I learned a lot, everything from mucking out stables to breaking them in."

"Right. I'll bear that in mind." Lara walks him to the door, giving him directions to the stables. "See you in the morning."

Sky ambles along the cliff path, heading toward a red brick building with a high gabled roof. Waves crash to shore, sending plumes of spray high in the air. He veers left, crosses a field, and pauses at the entrance to the stables. A girl stands inside, nuzzling a black horse.

"That's a good boy," she says. "Mmm ... mmm ... mm... I love you soo much."

Sky steps back and leans against the wall. The girl looks almost identical to Sol'aria. She has long, flaming red hair and speaks with the same exaggerated mannerisms. Anger rumbles in his gut. Sol'aria misled E'am about the launch of EmFire. She deliberately lied to him about the time and the place, and that cost him seconds with Time Blade.

"Oh, it's you." The girl peers outside the stables. "I thought I heard something. Back from Ruberah?"

"Who are you?"

"I'm Kate, Tamara's earthly helper. Lara Penrose is my mother. You must be Sky Blue Hunter."

Sky saunters into the old brick building, "It's Sky," he says. "Just Sky."

She nods. "Mummy doesn't know I'm here. I've been in France, but I got back early. How was Ruberah?" she asks, causally, as if he'd been on a vacation.

"Tragic."

Kate resumes smooching the horse's nose. "Do you want to talk about it?"

"Sure." He spots a wooden staircase near the far end of the stables, scoots past Kate, three more stalls, and climbs the stairs. "Come on up." At the top, he parts a wall of dark blue velvet curtains, and enters the loft. It smells freshly painted, white. The ceiling rises into a peak with wood beams. Sky opens the windows above the kitchen sink, airing the room out. He checks out the bathroom, tiny, with a stall shower. His backpack sits on the floor beside the bed.

Kate swishes through the drapes, and sits on the sofa. "Let's get this over with," she says. "I lived as Sol'aria in Ruberah. I've been back. I know all about it."

The awful memories of death and destruction plague Sky. "You blew up the world," he says, glaring at her, waiting for an explanation.

She folds her arms, and a forlorn expression crosses her face. "Living as Sol'aria, I believed EmFire would be good for the people. I was wrong. I'm sorry."

He feels cheated. He needs to get in the ring with her about this. She can't just fluff off her treachery with a few short sentences. He wants to ask if she felt remorse as EmFire destroyed their civilization, if she wrote a sacred future—a promise of recompense to mankind, and if she's paid that debt, but she unnerves him. She sits very still, staring at him—green eyes steady—as if locked closed to this terrible past.

"It's my turn now?" she asks.

"Your turn? For what?"

"Who was she?"

"Who?"

"The girl you made pregnant and left me for?"

He plunges into a chair beside the bed, thinking of Asari. *You are a beautiful man.* Those words had rocked E'am's world, and Sky senses that if he closed his eyes he could be right back there, swaying in E'am's shoes. He says, "You can't ask me about that."

"There you go, just like E'am, setting the rules."

"I answered that question at the time."

"And you're staying with that answer. You did it for Earth?"

"You slapped me across the face and told me never to come near you again."

"Who was she?"

Sky presses his fingers to his temples. Asari—a girl like no other. He can see himself as E'am, watching her walk toward him, carrying the iron pot with Luca's soul inside. He can hear her laughter and feel the tangle of her lashes as they had fluttered against his cheek. "She was no one you knew."

"You said having sex with her was a matter of genetics, predestined. Correct?"

"Uh-huh."

"Well ... if Gold, the Earth's heart, asked me to have a baby with an alien I'd do it, even if you and I were together. I wouldn't tell you either, and I certainly wouldn't ask for your permission. I'd say that's reason enough for you and I to leave each other alone."

"Are you're saying you understand why E'am did what he did?"

"I might, if you tell me who she was."

The orb spins, warning Sky to stay away from the subject. *Willingly*. He says, "You either understand or you don't."

She heaves a long and noisy sigh, just like Sol'aria used to do. "I've suffered many sorrows for my part in EmFire, and now I'm feeling the pain Sol'aria felt when she lost E'am to another woman. It's like it just happened. Your trip into the astral records disturbed my own."

Nights spent with Sol'aria at the Ruby Hot Pools invade Sky's thoughts—a sensuous prelude to love about to go wrong. So wrong that he'd stood ready to cut Time and expel her from the planet. "Look," Sky says, seeking a reasonable tone, "the human family was not very large at that time. We—"

"If it helps, I've been suffering the effects of my part in the destruction of Ruberah for centuries. Life after life, I encounter illness and tragedy, and then I die at age sixteen."

Sky shudders. "I'm sorry, Kate. I—"

"Don't." She holds up a hand. "Don't make any confessions to me. I turned sixteen a few weeks ago. This is my stuff. I'm just letting you know what's happening with me."

"Okay, but you must know that as E'am, I would never have hurt you by choice."

"It is as it is, and you can't do anything about it. That's going to be hard for you. E'am could solve almost anything. Now you'll become a lot like him. You will inherit his astral intelligence."

Having just spent five days as E'am, Sky could tell her E'am seldom felt like he had the answer to anything, especially Sol'aria. "You know," he says, "we spent a lot of time with Luca in Ruberah. We felt the light of his Sun Heart, and we were really tuned to the planet and its needs. Doesn't a little lovers' quarrel pale beside the evolution of mankind?"

"Don't get all bloody high-minded like E'am. You cheated on me." She slaps her hands on her thighs. "I trust you discovered how to raise Mt. Rube. T, Tamara, will let me know when you need me."

Need her—her, with that haughty attitude? He thinks not. Kate strolls over to the curtains, parting them slightly. She looks back at Sky. "You think you can haul a mountain up from the bottom of an ocean without the power of the Sun Flame?"

How does she still carry the Sun Flame, after using it to help launch EmFire? E'am did everything right with Time Blade and it left him. "Yeah ... well," Sky says, "I haven't yet remembered how to get Mt. Rube back to Earth. Every time I think about it, I see nothing but you and green fire and death."

Kate clutches the curtains with both hands, her knuckles turning white from the pressure of her grip. "I can't use the Sun Flame," she whispers. "I have to forgive myself for EmFire first, and I don't know if I'm going to get that done in this life."

CHAPTER THIRTY-ONE

Lezant looms into view, a stone-faced monastery perched at the end of a long and rugged headland. Sky pauses, shifting his backpack, which is getting heavier by the mile. He's hiked eight so far along the Coastal Path on the remote west coast of Cornwall. It's hot for England. Sun blazes on the cliffs, while a short distance out to sea rain pelts the ocean. He swigs down water, and trudges on, treading over wildflowers overgrowing the path.

The trail winds down the cliff, getting closer to the sea. Sky checks the map T left for him at reception. The path to Lezant splits off a short distance ahead. He folds the paper and tucks it in his jeans pocket. There won't be any cell service at the monastery. No Wi-Fi, just pay phones, and an Internet café two miles inland. T suggested Sky leave his devices in a staff locker at Penrose Hall. When he closed the door on them the air went out of his lungs, as if he'd pulled the plug on his life.

He stares at a sign: NO SWIMMING. HAZARDOUS CURRENTS. The notice is staked by the entrance to a bridge—rocks linked together with wooden planks. The sea rolls back and forth beneath the crossing, breaking onto a cove at the foot of the cliffs. Sky steps onto the first rock and then the first plank, spreading his arms for balance. The sun dazzles his eyes, and the sands on the cove flash silver bright.

"Asari!" The lilt of her laughter plays in the air, and Sky trips from this world to hers. He soars through space with her, side-by-side, weaving through times past and future. He's ultra awake in a place unmarked by custom and unattached to consequence. Free, until a massive wave whirls up from Earth and drags him back down—down into Sky.

The bridge sways beneath his feet, and he wobbles on the planks like a novice on a tightrope. Losing his balance, he falls to his knees and grips the boards with both hands. Waves swell, cresting and breaking beneath him. Foam spits in his face. Time whooshes by—a mass of filmy substance—tunneling back and forth across the cosmos. A tall, angular man with golden eyes walks through silver clouds. Sky runs toward him. "Master, I'm ready for class."

"Take control of your mind, Sky Blue. You have much to do in this life."

Wind whips Sky's hair across his face, and Master vanishes from sight. It doesn't matter. Nothing can take him down. He broke through the ether and met his teacher, and he'll do it again, and he will not crawl to Lezant. Slowly, spreading his arms, he gets back on his feet. Plank by plank, he inches forward, dipping with the sway of the bridge. "I have lots to do in this life, and I will do it."

The crossing gives way to a sandy stretch of beach at the base of the headland. He downs a bottle of water. The path to Lezant winds up the cliff face. He adjusts his backpack, and begins the climb.

T greets Sky at the top of the cliffs, swooping beside him in her body of sparkling light.

"Way to travel," Sky says, wiping sweat from his brow.

T smiles, eyes extra bright. "Everyone walks to Lezant. It's tradition."

"Why?"

"Lezant was originally built in the sixth century as a castle for a wealthy aristocrat. In the eleventh century it was used as a fortress against Viking invaders. Two hundred years later, a duke purchased the land and rebuilt it to suit his family. When his wife died giving birth to a blind and malformed son, the duke took off, leaving the boy in the care of a nurse."

T guides Sky toward the arched entrance to the monastery. "During this time," she says, "hundreds of pilgrims walked the Golden Triangle, a trail crossing Spain, France, and Cornwall. People spoke of a miraculous healing light that sometimes arose from those lands. Being a kindly soul, the sick boy's nurse gave shelter to these travelers. One night, a Breton priest called Jean Lezant arrived, and the sight of the crippled boy moved him to tears. Jean climbed to the top of the castle, fell to his knees, and prayed for the boy to be healed. Jean prayed for the boy every day, on the same spot, for hours at a time. One year later, a shower of golden light arose from the planet and fell over the child. His bones grew strong and he could see. When the youth's father heard of this miracle, he rewarded the priest by giving him the castle, and so Jean began the Order."

"That's amazing. Is it true or is it a myth?"

"It's true."

"What kind of monastery is it?"

"The Order does not belong to any religious sect. It serves Earth as directed by Gold. The monks come from different disciplines, many having lived in other monasteries around the world."

"How long will I be here?"

"Until you recall how to raise Mt. Rube back to Earth."

"Is this about Kate? I was rough on her. I'll apologize."

"It's about you, my darling child." T sets her soft aqua gaze on Sky. "Kate was not supposed to be at the Hall when you arrived. I warned her it would be disruptive for you to meet at this time. She did not heed my advice, but she has agreed with me now. I suggest you leave each other alone for a few years and stay focused on the work you've come to do."

"Yes, that's fine, but what happened to me, Tamara? E'am ran a huge energy company at my age, and he thought about mankind and the safety of the planet. I'm a mess."

"As E'am you lived beside my father for many years, and for two lifetimes in a row. You had full use of your jeweled intelligence. That will unfold while you're here. Just settle in and trust the routine."

Sky received a sheet of instructions about the routine. The monks meditate around the clock, changing shifts every four hours. The Friends-in-residence, people like Sky, may join them but must stay for the full four hours. Sounds daunting.

"It's an honor to be here," T says. "The waiting list to serve as a Friend is very long. Everyone works while here, helping to maintain the monastery."

"Is it all men?"

"The Friends are both men and women. The monks are all men. A sister order resides on the other side of the world in New Zealand. That Order serves Zan'drah, Goddess of Rubies. Between the two monasteries, there is always one Friend from every country on the planet. You will be the current representative of the United States of America."

"Me? Just me?"

T nods. "One person per country."

"What if I don't remember what E'am knew about raising Mt. Rube?"

T wraps her sparkling hands over his. "I am ever your guide, my darling child, but you will be assigned a mentor monk while you're here. It's to best work out any issues with him." She gestures toward the entrance. "Someone will greet you inside."

CHAPTER THIRTY-TWO

The gong sounds, a deep bass note, announcing the midnight service. The monks file into the Holy Square, where Gold healed the boy all those centuries ago. Located at the top of the monastery, the Square is open to the elements with views of nothing but sea and sky. Ribbed columns surround the hallowed ground, free-standing, like Roman ruins. Stars dazzle the sky, seeming close enough to touch.

Sky drops his cushion on the area designated for the Friends, and sits yogi-style, shivering. Wind howls across the great granite promontory. He huddles inside a woolen blanket, pulling it up around his neck. It's dark, and hard to tell if his mentor Ramon is among the monks. Monks and Friends wear the same clothes—black pants and a tunic, tied with a gold sash.

The monks chant OM, and Sky joins in, singing from deep in his throat. The word resonates through his body and on the air. His head feels heavy, as if drugged. A sphere of golden brilliance surfaces the planet and domes the Holy Square. His head flops forward. Everything goes blank. The gong sounds, trembling the atmosphere, waking Sky from a deep sleep. Feet shuffle past him, coming and going. He yawns. So much for meditation. He's slept through every one since he arrived a week ago.

The Friends depart the Holy Square, and bear left. The monks turn right. An electric cart pulls up beside Sky, driven by one of the grounds crew. "You have a phone call," he says. "Booth ten."

The guy drives off, and Sky jogs down a narrow road, winding around the monastery. The call must be from Lara Penrose. Sky told his mother he'd be travelling out of cell range for a while, but to call Penrose Hall in case she had to reach him.

Passing through reception, Sky glances at a wall with photos of the monks, fifty in total. Their names and how they arrived at Lezant are printed below. His mentor's reads: *Ramon: Walked from Spain*. It's the same for each monk. *Mustafa: Walked from London. Li Wei: Walked from Dover. Farrookh: Walked from Falmouth*, and so on, leaving Sky to presume most of them arrived in England by plane or boat, and then walked to Lezant.

He descends the stairs to the basement. The sports area lies to the right—squash courts, Ping-Pong tables, and a workout area with weights and machines. Booth ten is in the middle of a bank of pay phones on his left. He eases his shoulder against the old wooden bi-fold door, and picks up the receiver. "Hello!"

"Sky! Where the fuck are you?"

It's Zara! "How did you get this number?"

"My life stinks," Zara yells. "Reporters hound me all the time. I can't take it anymore. I miss Daddy so much." She sobs, sniffing and snorting into the phone.

"Just hold on, Zara. The media will move on to something else soon."

"No they won't. My mother is getting married again. He's twenty-two years old. I *hate* her."

"Zara ... calm down. Can't you just get out of there for a while?"

"Not without a gang of reporters on my trail. I'm their new poor little rich girl, pregnant and abandoned by you. What the fuck? I want to kill Cameron."

"Hey, come on ... you're not pregnant. That'll become obvious and—"

"I've got to tell you something."

Sky flattens his back against the booth. Zara had never been clear about whether or not she'd been pregnant. Her text—*we should talk*—haunts him. What if he'd been making out with Cameron while Zara was having an abortion? He drags a hand through his hair. "What is it?"

"I was going to tell you... but ... I don't know ... I was so confused. I thought maybe later." She breaks down crying. "Daddy left me so much money that Uncle Solomon insists I make a will. So I got to thinking, what if I die?"

"What are you talking about? You're eighteen. You're not going to die for ages."

"You never know. Daddy ..." She gasps. "Daddy ... oh my god ... I'm in his study, sitting in his chair, talking on his phone—the secure line he used when making deals. I'm trying to be strong like him, but I just want to be with him."

The desperation in her voice frightens Sky. "Zara, I can't imagine how painful this must be for you, but I know your dad would want you to live the best life you can. You have to do that. Do it for him."

"I've got to make a decision about something ... something that involves you."

"Me? Why?"

"This is going to sound weird, but it happened. I promise." She pauses, then lowers her voice, speaking softly, gaining control. "I was in the parking lot of the clinic about to go in for an abortion. I was totally messed up. It felt like my heart swelled up and got stuck in my throat. I rested my head on the steering wheel, closed my eyes, and I don't know ... I started speaking to the stars. I asked them if ... *it* ...was the right thing to do. I had a vision." She gulps a wheezy breath. "I saw a little boy running across golden sands. Then you appeared, and you lifted him onto your shoulders. He had your eyes. I looked into them—a vast blue space with stars behind them. I couldn't ... you know. I loved him already."

He bangs his fist against the booth, thinking of Zara dealing with this all by herself. "It's okay, Zara. I'll do whatever you ask. I'll come back, if you need me. We can work this out."

"No. I'm not pregnant. I did something different. I was still seventeen at the time, but I found a fertility clinic willing to help me. It's in Switzerland, and ... well, we have a frozen embryo."

It feels like someone whacked Sky on the head, whacked him so hard it opens his memories of Ruberah. He's E'am again, watching Mt. Rube sink into the ocean. Every detail becomes comes crystal clear: the square of luminosity that fell from space, the way it fluttered over Mt. Rube, then settled on the earth in a perfect round with twelve triangles inside. The way the land parted, and the jeweled mountain sank straight down through the planet and settled on the ocean bed, unharmed.

"Sky! Are you there? Did you hear me?"

Sky rubs his eyes, pulling himself back to the conversation. "Yes," he says. "That's cool."

"Are you stoned or something?"

"No." Sky leans against the booth. "What do you want me to do?"

"I listed you as the father and co-guardian."

Sky wipes his hand across his brow. "Why didn't you tell me, Zara? I would have helped you."

"I couldn't. Daddy was alive then, but I couldn't even tell him. The vision of the little boy stayed with me, but I just couldn't explain it."

"How did you manage everything?" Sky asks.

"It's called money. I wrote the fertility institute a big fat check against my trust fund, postdating it to my eighteenth birthday. That's why I was so scared Uncle Solomon wouldn't give me the money. I'm sorry I made up the story about buying property in Paris, but Cameron's blog on *Teens Dying for Love* totally spoofed me. She claimed I was pregnant by you, so I figured she'd found out. I was terrified."

He kicks his foot against the booth, furious that he'd let himself be played by Cameron. "I wish I could have helped you back then, Zara. You know I would have done anything you asked of me."

"You can help now," she says. "I chose to defrost the embryo five years from now. If I die before then, promise me you will make sure the baby gets born. There will be plenty of money. You'll be a great dad, Sky. I know that. Just find a kind girl to be his mom. Will you do that?"

Sky switches the receiver to his other hand, putting two and two together. "Zara, in the highly unlikely circumstance that you die of natural causes, I will make sure the child is born, and I will love him and be the best father possible. If you die of unnatural causes, any sort of overdose or suspicious looking accident, I will not do that. You saw this child. You're his mom. You've got to stay on the planet and take care of him."

She whimpers. "It's so painful without Daddy. I don't know if I can bear it."

"You've got to stay, Zara. That's the deal."

"I'm sorry, I'm such a mess."

"Hey ... you're Zara Bosche, *my* ex-girlfriend. Show some respect."

"You're stealing my lines."

"Is it a deal?"

She sniffs. "Fuck! We're going to have a kid together?"

He wipes sweat from his forehead. "I guess."

The laundry room, located in the sub-basement of the monastery, is humid and smells of hot air and bleach. Sky hauls the last sheet from the dryer, folds it into a square, and stacks it on top of a large rolling cart. A woman Friend arrives and grips the handle, ready to deliver the linens. She has graying hair, bifocals, and the kindly look of a grandmother. Everyone wears a nametag pinned above the heart. Hers reads: Livia/Argentina. His: Sky Blue/USA.

"Bonita!" Livia says, pointing to his tag.

"Thanks," Sky says. He's listed as Sky Blue in Astral Command and there's no changing it. He pats the stack of sheets. "Take it away."

Livia/Argentina wheels the cart down to the freight elevators. Sky scales the four flights of stairs to the room he shares with Hiroto, a really cool Japanese man. He finds Hiroto getting dressed for the day. He gathers his tunic about his small frame, as carefully as he might a ceremonial kimono, and then cinches the garment in place with the wide gold sash. Hiroto bows upon sight of Sky, clasping his hands and shaking his head like a bobbin on a spinning wheel.

"Arigato." Sky uses his one word of Japanese, which always delights Hiroto, and causes more bowing and head trembling. Conversing between Friends is discouraged. Silence is revered. That works for Sky and Hiroto. Something else passes between them—an understanding—so deep and multi-layered that Sky can't put it into words. It just feels good to be with him, like his life is on track. Hiroto bows again to Sky before leaving for the day.

The room is tiny, with whitewashed walls, two beds, and a small table between them. An oblong window overlooks the road that winds around the monastery. Sky changes into a clean set of clothes and heads for the monks' quarters. He swings through the dining room one flight up, and snatches a croissant stuffed with ham and eggs from the buffet. The Friends cook breakfast and lunch, and the monks prepare dinner, which is often great, as most of them cook dishes from their native countries.

Sky trudges up more stairs to the seventh floor. The gong rings, announcing the eight a.m. service. Sky knocks on the door to the meeting room assigned to his mentor. Ramon sits on one of two wooden chairs, the only furniture in the room. Sky takes the other, facing *Ramon: Walked from Spain*. With his muscular build, dark hair and facial stubble, Ramon looks more like a guerilla fighter than a holy man. No small talk passes between them. Ramon asked Sky some questions about his life when they first met, but that was not a formal session.

Ramon extends an open hand toward Sky, indicating the beginning of the session. Sky shifts his body on the chair. Before guidance begins, Sky must look Ramon in the eye. The Friends' handbook describes this "looking" as the Friend's consent. It gives the mentor permission to connect with the Friend's higher awareness and provide guidance. It's beyond weird. So far, Sky has not met Ramon's gaze long enough to begin a session. Since he's slept through every meditation to date, he's had nothing to talk about. It's different today.

Sky drags his glance up to meet Ramon's. Black eyes stare back at him, black but glowing with light. Sky shuffles his feet, and wills himself to keeping looking at Ramon. Slowly, like a stream of energy, he feels his mentor's gaze lock onto his own.

Ramon nods. "How may I help you?"

"I had a flashback to my life in Ruberah," Sky says. "I watched Mt. Rube sink into the ocean."

"Did you learn what you needed to know?"

"I saw a pattern of light fall over Mt. Rube. I think that's what I came for."

"Join the midday meditation today. Gold will show you what to do next."

"I haven't stayed awake in one of those yet."

"How are you progressing with listening to nature?"

Sky uncrosses his legs. He's supposed to listen to nature for ten a minutes a day. He hasn't made it past forty seconds yet. "I don't get the point of it."

Ramon remains quiet for a while—keeping his posture straight and his glance steady on Sky. He speaks. "The ancient Polynesians set sail on rafts in the Pacific, looking for land. They found it by watching currents in the ocean, reading the stars, studying shadows on the clouds—guided by nature. Few people could do that today. On average, we use about two percent of our brainpower, and mostly in response to opinions received from the world around us—noise that clouds the other ninety-eight percent. We're out of touch with the language of nature, and of the universe—the language of meditation."

Sky nods. He gets it to some degree. He listens to the sounds of the sea—to the currents and the undertow, waiting for the big wave. "I'll work on it."

Ramon stands, ending the session.

"Something else happened today," Sky says. "But, no. That's okay. It's nothing."

Ramon sits back on his chair, and opens his hands to Sky.

"It's a personal matter," Sky says.

"Proceed."

"I had a phone call from a girl I know. She told me something that took me by surprise."

"Do you love her?"

"Huh?" He thinks of E'am. One minute he was madly in love with Sol'aria and then he met Asari. "I'm not sure."

"I see."

Sky doubts that. Ramon may look like a guerilla fighter, but he was probably a saintly young man. *Walked from Spain.* "What do you see?" Sky asks.

"You have a deep spiritual connection to this girl. You love her on a level you're not yet aware of."

"What does that mean?"

"It is a cosmic love, a commitment made in the primordial, a promise for the benefit of Earth."

Sky thinks of Rae Blue, his most ancient self, bowing into Time, pledging his jeweled intelligence to serve mankind. Could this be another result of that? "Can you tell me more?"

"Consider all that passed between you and this girl. People reveal things about themselves in unlikely ways."

"She said she ..." He shuffles his feet, feeling awkward to the core. "She sometimes sees, like into the galaxy, when she looks into my eyes."

"What we see in others is a reflection of ourselves."

"So, she has stars in her?"

"We are a microcosm of the whole—the entire universe."

Luca used to talk about that, and E'am had understood. Sky needs to get with the meditation program. "She was pregnant," Sky says, the words coming without thought. "By me. It happened in high school. She just called to tell me. It's complicated."

"It usually is," Ramon says.

"She planned to have an abortion. Then ... she changed her mind. She told me she had the embryo removed and frozen."

"That's quite an undertaking for someone so young."

"It is, but not for Zara. She's got loads of money. Her father gave her a Gulfstream jet for her sixteenth birthday. Zara gets what she wants." Sky shifts his body on the chair, careful to keep his gaze on Ramon. "She didn't have an abortion because she had a vision of the child—a little boy. She said she saw me with him. We had the same eyes."

"How do you feel about that?"

"A lot better than if she had an abortion without my being there to take care of her. I had the flashback to Ruberah at the same time she was telling me about the frozen embryo. Seeing Mt. Rube as E'am had seen it … well, that blew my mind."

"That was a lot to absorb all at once, but it's helped to break up the messaging clouding your brain. Meditation should come easier today."

"What if it doesn't?"

"We take the best of our habits with us when we die," Ramon says, "and we place them in our soul. These are ours to command in future lives. You recently traveled into the astral recording of your life as E'am in Ruberah. Let his practices come back to you."

Noon

The midday meditation is the most popular, as it's the warmest part of the day. The Friends pile in, blanket free. Sky drops his cushion on the Holy Square, and spots his mentor among the monks on the other side. He wonders about Ramon's life before Lezant. However, it's so liberating to be a blank slate in his eyes, free of *Teens Dying for Love,* that maybe that's the point of anonymity. Sky Blue/ USA. That's his bio, and he likes it.

Sky sits cross-legged on his cushion. Livia/Argentina and Hiroto/Japan are parked a couple of rows in front of him, although not together. No one is together, but nametag checking is fair sport. Sky leans forward slightly, glancing at his neighbor to the right. Bjorn/Norway— male, fiftyish, balding head, blond sideburns. To his left, Samira/Kenya—female, gorgeous, long lithe body, and young as far as the Friends go, on Sky's side of forty.

Samira catches Sky's glance, smiles, and points at his nametag. "Love it."

He says, "I bet you're really good at listening to nature. Could I join you sometime?"

"Get away with you," Samira laughs, digging her elbow in his side. "I'm old enough to be your mother."

He laughs. She's hot, and it's not a flat-out no. He'll give it another go, if chance permits. The monks begin to chant. Samira closes her eyes, and a serene expression settles on her face. Gone, just like that, connected to astral awareness.

The wind lies low, and the atmosphere hangs heavy over the headland, holding the echo of the gong, soft and lulling. Sky's head drops forward, but he catches himself at the brink of sleep and jerks his head up straight. He joins in the chant, singing OM, holding the sound on one note. He recalls Luca saying OM creates a play of sounds that wave against the matrix of time, opening a space to go beyond.

Sky looks inward to the sparkling orb centered in his frontal lobes. He bows, mentally, as E'am had done. *I come to serve.* Thoughts persist, like the closeness of Samira's knee to his. Sky inhales and exhales to the count of four, focusing on the pause between the breaths. Chanting and breathing, his worldly thoughts fall silent, and the space between the breaths gets bigger and bigger.

Fiery rays shoot up from inside the planet and dome the Holy Square with golden light. Inside the dome, Sky can see the interior of Earth. First, the crust that holds the elements that support life, then, the mantle—a dense complexity of rocks, iron, and aluminum. Finally, the core—the molten gold beauty of the Earth's heart— an ever-expanding radiance emanating from the Lord of Love.

One golden ray points downward and lights up a body of water, lying far beneath the other oceans of the world. Mt. Rube rests there, tinting the sea pink. A circle with twelve triangles surrounds its base—the astral pattern for the mountain—just as E'am had seen it.

A bolt of darkness blots Sky's view—the unmistakable blackness of Dark Master.

I told you I would be back for you.

The tinny, hollow sound of the ruler's voice evokes painful memories of E'am's last fight with him.

Get away from me.

Dark Master swivels his head, a black-hooded mask planted on his shoulders. *The ruby mountain is mine, and the powers of Rube belong to me. Join me in my kingdom, and I will share the riches of the world with you.*

Never. I will raise Mt. Rube back to Earth, and its forces shall serve all people, as is rightfully so.

The ruler laughs, flashing the lining of daggers inside his cape. *You're the same fool you've always been. You lost as Master for the planet. You lost in love, and you lost Time Blade. You'll never defeat me.*

The gong booms over the headland, and Sky jerks awake, his butt aching against the hard stone of the Holy Square.

Three weeks later, Sky flops on the chair opposite Ramon, soaked from a four-hour meditation in the drizzling rain. "Same thing," he says. "I got up close to Mt. Rube and Dark Master bugged the shit out of me. Sorry for the language, but this has been going on forever."

"We suggest taking a rain cloak to meditation in this kind of weather."

"I need help," Sky says. "Where's Tamara? She's supposed to be my guide."

"Have you called her?"

Sky chuckles. "Does she have a phone now?"

Ramon shakes his head. "You're angry, and that's clouding your thinking."

"Yes, I'm angry. I set out to see the world and I've been in a monastery for a month. That's not what I had in mind."

"Remind me, how did you envision your journey?"

Sky folds his arms, keeping his focus on Ramon. "Traveling around, working as I needed money."

"Are you in need of money?"

"That's not the point. I—"

"I think it is. When we first met, you told me you were traveling by the hand of chance."

"That's just an expression. I was being a smart-ass kid."

The patter of rain falls against the window, and Sky fidgets, uneasy on his chair.

Ramon speaks. "I was impressed with the way you spoke about your journey on the first day we met. You explained the difference between a traveler and a tourist. You said a tourist leaves home, knowing when he will return, and so he buys a round-trip ticket. A traveler buys a one-way ticket, because he has no idea when he will return, or if he will. A traveler stays in one place until another calls him. Therefore, I must ask you, are you called to another place?"

"I didn't come up with that stuff. I found it on the Internet."

"And in so doing, you identified with the traveler, which legitimized your calling. I expect that was quite exciting at the time."

Sky blinks. The guy must be physic. That's exactly how he'd felt.

Ramon stands. "I'll see you at the four a.m. meditation."

Four a.m., and it's cold, dark, and chucking down buckets, as the Brits say. The gong rings as Sky enters the Holy Square. He sits on the black cushion and flaps the rain cloak, spreading it to cover his legs and feet. To add to his misery, Hiroto left the monastery yesterday. Sky didn't find out until he returned to his room and discovered another guy had already moved in. He'd dumped his bag on Hiroto's bed, his clothes spilling out of it like the innards of a ravaged animal. Despair took Sky over. He didn't know where Hiroto lived or how to find him. The Friends' Handbook stated clearly that the monastery would not divulge personal information about the monks or Friends.

The monks file into the Holy Square, at least forty of them, and the chant begins. Sky does the breathing exercise E'am had used, focusing on the count of four and watching his breath. Golden light showers up from the planet. Sky's orb shimmers in his frontal lobes. He bows to it. *I come to serve.*

Straight away, the light pattern at the base of Mt. Rube comes into clear view. No Dark Master, no disturbances of any kind. People stand on the rim of the circle with the twelve triangles inside. Sky tries to see who they are, but Tamara dives into the golden dome, the light of her Sun body blinding him to all else.

"Well done, my darling child. This is what you came for. You may return to Penrose Hall."

CHAPTER THIRTY-THREE

Sky drops his backpack on the ground, and gazes at Penrose Hall. The sun passes in and out of clouds, highlighting the crystalline structure in the sprawling granite house. Gulls swoop low in the air, squawking, and the pink mists of Ruberah swirl over the turrets of a round-shaped tower. A sense of belonging to something wonderful sweeps over Sky. He recognizes it as the happiness of rubies—the feeling E'am experienced when Rube healed his wounds. He's about to close his eyes and direct pink mists of love and healing to cover the planet, when T arrives.

"The Goddess is pleased with you, my darling child." She takes Sky's left hand in hers, and slides her palm over his. His astral disk shimmers to life. "It's the same version E'am used in Ruberah," T says.

Sky takes a deep breath, gazing at the disk. The losses he suffered as E'am fade back into his ancient memory. He feels whole again—ready for the challenges ahead. The icon for SunVision pulses silver-gold in the center of the screen. "Can I reach your father?" he asks.

"That's between you and him."

"Like—"

"Like ... however you can make that work." T smiles. "It's time to go forward with your travels, Sky."

Sky tells T about this roommate at Lezant. "I'd like to visit Hiroto. How can I find him?"

T shakes her head. "Anonymity is sacred at Lezant. You'll find a way."

"So, I just take off. Is that it?"

"Not quite. We call the astral pattern for Mt. Rube the Ruby Ring, and it must ascend to the surface of the planet before we can raise the mountain. Twelve people serve on the Ring. You stand at midnight. When the Goddess decides, I will gather everyone together and we will lift the Ruby Ring per her instructions."

"Who are the others?" Sky asks. "Do I know them?"

"You can study the Ring on SunVision, although not all the servers are in place yet. When they are, you must be at peace with each one, including yourself."

"Do I have a problem with that?" Sky's mind races in multiple directions, his dad zinging front and center. He's not exactly at peace with him, but Clive Hunter couldn't be on the Ring. He's just too unlikely.

T taps her astral disk, and a SunScreen pops up in front of Sky—a huge square of silver light. The Ruby Ring with the twelve servers comes into view. T zooms in on the seventh triangle, but Sky can't make out who stands at that point. It's covered with a cloudy substance.

T swipes the fog away with her finger, and Sky takes a step back, shock prickling his scalp. "Seriously?" he says. "Cameron is on the Ring!"

"She could be. It's up to you, Sky. It has to do with your life as E'am. Go over the five days you just spent in Ruberah and reason why that is."

CHAPTER THIRTY-FOUR

After three years on the road, T called Sky to work for Earth-Astral in New Zealand. He'd covered a good portion of the world, but far from all of it. He spent the first year and a half in Europe. From Paris to Barcelona, in coastal towns along the Mediterranean, up through Italy, Austria and Germany, he cleaned kitchens, waited tables, and learned bartending skills. He often bunked in with other waiters, found cheap hostels, or slept outside on a bed of grass, gazing at the stars. As winter approached, he headed for the French Alps and landed a job, shoveling snow and delivering room service to private chalets at a five-star resort beneath Mt. Blanc. One day a ski instructor failed to turn up for an important guest, and Sky stepped in. The client gave him a glowing reference. He kept the ski instructor job for the season, raking in five-star tips. He also met Gina—a gorgeous Italian girl who worked at the spa. It was hot from the start. They moved in together, and he tasted the possibility of love and a future with Gina. However, he didn't tell her about his mission in life. It just didn't jive with who they were together. Time Blade fell quiet in his mind and raising Mt. Rube back to Earth faded—almost into oblivion. It scared him. He had to meet his sacred future. No other cause could come before that.

He broke up with Gina. It hurt—flipped his heart inside out, but chance swayed in his favor. He'd been hired by a wealthy man from Morocco to ski with his son Ayat in the high, glacial terrains of Mt. Blanc. They hit it off as ski buddies, and Ayat had suggested Sky fly back to Rabat with him on his father's jet and spend some time in Morocco. Sky took him up on that. He spent the next year working his way along the north coast of Africa, down to Egypt, and then over to India.

He'd turned his hand to hard labor to survive these journeys, and he continued that pursuit in India. He worked on road repairs, shoveling asphalt and cleaning up building sites. Jobless in Mumbai, he joined the homeless living in the slums. Humanity sprawled the streets, husbands and wives, children, the aged and the newborn, all crammed under tents made of tattered but colorful fabrics. His insides crawled with shock and shame, and his lungs constricted and his breath came in slow, soft whimpers. These were the people whose lives would change the most when Rube was back on the planet. Fresh water, education, and healing services would be free for everyone. He had to do something about that right away.

As a young white guy scouring the back alleys for a place to rest his bones, Sky raised suspicion. He felt it—negative vibes—clouding his thoughts. He programmed his astral disk to the ruby sphere, and then directed rays of love and well being into the crowds as he walked by. Finally, an old man caught his glance. Sky bowed to him. The old man patted the pavement beside him. Sky laid down a large square of cardboard he'd purchased from a street kid, and then sat on it.

Traffic lumbered by close enough to take the skin off his toes. He crossed his legs yogi style. Construction noises banged in the background—drilling and hammering—new luxury apartments—rising up a few streets away.

He'd not connected with his sapphire intelligence for some time, but he did then. He gazed inward to the orb. *I come to serve.* He did this over and over—day in and day out until he no longer heard the din of life. Time opened, and he soared into *I am*—his atom of brilliance amongst the multi-billions that make up Time. The astral records of Ruberah stretched out before him. He re-entered his life as E'am—the part where he studied with Luca. This time he retained some awareness in his present-day life. It was the most incredible experience ever. He re-learned the knowledge Luca had passed to E'am—about the astral energy of jewels and the Laws of Time. He maintained this same practice every day for six weeks, sitting on his square of cardboard on a street in Mumbai. When he came back from these meditations, his face would be wet with tears, and he'd find water, food, and flowers scattered at his feet.

The moment he completed his lessons with Luca, T swept to his side and led him back into his worldly mind. She congratulated him in her usual loving way, and said the Goddess would soon call him to work in the matter of raising Mt. Rube back to Earth. If there was any place he wanted to visit but had not yet done so, he should go posthaste.

Sky headed to a surf camp on the southeast tip of Java, and lived his teenage fantasy life. He surfed by day and partied at night with free spirits—roaming the world like him. He lived in a hut at the edge of the jungle, where the beach stretched down to the sea. Late at night, when the party ended, he pulled up the Ruby Ring on a SunScreen. Except for Lara, Kate and Cameron, Sky had not yet learned who else was on the Ring. One night as he stared at the fifth triangle, Hiroto's face appeared. Sky's mind spun at the verge of revelation, and he held his gaze steady on his friend's image. Slowly, Hiroto's features disappeared and Nett's face emerged, smiling back at Sky. Memories from Ruberah welled up, and he took a shuddering breath. No wonder he'd taken to Hiroto like a brother at Lezant. The order of his life's journey awed him—the maze of events that led him to this moment. The years of travel, the people he worked with, the friends he made, and the girls he might have loved but left in favor of his life's mission. All had added to him— had helped him remain faithful to the sacred future he'd written eons ago in Ruberah. He recalled Asari telling E'am SunVision stayed with a person for as long as they lived on Earth. Nett had used SunVision.

Sky entered Hiroto/Nett in the search bar on his astral disk. A silver-gold dot pulsed to life on the map of Japan. The next day, Sky traveled by plane, train, and bus to the Kii peninsula in Japan. Following the silver-gold dot, he hiked dozens of miles around the foot of the Kii Mountains and found Hiroto in a deeply wooded area. His old friend stood on the deck of a small house, smiling and nodding. Sky ran up the steps, swept him off the ground, and spun him around and around.

Hiroto had lived as a monk in a local monastery for most of his life, but he always knew he would one day be called to another job. When Hiroto met Sky at Lezant, he recognized him as having lived as E'am in Ruberah. Then he knew they would work together just as they had in Ruberah. Hiroto said nothing, because they were at Lezant to serve Gold. Upon his return to Japan, Tamara appeared to Hiroto and restored his astral disk to life. Hiroto moved into the house in the woods and waited for Sky to find him.

If T had asked Sky where he would like to live most in the world, he might have chosen New Zealand. He rents a bungalow overlooking Manu Bay—home to some of the best surfing on the planet. Hiroto has moved into an apartment in Auckland. As Executive VP of Earth-Astral, Hiroto runs the office with devotion and efficiency, just as he had in Ruberah. Sky works mostly from home via SunScreen. Using the holographic view, he attends meetings and consults with co-workers in virtual reality. Zan'drah, Goddess of Rubies, presides over the raising of Mt. Rube back to Earth. Sky answers to her. Not everything is perfect.

A SunScreen lights up in his living room, and T appears, as she often does.

"How are you, my darling child?"

"Good. What's up?"

"Everyone who lived in Ruberah is back on the planet—the last, a little girl, was born at four this morning in Stockholm. Events will move rapidly now." T grins. "You're president of Earth-Astral, my darling child. It's time to get a haircut and dress the part."

"Come on, Tamara. People don't care what I wear."

"The Goddess does. She watched the World Symposium via the Ruby Satellite. She praised your presentation on astral energy, but you know she has an eagle eye.

She spotted a hole in your T-shirt. You're going shopping. A stylist awaits you in Auckland."

Sky cuts left and then right, dodging sightseers and the lunch crowd filing into restaurants. Auckland has a few glitzy buildings. The Sky Tower spirals high above the city, like a needle piercing the clouds. Earth Inc., the umbrella company for all Rube-related companies, occupies a laid-back structure in the hub of downtown. Sky ducks inside, swinging through the revolving door. The atmosphere is dingy, like a tourist office in a town on the edge of bankruptcy.

"Hi. It's me." Sky waves at Muriel Backer, receptionist and avid biker woman with a racy red Honda parked outside.

Muriel tugs on a tuft of her dark spiky hair. "Blimey, mate. You clean up nice."

"You think?" Sky pats the lapels of his jacket. "Italian, and designer jeans ... three hundred bucks a pair. Would you believe?"

"Looks great, darlin'. You'd better have a suit too."

"Being altered."

Sky lays his left palm against an eye embedded in a plaque outside the elevator. The door slides open, and he steps inside. He gets off on the eighth floor, and it's like stepping back in time to Rube Enterprises in Ruberah. Huge monitors line the walls of a long, lofty room. The Ruby Ring fills the main screen. Employees gaze at computers, charting the rise of the Ring to the surface of the planet. Dozens work at desks spread across the room, the best techies in the world, some doing the same job they did in Ruberah. Sky moves among them, checking progress and answering questions.

Joe Simmons bounds down the office. "Sky, my man." He claps his hands. "Crikey, mate. You look like a bloody film star."

"Yeah, right."

Joe is an Aussie, big, fortyish, with a thatch of blond hair. He was called Ki'an back in Ruberah. He managed Rube Operations back then, and he is preparing to do that job today.

"Come in." Joe steers Sky into his office and gestures to a futon about as shabby as the one Sky had in Valhalla. "Got everything programmed, have you?"

"What? Astral Command or the Ruby Satellite?" Sky asks, jokingly.

"Yeah ... I don't how you work with the Goddess at all. She's so busy multi-tasking the universe I can't understand a bloody thing she says."

Sky laughs. "I don't have to worry about that. Sun-Vision perceives my thoughts as she speaks, and then translates her responses for me. SunVision is light years ahead of jeweled intelligence."

"Well, rather you than me," Joe says. "Still, the old girl is a bloody wonder. She handles Astral Command by herself, a job that all six goddesses shared in the Time of Ruberah." Joe scratches his head. "She wants the Ring on the planet by the end of the month. One week from today, but I guess you know that."

"Yeah. I'm ready."

Joe struts the floor, back and forth. "It forces the situation with the Seven on the Ring." He darts Sky a piercing look. "Cameron is in New York. You have to make nice with her, like yesterday."

Sky's mind knots in the twist of angst associated with Cameron. "I thought that was make peace."

"Whatever it takes, mate."

Sky has done as T asked. He reviewed his life as E'am and figured out why it falls to him to offer Cameron a chance to serve on the Ring. He's put it off, as he can't picture himself doing what he has to do. He sighs. "So ... fill me in. What's Cameron up to these days?"

"She wrote for various online venues, trying to peddle her moment of fame into success. Didn't work. Then she created Vera Star, a character who spends a lot time in her closet, deciding what to wear to attract him, bed him, beat him, kick him out, or keep him. She scored big with this, and began her own online magazine *VERA STAR*. Two years ago, she moved to New York, hoping to launch a print version. She struck gold when she met billionaire Peter Holt of Holt Capital."

"Holt!" Sky says. Nothing about Cameron surprises him, but Peter Holt is a menace. He opposes astral energy. He claims Earth is in the grip of malicious alien forces. "I keep close tabs on Holt. He's married to a high-profile New York socialite. Is it strictly business with Cameron?"

Joe sits beside Sky. "We've had surveillance on Peter for some time, due to HoltTech. He has a fling here and there, but this thing with Cameron is chancy for him. Cameron is living in the penthouse of one of Holt's buildings in Tribeca. She's either the best fuck on the planet, or Peter has discovered her ancient history and knows she could be a player in bringing about a world powered by astral energy."

"What's your take?" Sky asks.

"Our recent ad campaign, emphasizing the choice factor with Rube—*If you like your electric company you can keep your electric company*—has kicked the shit out the alien takeover theory. The ads are funny. People love them. Would Dark Master know Cameron lived as Ka'rine in Ruberah?"

A chill creeps over Sky. *Cameron had been Ka'rine.* It still shocks him, although it shouldn't. They had certain similarities. "Yes," he says. "Dark Master would know that."

"And could he unblock Cameron's ruby intelligence?"

"No. Tamara is the only person who can restore that." Sky stretches his arms over his head. "But Dark Master has developed instruments capable of extracting jeweled light from the human brain."

"And HoltTech has a new brain scanner in development." Joe grins. "What are you waiting for, mate? Off you go. Rescue the fair maiden. From what I hear, you won't have a problem making a date with Cameron. She was overheard talking to a girlfriend. She still carries a torch for you."

"That's not a torch, Joe. That's a sniper rifle."

Earth is a mistress more terrible than any woman. We can't live without her. — Leah, Queen of Ruberah

Earth became Sky's mistress the day he crossed the River Tamar and met Tamara. He inherited her from E'am who inherited her from Luca, but the love affair began with Rae Blue on the day Earth was born. Sky has visited that event so often that he's bookmarked it on SunVision. He taps that symbol as he walks toward Cameron's apartment.

A SunScreen pops up, shimmering with the silver-blue light of planet Miron. There he is, living as Rae Blue, a man giddy, joyous, ecstatic, gazing at Earth spinning to life: *I will love you and defend you for all the days of all the lives I shall live.*

Sky takes a deep breath, buttons his jacket, and pushes the bell to Penthouse A. He hears the clacking of heels on hardwood floors. The door swings open. Cameron gasps, eyebrows scaling her hairline. "What the fuck? How did you get up here?"

"That was the easy part. Am I coming in?"

Cameron darts a nervous glance down the hall. "I'm expecting company."

"Okay, later tonight?"

"You're the last person I expected to see. Why are you here?" She ushers Sky inside. "Just for a few minutes."

"Nice digs." Sky takes in the spacious room with sweeping vistas of the city and a terrace overlooking the Hudson River.

"If you've come to punish me, forget it. I did my time in therapy, and I've moved on."

She sure has. Diamonds dangle from her ears, and she wears a black dress slit to her thigh, and red suede ankle boots. Her hair is scraped off her face and twisted in a knot on top of her head, a style that accents her pointed chin and high forehead.

A phone rings. Cameron dashes to an island between the kitchen and living room. She snatches the instrument to her ear. "Oh, of course, darling. No. No. It's fine. Yes. Tomorrow."

"Change of plans?" Sky says.

Cameron stalks down the room to a bar near the windows leading onto the terrace. "We can have a drink. Sit down."

She drops her shoulders and speaks in a less brittle tone of voice. "You're looking hot, Sky Blue Hunter ... nice threads ... who would have thought?"

Sky eases onto a barstool, keeping his focus on Earth—his mistress—a romance that works better in metaphor than reality. Cameron shovels ice into a couple of large on-the-rocks glasses and picks up a bottle of Chivas Regal.

"Scotch. Okay?"

He nods. She slides a glass toward him, half full, no offer of water or soda. "How was the world? You were gone for ages, I hear."

"The world is great, and I'd like to keep it that way."

"Hah! You were always hard to read."

Cameron perches on the stool next to Sky, lifting her leg so the slit in her dress falls open, exposing her thigh—very Ka'rine-like.

"You were seen with Zara in Sydney just last week," Cameron says, "all the way on the other side of the world. That tells me it's still a thing with you two, so let's cut to the chase. Yes, to whatever you came here for, but only if you can get Zara to do a cover shoot for *VERA STAR.*"

Sky slugs on the scotch. He'd like to tell her off but good. Her blog on *Teens Dying for Love* changed the course of Zara's life. He holds his temper in check, and chooses his words carefully. "If you can't get Zara's agent to book her for your magazine, then I guess it's not the right thing for either of you."

"Don't fuck with me. I made supermodel Zara. She skyrocketed to fame on my back. She's on the cover of every fucking magazine in the world except mine. How is that fair?"

Sky twists his glass, shaking the ice, trying to keep his head straight. "I'm not here to trade favors, Cameron. I'm here to make you an offer—a gift that is due to you by a fault of mine."

She drains her glass, refills it, and tops his off. "What are you talking about?"

"I work for Earth-Astral, in charge of energy conversion. That means I can switch your computers, lighting, heating, cooling, everything powered by electricity, oil, gas, etc., to astral energy."

Cameron smirks. "Don't tell me you believe in that crap. If there actually is a mountain made of rubies and if it ever surfaces from wherever the fuck it's hidden, it'll be nuked. All that alien spawn inside will go up in a cloud of plutonium."

"Sounds like a Tweet from Peter Holt."

"He's a very smart businessman."

"I know about your relationship with Peter. Did he ever take you to HoltTech and scan your brain?"

Cameron strokes Sky's cheek with the back of her hand. "We had some hot sex, didn't we?"

He yanks her hand off his face. "Most corporate leaders are not threatened by the idea of astral energy," Sky says. "Free power for everyone won't shrink profits. Funds saved from the cost of fuel will be available for investment in new businesses, and the money saved by consumers will go back into the economy."

"Peter invested in *VERA STAR*, and we fuck. So what? I know he's married. I'm not some stupid girl waiting for him to leave his wife for me. I'm going to build a publishing empire, and he's a step along the way."

So much for therapy. Sky's mother had fought for Cameron after the *Teens Dying for Love* fiasco. She insisted Cameron and all the girls on the website needed help, not reprimand. "I'm not referring to your personal relationship with Peter," Sky says. "Has he ever taken you to HoltTech?"

"Why?"

"I think he's using you, drawing energy from your brain."

A loud buzz crackles the air, and Cameron flees to an intercom in the kitchen. "Yes."

"Mr. Holt is on his way up."

"Shit!" She dashes back to Sky. "You've got to get out of here. Go on the terrace and hide. Take your glass with you." She waves a finger at Sky. "Don't make a sound, and leave the instant I take Peter into the bedroom."

"For god's sake, Cameron. Can't you have friends?"

The doorbell rings. "Go!"

Sky slips outside but leaves the doors open. Tall shrubs line up next to them. Sky hides behind one, pushes the leaves apart, and peers inside.

"Oh, darling." Cameron throws her arms around Peter's neck. "What a lovely surprise."

"I hope so. I canceled a meeting to be with you." Peter swaggers into the room, like a gangster with a gun stashed in his belt. He goes straight to the two barstools out of alignment with the others. "Drinking alone, or did you have company?"

"Mindy stopped by, wanting my input on a layout." Cameron laughs. "Good thing she had a date or I would have gone out to dinner with her and missed you." She swings in behind the bar. "Would you like a drink, or would you rather whisk me into the bedroom and—"

"Vodka." Peter sits on the barstool Sky just vacated, and drums his fingers on the marble countertop. He stops suddenly, and guffaws, taking on a good-natured attitude. "I guess I'm like a kid. I want to impress you. We've improved that brain scanner I showed you. I want you to see it again."

Cameron doesn't flinch. She pours the vodka and places the glass in front of Peter. "You impress me every day in every way, my darling." She sidles to his side. "And I want you to do that right now, in bed."

"That'll have to wait. I've got to show you my new baby. This scanner can assess your IQ. You're so smart, and it will figure how much I should invest in *VERA STAR*. Get your coat."

Cameron tilts her head, and Sky can almost hear the cogs of her brain turning. "But I need you, Peter. I—"

"Now!" Peter grabs Cameron's arm, agitated, like an attack dog straining at a leash. Sky stands ready to rush in and tackle Peter, but holds back, sensing Cameron might be used to this sort of thing. He's right.

She raises her hand in front of Peter, spreading her fingers wide, as if in an agreed upon safe signal. "Peter," she says in a firm voice, "I will come to HoltTech tomorrow at noon."

Peter hunches his shoulders. "Bitch. You're not getting laid tonight."

Sky looks away, and moves to the edge of terrace. It's a crisp autumn night. Stars glitter over the Statue of Liberty and tugboats cruise the Hudson. He reviews his reason for being here.

Cameron had lived as Ka'rine in Ruberah, and E'am had been her boss at Rube Enterprises. Overt flirtations were not to be tolerated in the workplace. An offender should be issued a warning, and if they continued, be dismissed. Ka'rine flirted with E'am at every opportunity, but E'am did not fire her because he still got off on his old schoolboy crush on her. When the EmFire crisis struck, E'am needed to work alone with Time Blade. Ka'rine wanted to stay. Desperate to get her out of the office, E'am shoved her through the door. In parting, Ka'rine said he'd pay for that. Sky checked his recollections out with T. She said Ka'rine had died with thoughts of punishing E'am. Consequently, she was born as Cameron today, and did what she did to Sky. It's a tough nut to swallow, but if Sky doesn't clean up this mistake he made as E'am, Time Blade will not return to him.

Cameron storms onto the terrace, shaking a fist at Sky. "Don't say a fucking thing about Peter. What do you owe me?"

She shivers, maybe with fear, maybe from the cold. Sky removes his jacket and places it over Cameron's shoulders. "Remember when you thought I was smarter than I let on, back in high school, like when I did my homework just before class?"

"So?"

"You were right. I had astral intelligence. I've always had it. I can look at a question and know the answer. You could do that too, back in Ruberah."

"Oh, for fuck's sake. I don't believe in that stuff about some civilization that could use astral intelligence. Jesus, Sky. Give me a break."

"Why do you think Peter wants to scan your brain?"

"I don't care. I need him to make payroll next Friday, but if you can deliver Zara for a cover shot, I could score enough advertisers to carry me over."

"This is between you and me, Cameron. In those blogs you wrote for *Teens Dying For Love* you talked about the beautiful and brilliant girl you were in your dreams. Well ...back in Ruberah ... the time you don't believe existed, you were that girl."

"Stalemate." Cameron hands Sky his jacket, and strolls inside.

Okay. He tried. She's not interested. He can't force her, but he can't quit either. He treks back to the bar. Cameron pours another drink. Sky draws up a SunScreen. The square of light floats between them, but Cameron can't see it yet. Her astral awareness still sleeps.

She pushes the bottle of Scotch toward Sky. "Help yourself."

"No thanks." He runs the forces of sapphires into his hands, reaches over the bar, and touches Cameron on the forehead. The glass drops from her hand and smashes on the bar. She doesn't notice. Her gaze freezes on the Ruby Ring, filling the SunScreen between them.

"This is the Ruby Ring—the astral form for Mt. Rube," Sky says. "Twelve people stand at the edge of the circle, and each has a job to do to bring about the new Age of Jeweled Intelligence." He points directly to the Seven on the Ring. The girl previously hidden in darkness stands free and clear—Ka'rine with her lush dark hair, creamy skin, and curvy body. "This was you," Sky says, "a beautiful and brilliant girl who lived in the *Time of Ruberah.*" Her name was Ka'rine. You could inherit her talent and intelligence today. Do you want that?"

CHAPTER THIRTY-FIVE

Despite a quick leap to the side, the thug lands a brass-knuckled fist in Sky's jaw. Lights flash at his temples, and a searing pain shoots through his head. He stumbles. His assassin comes at him again. Sky manages to knee him in the groin, leaning in with his whole weight. The thug winces, bending at the waist. Before he can straighten up, Sky forms a SunShield, a banner of light, his favorite weapon of defense. The guy charges Sky again, face scrunched in anger, aiming his knuckles at his chin. Sky dances around him, fielding him off with the banner. After a few thrusts—hitting nothing but air—the thug flees.

Sky shouts after him. "Give my regards to Peter."

He feels a flap of torn skin hanging from his jawbone. Blood spurts from the wound, and pain hammers on his brain. Sky wipes his chin with the sleeve of his jacket, and strides up Broadway looking for a quiet spot to do some repair work.

A text arrives from Zara. *Where r u?*

B there in 5

He steps into a darkened doorway between a Thai restaurant and a deli. People pass by, engrossed in conversation or music flowing through ear buds. Looking into a SunScreen, Sky checks his wounds, using the x-ray feature. He flinches. No wonder his whole head throbs.

His jaw is cracked in several places. He selects HEALING. MALE. FACIAL. The map of a man's face appears. Sky slides the cursor to the jaw, indicating the damaged area on his own. PROCEED. His orb floods with the silver-gold light of the Sun Kingdom. He hits CONTACT, and a warm energy spreads through his face, buzzing like a bee at a hive, knitting his bones and skin back together. The searing pain subsides. He lets out a breath of relief, mingles back into the crowd, and strides north on Broadway.

Two years ago, Earth Inc. began releasing information about man's ancient history in Ruberah, and the coming of the new Age of Jeweled Intelligence. At first, people thought it was a hoax, but as Earth Inc. streamed programs on the Internet, showing people how they would use astral intelligence, the conversation changed. The reveal of ruby-powered spaceships, cars, and grids—for a worldwide network of ruby light paths—created mass excitement. These products had been under manufacture for dozens of years and would become operational the very day Mt. Rube was raised back to the planet. All this threatened Dark Master's power on Earth, and he riled up the dissenters—the alien takeover theorists. None of it mattered. The Lords for Earth hold covenant over Earth, and Mt. Rube will be raised when they say so. When Sky was appointed President of Earth-Astral, Dark Master upped surveillance on him. Thugs like the last one appear out of nowhere, and beat him up. But for the SunShield and healing powers of SunVision, he'd be long dead.

Sky veers right on Canal Street, left on Mercer, and turns into the entrance to Zara's building. It's been a wild ride with Zara these last four years. She's often called Sky, sobbing, reliving the death of her father, wanting to die and be with him. That changed six months ago, when Tamara appeared to Zara as her spirit guide. T told Zara she'd come to Earth to do a special job, and Zara has been on cloud nine ever since. So what's her urgent need of him tonight?

The elevator opens into Zara's loft, and she's right there as he gets off. "What's up?" Sky asks.

Zara grips the lapels of his jacket and hauls him toward her. "Ugh." She flicks her fingers. "Blood. What happened?"

"Nothing serious."

"You've been attacked again. This has to stop. Nanny-mein!" Zara yanks the jacket off Sky. "Come here!"

Sky cringes at the way Zara orders her old nanny around. Story has it the Austrian-born woman tried to teach a very young Zara to say my nanny in German. Instead, Zara insisted on Nannymein, as in hers and hers alone. Zara takes Nannymein everywhere with her, like for the abortion she didn't have, and to the clinic in Switzerland where she had the embryo extracted and frozen.

Nannymein shuffles into the vestibule, eyes placid behind black-rimmed glasses. Sky nods at her, a token of shared understanding, the kind parents exchange when dealing with a difficult child.

"Call the concierge, Nannymein." Zara dumps Sky's jacket in her arms. "Tell him to get this cleaned and returned within the hour. It's bloodstained."

"I do it myself. I clean plenty of blood in my life."

Zara's loft occupies the entire top floor of the building, with a stainless steel staircase that zigzags up to a roof garden. The ceilings are high, and the furnishings sleek and sparse, with an occasional mix of antiques. The space might be too cold or too big for any one person other than Zara. Slight as she is, willowy as the trunk of a coconut palm, she prances through the wide-open rooms. Her chestnut hair bounces about her face, and she spreads her arms wide, as if pushing the walls out, needing yet more space.

"How's it going with the foundation?" Sky asks.

"It's coming together." She flings her arms above her head. "I've given the entire fortune Daddy left me to the Simeon Bosche Foundation. I'm a working girl." She grins. "Totally self supporting."

"Your father would be so proud of you, Zara."

"Know this, Sky Hunter, if I ever have to tap my friends for a helping hand, you'll be at the top of my list. You must be loaded now ... CEO of a huge company. I bet your stock in Earth Inc. is worth a fortune."

"You'd better hold onto your rich boyfriends, Zara. Earth Inc. belongs to the people. Profits go back into the planet."

"Only you could land in a situation like that, Sky." She scowls at him. "I hope they pay you well."

He laughs. "I get by."

Zara steers him to a butter-colored leather sofa snaking down the room. The media hounded Zara for months as a result of Cameron's blogs on *Teens Dying for Love*. Then reporters discovered Simeon Bosche had left Zara half of his estate, the rest to be divided among her siblings and her mother. The Bosche family feuded and tried to contest the will. A gardener wrote a tell-all book about life in the Bosche mansion. Zara landed back in the tabloids, making headlines for weeks on end. Finally, she decided to get in front of the cameras on her own terms. She'd received many offers to model and work in movies. Zara never studied art history at the Sorbonne. She moved to New York, and took up modeling.

"Well," Zara says, sitting on the sofa. "Spill it. Is Cameron on the Ring? Not that she deserves to be even considered. Bitch."

Sky doesn't know what happened with Cameron, because T swept in after he showed her the Ruby Ring. He beat it out of there. Cameron's transformation held no joy for him. He's not there yet. "Zara, if we're going to talk about the Ruby Ring, you'd better connect with your Star Intelligence."

"Oh, Awesome Balls, you're so commanding these days." She wriggles like a little girl, winning him over. "Bring up the Ring on the SunScreen. Please, please, please."

Sky leans back, relieved to find her happy and playful, but that can be an act. "Tell me," he says. "Why am I here?"

"You look wonderful." Zara cradles Sky's face in her hands. "All shaved and cleaned up. My baby daddy gets more handsome by the day."

She dips her body so the strap of her long, tank-type dress slips off her shoulder. They've been lovers on and off through the years, falling into bed after Sky ran to her rescue—under Nannymein's threat Zara would die unless he came at once. When Sky got ready to leave, Zara would dive back into the memory of the day her father died—into a seemingly bottomless well of grief.

Sky places the strap back on her shoulder. "We decided not to be lovers anymore. Remember?"

"Um ... but it's different now that I know I'm a star being." Zara hugs Sky, then holds him out at arm's length, smiling. "Tamara explained how my separation from the great whirl of the galaxy was at the root of all my sadness. Every little sorrow led back to the day when Time called me to leave my star mate and come into this life. I first met you back then, at the birth of the galaxy, back when you lived as Rae Blue on planet Miron."

She gasps and drops her voice, as if to impart a secret message. "Rae Blue was like the poetry of what a man should be. He was beautiful and strong and gentle, and he had luscious, long flaxen hair." She runs the tip of her tongue over her plump bottom lip. "I, as my star being, trusted Rae Blue at first sight," she whispers. "He wore a band of magnificent sapphires around his head. I remember being touched by the resonance that drifted off them—a whispering of celestial wisdom." She leans back a little. "So ... when Rae Blue ... you ..." she says, rapping her knuckles against Sky's chest, "bowed into Time and offered to serve mankind as needed, I did the same thing, offering my Star consciousness. I did that because your celestial wisdom told me that Rae Blue—you—Sky Hunter today, would find me on Earth and take me home to the stars where I belong. You're why I'm here."

Sky doesn't doubt Zara's memory of Rae Blue, but he has no recollection of meeting her as a star being. He enters the astral record of Rae Blue's life on a very selective basis. Rae Blue's descent into anger with Luca baffles Sky, and he does not want to experience it firsthand. It's a relief to know why Zara got so emotional whenever he left her—at least it wasn't due to him. Sky thinks of how Rae Blue, inspired by Asari's leap into Time, followed her. Zara must have been right behind him. Now here they are bound to one another by a cosmic promise—love for mankind—love too big for mortal consumption.

He makes light of things. "At least you got the looks this time."

"No, no. My baby daddy is scrumptious. Let's go to the cinema. It'll be wonderful in there."

"What will be wonderful in there?"

"Why ... the Ruby Ring," Zara says, as if any fool would know that. "Bring it up for me. Just for a little bit so I can visit my star mate."

"Is this why you wanted to see me?" he asks.

She drags Sky off the sofa, humming, pulling on his arm.

It's dark with soft lighting inside the cinema, never to be called a screening room—too L.A. Zara leads Sky to one of the lounge chairs designed for two. She presses a button, and the curtain whooshes up, revealing a super-sized screen.

"I love you, you know," Zara says, her big violet eyes misting over. "I don't mean I love you, like in I love you, like with all the strings and plans and confining things that go with that statement. I mean I really love you, really, really, really, like big as the universe. Do you love me that way too, or am I such a pain in the ass, you wish you'd never come to play tennis with me that Saturday morning four years ago?"

Cosmic references have always been Zara's style. Back when she'd watched him surf a big wave she called him a wind god. She'd seen the galaxy in his eyes and claimed he was so far out he must come from a planet with many moons. Ramon was right. She had revealed herself—her star consciousness—in her everyday conversation. He says, "It's always very special to be with you, Zara. And I wouldn't have missed all that sex in the pool house for any reason."

She giggles. "That was fun wasn't it? I loved high school. I didn't have a care in the world, and Daddy was alive." Her glance strays to the side. Sky holds his breath, waiting for the tears to start, but they don't. She bounds to her feet. "I'll get some popcorn while you bring up the Ring."

Sky covers the movie screen with a square of light from the Sun Kingdom, and magnifies the One on the Ring. He hadn't known Zara was the girl inside the stars over the One, until six months ago when T told her she'd come to Earth to help raise Mt. Rube back to the planet. It's hard enough to believe he's a player on the Ruby Ring, let alone Zara, and now possibly Cameron.

"Ohmigod!" Zara clutches a bag of popcorn against her chest and gazes at the beauty of the Milky Way as it fills the screen. Sky opens HOLOGRAPHIC VIEW, and the stars float all around them. Zara dumps the popcorn, and runs into the whirling depths of the galaxy, vanishing from sight. Her laughter fills the room, hers and her star mate's—blending with the harmony of the universe.

"Come back, Zara. Tamara is calling me. I have to close the Ring."

Sky taps END on his astral disk, and the SunScreen folds back into space. Zara throws herself on the seat beside him. He reads Tamara's message.

Cameron has been accepted on the Ruby Ring. Go to England tomorrow. Return to Penrose Hall.

"What does Tamara want?" Zara asks.

"Have I given you what you wanted?"

"Mmmm." She retrieves the popcorn from the floor and palms a handful into her mouth. "Since the Goddess will raise the Ruby Ring in the next few days, I was thinking," she says, munching. "It's so hard being without my star mate. You understand. I know, because you're so kind and—"

"I understand, Zara. Just tell me what you want."

"The ruby mountain will probably be raised soon after the Ring." She dumps the popcorn back on the floor, and climbs on top of Sky, curling up with her head against his chest. "He's frozen," she whispers. "Our little boy is on ice. It's too awful. I can't bear it any longer. I want to have him now."

It's not the first time this has come up, but images of a frozen baby usually come with the grief and hysteria associated with her father's death. Sky says, "You know I can't be a hands-on dad for another two years. I've not been informed when Mt. Rube will be raised, but Tamara told me I'll be traveling the world for at least a year after that, overseeing the flow of astral energies into cities and homes."

Zara slides off him and onto her side of the seat. "It's wonderful to know I'll return to my star mate at the end of this life. Meanwhile, I'm stuck here. I live for little Simi. Don't take him away from me."

She looks sad and lonely, like she did on the day her father died. Everything changed then. The playground of teenage love blew up in their faces and scorched the threads of what might have been. "I won't stop you from having the baby, Zara. I'll sign the release forms as the father, but I can't be there on a regular basis until the worlds run smoothly on astral energy."

"But I need you."

Sky massages the back of her neck, and speaks softly. "Rae Blue, the guy you described as the poetry of what a man should be, thought and acted from the highest planes of his soul. He made promises that were realistic to him, like to love and defend Earth for all the lives he would ever live, and to serve Time as needed. I'm just me, Zara ... Sky Hunter ... a surf bum at heart, trying to keep his word."

"Wind God," Zara says. "I'm seeing the guy who rode that huge wave in Santa Rosa. He wouldn't leave a little baby alone and frozen."

The tremble of a sob rattles in her ribs, and Sky says, "He's not frozen. He's a beautiful little spirit, playing in the golden sands of the primordial."

"How do you know?"

Asari is a place of solace for Sky. Alone at night, he opens SunVision and views the videos she took of E'am and her in Ataleah. It feels to Sky like he's inside E'am's skin, falling in love with her all over again. Sky pulls Zara into his arms and tells her the story of E'am and Asari. Then he does what he has not done before. He opens the video of E'am, gazing into the golden sands of the primordial, watching his unborn twins chasing each other around, playing tag.

"Oh!" Zara gasps, tears flooding her eyes. "They're so beautiful, and you never knew them?"

Seeing the children takes a toll on Sky, tearing his heart at the seams. He speaks softly, his voice trembling with emotion. "EmFire destroyed the world, but Asari and the entire Atal tribe survived."

"And the twins?" Zara asks.

"I'm sure they grew up loved and happy," Sky says, comforting himself as much as her. "The human family would not be here but for the Atal, and the Age of Jeweled Intelligence can't restart without you, Zara. You're a star being. When we raise Mt. Rube, you will bring in the power of the galaxy."

Zara crawls back onto his lap. "You love Asari. I can tell. You love her like I love my star mate."

"It was a long time ago."

"But it's love from the other side of time. It never dies."

"Maybe. Meanwhile we're here on Earth, and I don't want to be an absent father."

Zara takes his hands in hers. "I'll wait to have the baby."

"Are you sure? Will you be all right?"

"Stay over."

"I can't, Zara. Tamara wants me in England tomorrow, and I've got a lot to do before I leave."

"You need to sleep somewhere."

He heaves a sigh, sorely tempted. "The Ruby Ring is due to be raised in a few days and I don't have Time Blade yet. I can't do my part without it."

"Where is it?"

"I don't know, but it won't come to me unless … well … there are rules for the man who carries the Blade. I have to live by those standards." He pauses, dodging her scrutiny. "It doesn't feel right for me ... for us to sleep together, right now."

"Why not?"

"There's a Pure Heart rule. I don't remember how it's worded, but it boils down to doing the right thing. I want to be with you, Zara, but I can't afford to ignore the feeling that I shouldn't, not tonight."

"Is it about Umi, my star mate?"

"Maybe. He's the Two on the Ring. He'll be here, Zara, right beside you when we raise the Ring. I just heard you laughing together. You sounded so happy, so perfect together. That's something to treasure, isn't it?"

"Umi wants me to have whatever I need to be happy during my time on Earth. Nothing I do here will change what we have in eternity. Don't you think Asari feels the same way about you?"

"Zara, you have a one-lifetime contract with Time. I don't. What I do creates consequences. To be with Asari, I have to earn the Sun Heart and transcend to that Kingdom. That means making the right choices." He holds her by the shoulders. "I want to stay, but I have to go."

CHAPTER THIRTY-SIX

"Sky!" Lara Penrose strides across the reception hall. "It's so good to see you," she says, wrapping Sky in her embrace. "How the years have flown by." She blinks tears from her eyes. "Tamara told me you're working for the Goddess. I'm sure that's demanding. Even Luca had to power up to deal with her."

Being with Lara defies time. Sky feels every bit as close to her as E'am had felt to Queen Leah in Ruberah. "The Goddess is a tough taskmaster," he says, "but I just tremble in my shoes and do as I'm told."

"Good practice for marriage, then."

Sky gives that subject a pass. He'd come close to love a couple of times after Gina, but backed off. His life as E'am is never far from memory. The trouble he had trying to balance work and love remains a lesson well learned.

"How's Kate?" he asks.

"She's good. You'll see her later." Lara passes through the French doors onto the terrace. "You're in the Tower Suite."

The circular tower stands tall and solid. Pink mists swirl around the turrets—vapors rising up from the Ruby Ley Line buried deep in the earth below.

"We keep the Tower Suite for the traveler—the one who journeys alone. Should suit you well." Lara crinkles her nose. "I want to hear about your adventures. I had a few phone enquiries, people checking on your references, mostly from luxurious resorts in exotic places. That must have been fun."

"Thanks for the thumbs up."

"Ah, to be young, strong, and fearless. Come to dinner tonight, Sky. The family is all here." Lara smiles, a wistful look in her eyes. "I miss him. It helps when you're around."

"I'll be there."

She points to a wooden door with black iron hinges. "It's open. Go on in."

Sky climbs a flight of stone stairs and enters the living room. Large tapestries soften the granite walls. A seascape of finely stitched blues, grays, and greens fills the entire rear curve of the room. Sky sets his computer on a table by the front-facing windows. Views of the coastline stretch for miles around. A person could sit here forever and never feel alone. The quest of the traveler is everywhere, the seeking and the finding. The magnetic pull of the next place, coupled with the realization of why you came to the destination you're in. The moment of wondering what it would be like to stay and reap the comforts of that, but not for long. The magic of travel—discovery— would call him on.

Sky sits on the one chair at the table, and opens his computer. SunVision appears without his command, and a letter floats on the screen. The jeweled emblem of the Emerald Kingdom shimmers on the masthead.

Beloved River,

It is the night prior to my meeting with the Princesses Li'ram and Sol'aria of the Ruby Kingdom. Tomorrow, with their help, the human race should be the beneficiary of a force of power from our sacred Emerald Mountain, an energy that will afford our civilization a tremendous leap forward in evolution.

The greatest scholars of our time and my people have expressed an overwhelming enthusiasm for me to ignite the Emerald Force. There was but one voice of dissention—that of Li'ram's father, the late king of the Ruby Kingdom. However, he was said to be failing in health and in cognitive thought. Therefore, I remain assured of my decision to proceed.

I have not sought your advice on this matter, as I am not able to believe in you to the extent that I would follow your guidance, should you even answer me. In the sadness of my childhood, you remained hidden to me. Why, when other children claimed you appeared to them and helped them? I am deeply wounded by this, and yet I write this letter as I might call out to you with my dying breath. But I write for a reason more terrifying than death. Should my effort to ignite the Emerald Force prove catastrophic, I do, for lack of knowing what else to do, cast my fate into your hands.

I commit these words into the Cycles of Time to follow me through my eternity. If one day we read them together, then I will have wrought a great calamity upon the human race and you will find me the

most desolate and wretched of men. If mercy be your
nature, as so many believe, I would ask one thing of
you. Let me do no further harm. Destroy me for all
time to be.

I am in truth,
Da'krah, Prince of The Emerald Kingdom

Sky slinks down on the chair, feeling wretched.
E'am had not known his enemy as well as he thought
he did. What if E'am had reached out to Da'krah, tried
to befriend him? Sky stabs DELETE. The letter remains
vivid on the screen. He hammers his finger on the key.
Nothing budges.

A sparkling hand touches the screen, and the letter
disappears. "E'am knew Da'krah," T says. "He met him
in his star being when he used Time Blade to still Dark
Master's influence on the prince."

Sky nods, remembering the compassion E'am had
felt when he looked at Da'krah through the eyes of his
own atom—*I am*—in Time. It's a travesty. The Goddess of
Emeralds chose Da'krah as guardian of the rise of EmFire
on Earth, but Dark Master blinded him to that at birth.
"You know," he says, thinking back to EmFire. "Time
allowed EmFire to happen. Why? E'am still had some
fight left in him. He could have stopped it."

T rests her hands on his shoulders. "When my father
first arrived on Earth with the Atal, the Lords for the
planet allowed him to create a SunShield to protect the
tribe for five hundred years. That time ended, just before
EmFire was about to destroy Ruberah. If E'am had cut
Time and expelled Da'krah, Li'ram, and Sol'aria from the

planet it would not stop Dark Master from continuing his quest to ignite the emerald force. The ruler would go after the Atal to help him. The tribe had no experience with the ruler's ways of persuasion, but they were powerful. They could intuit energy from the Sun Kingdom. Without the SunShield to protect them, Time could not rule out the possibility that one or two of them might fall victim to Dark Master's schemes."

"No." Sky bangs his fist on the table. "Asari would never have let that happen."

T leans closer to Sky, and the tangled trails of her hair fall over his body. She says, "If the Atal had drawn energy from the Sun Kingdom to launch EmFire, it would not only be the end of the human family, but the planet too."

Sky sinks his head into his hands. Time feels like a monster, rolling the dice, betting millions of lives against questionable odds. And he still doesn't know what happened to Asari after Ataleah fell to sea level. The astral records of Ataleah do not appear in Earth's Cycles of Time. They're in the Cycles of the Sun Kingdom, and can only be accessed via the Sun Heart.

"I know it hurts," T says, "but as E'am, you obeyed Time. You died as requested. Now billions of people live on the planet, and the Lords for Earth have sanctioned a new Age of Jeweled Intelligence. You have work to do, Sky. I need you to concentrate on the Ruby Ring. Can you do that?"

"Sure."

"I restored Ka'rine's ruby intelligence to Cameron," T says, jumping right in. "She's every bit as imaginative with Rube today as she was in Ruberah. I'm not sure what she will want to do, but should she ask to work for Earth-Astral, would you consider hiring her?"

Sky's first instinct is no, no way, but he doesn't have Time Blade. This could be a test. He says, "If Cameron has the talents we need, I'll work with her."

T flashes Sky her most dazzling smile. "That's my darling child," she says, enfolding Sky in her sparkling arms.

"I know. I'm a great guy. What next?"

"The twelve servers of the Ruby Ring will be at the Hall by tomorrow. The Ring is due to surface the planet at noon the next day. I will keep Dark Master at bay while all this is happening."

"And?" Sky says.

"You must review the laws for the man who carries Time Blade and make sure you fit the bill. That's the only way the Blade can find you."

"What if I don't fit the bill?"

"That's not an option."

Sky opens the file for the Laws of Time Blade on his computer, knowledge he relearned during his meditations on the streets of Mumbai.

The man who carries Time Blade obeys Time without question.

The man who carries Time Blade meets his every responsibility.

The man who carries Time Blade treats all men as equals.

The man who carries Time Blade communicates with each person at the level of his understanding.

*The man who carries Time Blade finds his worth in
service to others.*

*The man who carries Time Blade is not reckless in his
dealings with life. He is well thought out, law-abiding, and
careful in all matters.*

Sky leans back, clasping his hands behind his head.
He can either sweat this out, or respond off the top
off his head and see how he stacks up. He chooses the
latter.

1. *Obeys Time?* That's easy. Time hasn't asked him to
   do anything yet.
2. *Responsible?* He's pretty good with that.
3. *Treats everyone as equals?* He doesn't think he's
   better than anyone else.
4. *Communicates with others at their level of understanding?* He gets along with people.
5. *Finds worth in service to others?* Sure. He likes helping people.
6. The Pure Heart rule. *Reckless?* Obviously he was
   as a teenager, but not so much now. *Well thought
   out, law-abiding, and careful?* That language is too
   ancient for today's world, but he's passable by current standards.

"Sky!" Her voice travels up the stairs. "It's Kate. Are
you busy?"

Sky rushes to the top step. "Hey! Come on up."

She rounds a curve, coming into sight. "Whoa!" Sky
does a double take. Kate has shaved her head. There's

just a scrub of flame covering her skull. "What's that about?" he asks.

"You've been tidied up yourself, Mr. President of Earth-Astral. I watched you on the World Symposium from Sydney. Impressive."

Kate strolls around the room, running her fingers over the tapestry of the sea. Per T's request, they've not seen each other or communicated for four years. Gone is the ramrod girl of sixteen. Her carriage is gentler now, broken in by life.

"Mum told me you're coming to dinner tonight," Kate says. "I wanted to fill you in on a few things before you stepped into what could be a bit awkward."

Sky laughs. "My mom is known as the Happiness Guru. I've got awkward covered."

Kate starts flipping through photos on her phone. She stops, and holds the phone up to Sky's face. "This is what I came to talk to you about."

A baby's face appears on the screen—a little girl with green eyes, red hair, and skin the color of a latte. "You have a child, Kate?"

"Yes, but she's not mine."

Kate breathes in a definite rhythm, like Sky does when he's trying to control his feelings. "My brother and I are very close," she says. "I think I knew Christopher was gay before he did. When we were children I'd tell him it was okay, that he'd grow up and fall in love with a wonderful boy and be happy. I said I would have a baby for them so they could be a family." She turns the phone over again. "This is that child."

"She's beautiful. How old is she?"

"Four months. Her name is Glory. Chris and his partner Raji are here with the baby. They'll be at dinner tonight."

"That's an amazing gift," Sky says. "Are you okay?"

Kate folds her hands neatly in her lap. "'T made it clear that if I did this, I must do it without strings. I should step aside as Glory's mother and allow Chris and Raji to raise her. I should simply be her Aunty Kate." She huffs a breath. "Luca used to say humility enables the Sun God within to act through you. I wanted to do something to remind me of that. Buddhist monks shave their heads as an act of humility, and so I chose that."

"Kate, I can't even imagine how—"

"No, you can't. Nothing is ever like you imagine it will be, but my love for Glory is greater than my grief over EmFire. The day I signed the adoption papers, the Sun Flame came alive in my heart."

The look on her face is solemn, telling Sky there is no right thing to say. He says, "Blimey," imitating Joe's Aussie drawl.

Kate spurts a laugh. "You can't say that. Say something American."

"Motherfucker."

"Brilliant." She gets up, and heads for the stairs. "The inn is closed to the public for the weekend. I've got to help set things up for our co-servers on the Ring. See you at dinner."

On the Atlantic Terrace, Lara cuddles her grandchild while her husband Lance dawdles over drinks at the bar. Kate's brother, a younger version of his dad, clinks glasses with his partner, the darkly handsome Raji. Kate sets a tray of appetizers on the bar.

"Come on up." Lara waves Sky onto the terrace, and introduces him to Chris and Raji. "Cocktail, wine, or beer?" Lara asks.

"Let's have martinis," Chris says. "Move over, Dad. I'll make them."

Raji takes Sky's arm, drawing him aside. "Chris and I watched every minute of the World Symposium, all three days of it, over and over again," he says. "The panel was amazing. I loved your presentation about how we will explore the universe in our astral bodies. I want to know—"

"Raji!" Chris scowls at his partner.

"I don't mind," Sky says.

Raji continues. "About our astral forms. Are we going to be able to get into them and just go and explore space?"

"As long as your intention is in harmony with your ruby intelligence."

"Ah, yes," Raji says. "That's the part where I close my eyes and look inward to here." He points to his forehead. "That's easy for me. I'm Hindu. I've been meditating all my life. That's like looking into the Third Eye."

"Right," Sky says. "Once Rube is on the planet, you'll see a pink glow there, about the size of a dime. That's your astral intelligence."

Raji claps his hands. "I love, love, love it."

"And we have to talk to that pink light?" Chris says, screwing his eyes into slits.

Raji assures Chris it won't be weird. "You will bow to that light," Raji says. "It's a mental action, and you'll want to serve it, because it's like being held in the arms of never-ending love. Then it'll just happen. Wherever you want to go, you will go with that love in your heart."

"I think you should be on the next Symposium," Sky says.

Raji bows. "At your service."

"About virtual reality," Chris says. "Can we really build virtual worlds on other planets, still live on Earth, and visit our virtual lives?"

"Sure. Gems retained their astral consciousness when they migrated to Earth. We begin by using the power of rubies because rubies enhance creative ability. We can set goals and achieve them, which brings happiness. Your ruby intelligence will never harm another living creature. In a virtual world, we can live on other planets and study and understand their life forms, without inflicting or catching life-threatening viruses."

Chris says, "But life was like that in Ruberah, yet someone brought that world to an end."

Kate moves to her brother's side. "That was human error," she says. "Back then people filtered the astral forces of rubies into the planet. Today, Rube will be distributed by computers in Astral Command, untouched by human hands."

"Good heavens," Lance Penrose says, "I don't want to be ruled by a computer, and I don't want an electronic gadget on my hand."

"Daddy," Kate says. "I explained. You can select to not have the disk."

"Select suggests it's already there and I have to get it off."

"No. I will pre-register your choice."

Another round of martinis, and the conversation flips to favorite places, restaurants, and movies. People ask Sky about his travels. He talks about the highlights—things everyone relates to—scuba diving at the Great Barrier Reef, visiting the Taj Mahal, and exploring the pyramids.

"Kate has been in film school," Lara says. "We're so proud of her. She just graduated and—"

"Mummy! I'm right here." Kate glares at her mother, then ushers everyone in to dinner.

They eat the traditional Brit meal, roast beef, Yorkshire pudding, and veggies, served family style. Lara and Lance head the table, and Sky sits next to Chris on one side, facing Kate and Raji on the other. Red wine abounds.

Lara gives a toast. "To everyone we love and to all we have yet to love."

It was Luca's toast, and Lara smiles a brave smile. Sky gulps, as he always does at the mention of Luca.

Chris and Raji expound on the joy of being parents. "Guess what?" Raji says. "We've decided to grow our family. My sister Aditi has agreed to have a baby for us. Chris's baby this time." Raji stands, and raises his glass. "Aditi lives in New Delhi, and the sperm is in the mail!"

"What?" Lance Penrose says, looking confused.

"Oh, that's lovely, Raji." Lara smiles, sipping wine."

Sky raises his glass. "Here's to the sperm in the mail."

Kate scowls at him, mouthing *motherfucker*.

Lara says, "We're renovating the East Wing. It's so dilapidated that it's been closed for years."

"This is all well and good," Lance says, "but we can't go on rebuilding this old pile. We should consider the offer from the National Trust."

"Lance, darling, it's time to expand. Bookings are pouring in. We—"

"Dessert," Chris says. "In the kitchen. Let's go."

The group breaks up. Chris and Raji leave first, as they're driving to London early in the morning. Kate and her dad follow, claiming the need for sleep.

Sky sits over coffee with Lara at the counter in the kitchen. "Are you okay?" he asks.

Lara twists her mug in her hands. "I have a feisty stallion named Luca. I ride him every day. He tries to throw me, but I whack him with my crop and let him know I'm master now." She laughs. "I put him out to stud, and that's the sweetest money I'll ever know. All this to combat old grievances over my life with Luca in Ruberah, and yet if he walked into my world today, I'd give him my heart." She looks at Sky. "Please don't mess Kate up."

He's taken aback. "There's nothing going on between us."

"Kate is living with a man in London, Carl. She moved in with him when she got pregnant. This sort of thing is beyond my understanding, but he took care of her. Trust me, Sky. That was a roller coaster ride. Did she tell you about Carl?"

"No. We met briefly before dinner. She told me about the baby. That's all."

Lara smiles, a mystical look filling her gaze. "As a little girl, Kate talked about having a baby for her brother.

She'd always be the mummy. You know, two men ... they'd need her." Lara shakes her head. "She held onto that all through her pregnancy. I could tell, even though Tamara advised her differently."

"Lara, you know children come to parents by vibration—by the sounds and lights of attracting souls. Chris and Raji are Glory's parents because they have what she needs to meet her fullest potential. Kate would not have been challenged to step aside as her mother, if that were anything but true."

Lara rests her elbows on the counter. The light of amethysts glows around her, the strength of will—the volition she had used to help Luca run the Kingdom of Ruberah. "How are your parents?" she asks.

Sky runs back to the tower, races up the stone steps, and grabs his computer. He opens Skype. "Be there, Dad." Why had he left this to last minute? What was he doing, telling Lara how kids find their parents, when he's never applied that to his life, his dad? He glances at his watch. It's eleven at night here, three in the afternoon in L.A.

"Hello, Sky."

His father's secretary appears on the screen, the devoted, long-suffering, Anne. She tells Sky his father is coming out of a meeting. Hold on. She'll get him.

Sky runs his hands through his hair, frantic. Where will he start? He's never known where to start. His visits home have been short. He always itched to get back on the road.

"Sky." Clive Hunter plunges into the swivel chair behind his desk. "What's wrong?"

"Nothing. I wanted to talk with you. Is this a good time?"

His dad frowns. "What is it?"

"Um ... as a kid ... um, I thought you weren't around very much, and I just wanted to say now that I'm working all the time, I look back and see how often you were there. I don't know how you managed that."

His dad leans back. "Are you in trouble?"

"No. I'm trying to say thanks, Dad."

Clive Hunter looks surprised, like when he's confronted by a twist in a case. He rubs his earlobe, glancing down at his desk. "I fell short as your father in many ways," he says, lifting his gaze back at Sky. "I hurt you when you were very young. I should not have implied you were not a normal kid. I've regretted that time and time again."

"I wasn't a normal kid, Dad. Someone had to clue me in. I couldn't have found my way into the job I'm doing without your influence. I sneered at the way you worked, but now I'm that person."

His dad shakes his head. "I can hardly believe you're my son. It seems you went from being a spaced-out teenager to the man in charge overnight."

"There are a lot of people in charge." Sky laughs. "Let's be glad of that."

His dad leans in close to the camera. "I should have been the one to make this call. I've thought about it a hundred times, and then—"

"I punched you in the face, remember?"

"You were a hell of little kid." His dad laughs, caressing his chin in the place where Sky's five-year-old fist had landed.

"By the way," Sky says, "did Simeon Bosche ever talk to you about me?"

"Simi?"

His dad's voice quavers, and he fiddles with a pen on his desk. Sky thinks of the change in his dad, the way he'd responded to Sky's part in the *Teens Dying for Love* scandal. No criticisms. The dreaded truth hits home. Simeon Bosche must have talked to his father about Sky before he died—told him he thought Sky was very smart and he wanted him to come and work for him. "Dad," Sky whispers. His voice trembles as regret pounds on his conscience. "I'm sorry."

Clive Hunter looks up. "I broke the sacred trust between father and son, Sky. I hope you can forgive me. I'd like to earn it back."

"You have earned it back, Dad. You told me you believed in me, when I needed you the most. You sent me into the world with your blessing."

"Your mother always knew. She told me you'd come to do a special job in the world. I blew her off."

"Dad ... Mom says that about everyone."

Clive Hunter laughs. "I wouldn't have amounted to much without your mother, you know. I don't know what I did to deserve her?"

"Plenty, if you listen to her."

His dad scoffs. "When will we next see you?"

"Soon. I'll stop over on my way back to New Zealand."

Sky climbs the stairs to the second floor of the tower, feeling lighter, free of a nagging guilt about his dad. He stops short as he enters his bedroom. Kate lies on his bed.

"There's a knife under your pillow," Kate says.

He would snatch the Blade and leap for joy, but it would appear he has one more test to pass. Kate. Sky bends over her, slips his hand beneath her head, and withdraws Time Blade. The gems in the crossguard sparkle, and the astral fire of jewels shoots through his body. He strolls to the window, clutching the Blade to his chest. *Whatever you ask of me, I am.* Those words warm his heart, and he cherishes the trust placed in him by Time. He lays the Blade on the windowsill, and sits on the edge of the bed. "What do you want, Kate?"

"What if it's still there—the chemistry, the fire, the love?"

"Your mother told me you're living with a guy in London. Carl."

"Bloody hell." Kate balances her body on her elbows. "She has no—"

"She's looking after you, Kate."

"I am not Sol'aria. I'm not going to fall apart over any man."

Sky folds his arms across his chest. "If you love Carl, you—"

"I don't know if I love him. I keep diving back into the astral record of my life as Sol'aria. I feel the passion we shared. It's like the whole world existed just for us to love one another. I've never felt that with Carl, or with anyone else."

Her gaze bores into Sky, intense and unwavering. Traces of the love E'am had felt for Sol'aria ripple his memory. He could be interested in Kate under different circumstances. She's courageous to the core—a woman who will make her

mark on the world, but everything in him knows it would
never work between them. He still loves Asari.

"What's Carl like?" he asks.

"Weird. Funny. I met him at film school. He's a writer/
director, an aspiring auteur, demanding on the set, but
cool with me, odd as I am."

"You light up when you talk about him."

"Sometimes, we carry love over from one life to
another."

"A man who looks after a girl who is pregnant by
another man loves her."

"Bloody hell! What world do you live in? I'm brilliant
script material."

Sky leans back a little. "Okay, so call Carl and tell him
you want to take a break from your relationship. Or isn't
it that kind of script?"

"You know what?" Kate swings her feet to the floor.
"Fuck you!"

She's halfway down the stairs, then she turns, climbs
back up, and slaps him hard across the face. "That's for
fucking with Sol'aria."

"You did that at the time," Sky says, clenching his fists.

"Well, it wasn't hard enough."

Kate dashes down the stairs, fury trailing in her
wake. Sky picks up Time Blade, slides it back under the
pillow, and lies down on the bed. *I give you my mind, my
body, my heart, and my soul. Teach me what you would
have me know.*

CHAPTER THIRTY-SEVEN

Tamara calls early in the morning, swooping over Sky as he works on the computer. "Everyone is at the Hall," she says, "and I will take care of matters big and small with each person."

Sky taps the face of Great Grandfather Leo's watch. He's worn it all through his travels, winding it every morning. He smiles, remembering how he used to imagine time, encased in the watch, falling under his control.

"You still have the Three and the Nine to meet," T says. "That's Mitch and Miriam aka Da'krah and Li'ram in Ruberah. Are you ready?"

Sky glances out the window. T told him Mitch and Miriam have suffered greatly for their part in EmFire. Both have met sacred futures and paid their debts to humanity. In consequence, they are happily married today. Sky gets a grip on himself, banishing old resentments toward Da'krah and Li'ram. He looks back at T. "I'm ready."

Sky is still winding the watch, when Mitch and Miriam walk into the room. He leaps from his chair. His gaze lands on Mitch. Except for his dark, close-set eyes, he bears no resemblance to Da'krah. No trace of swagger. Middle-aged and graying at the temples, Mitch offers Sky a tentative hand. Their feud of ages past weaves in and out of Sky's thoughts, but Da'krah's letter to Tamara takes precedence. Sky imagines Da'krah writing it, facing the possibility that EmFire might wipe out the world. *Destroy me for all time to be.* The shared weight of loss compels compassion. Sky lifts his left hand toward Mitch, palm forward, in the tradition of Ruberah. Mitch rests his palm against Sky's. The diamond glow of his astral disk meets the sapphire light of Sky's. Hand to hand, easy as the tide turns, they pass forgiveness and goodwill.

Miriam greets Sky with the same zest for life she had as Princess Li'ram. She flings her arms around Sky. He feels the love of rubies streaming from her heart to his— the blessings of creative power and happiness.

CHAPTER THIRTY-EIGHT

The columns stand tall and elegant, as if keeping watch over the Holy Square. It's a bright October day, not too windy, and the midday sun warms the air. The Friends-in-residence file in, and the monks follow. Ramon steps forward and greets Sky. *Walked from Spain,* that's still all Sky knows about his old mentor. That, plus he's the Eight on the Ring. Ramon's handshake comes firm, like his devotion to the planet.

The Ruby Ring glows on the surface of the Holy Square, filling the entire space inside the pillars. Tamara guides each of the servers to their correct number. Sky goes over them by name in today's world and in Ruberah, if applicable, and by jewel kingdom.

One: Zara/The Milky Way
Two: Umi, Zara's star mate, not yet here
Three: Mitch/Da'krah/Diamond
Four: Lara Penrose/Queen Leah/Amethyst
Five: Hiroto/Nett/Sapphire
Six: Kate/Princess Sol'aria/Pearl
Seven: Cameron/Ka'rine/Ruby
Eight: Ramon/Gold
Nine: Miriam/Princess Li'ram/Ruby

Ten: Joe Simmons/Ki'an/Diamond
Eleven: Samira/Emerald
Twelve: Sky/E'am/Sapphire

Sky catches Samira's smiling glance, directly to his left. They spent time together during the World Symposium in Sydney. Married, with two teenage daughters, Samira heads up Astral Education for high school kids. She's quick-witted and very outgoing. They laughed over the pass Sky made at her four years ago, right here in the Holy Square. Could he listen to nature with her?

Cameron steps onto the Seven spot. They talked last night over a buffet dinner at the inn. Ever the opportunist, Cameron had made a deal with Earth Media to create a magazine—*Ruby Smart*—for the entrepreneurial woman. Old grievances stirred, but Sky aimed for the high road. Cameron came from a broken home. She never knew her father, and Sky had been complicit in the karma she inherited from Ka'rine in Ruberah. He wished her good fortune, and he meant it.

He shifts his glance to Kate, standing on the Six. She trekked into the tower early this morning. "S o r r y," she yelled, as she mounted the stairs to the living room. "Ugh!" She came to a halt and shuddered. "I've got the temper that so famously goes with the hair I don't have anymore," she said. "I didn't mean the awful things I said last night. Well, actually, I did, but you're who you are today, and I'm going to try to let you off the hook." He recalled how E'am had suffered, carrying the vestiges of Rae Blue's anger toward Luca. Kate was in the same boat, dealing with Sol'aria's heartbreak over E'am. "Let's hug it out," Kate said, "for the sake of Mt. Rube." Not exactly a clean slate, but a start.

Zara stands on the One, a couple of feet to Sky's left, making the monk's outfit look worthy of a *Vogue* cover. She arrived very late last night, and they talked briefly, making arrangements to fly back to New York together tonight.

T approaches Sky. "If all goes well with the Ruby Ring, the Goddess will direct you to raise Mt. Rube," she says.

"The mountain itself!" Sky's voice scales the heights of surprise. "I thought we were just raising the Ring."

"You're ready for this, Sky. Remember the astral pattern for Rube, as you saw it in your life as E'am, and do what you do with Time. Oh, and one other thing, my darling child. If the Goddess gives you the order to raise Mt. Rube, I must release Dark Master from the SunShield I created to keep him at bay while the group gathered at Penrose Hall."

"Why? He'll attack me."

"Mankind gave Dark Master his place on the planet. Man can only evolve by overcoming the weaknesses that tie him to the ruler. Deal with yourself, Sky."

T takes her place on the black dot in the center of the Ruby Ring. The gong booms, echoing over land and sea. The monks chant OM. Sky pulls on the focus of his double sapphire, until the clutter of his worldly minds falls silent. He sings with the monks. His voice rides on the resonance of OM, moving him into the space between the breaths. *I come to serve.*

The Golden Dome arises from inside the planet and lays over the Holy Square. The stars of the Milky Way

appear, as if under the dome—swirls of crusty light—
whirling around Zara like rivers of snow. A star being
strides forth from a blue glow at the center of the galaxy—a man with similar features to Zara's but with silky
dark hair. He takes the Two next to Zara. She tucks her
hand in his, a gesture of love and belonging. Sky looks
away.

The Ruby Ring bursts through the crust of the
planet—a circle of red fire that spins across the globe
and settles in the middle of the Pacific Ocean. A landmass
forms inside the fiery rim, causing the seas to swell and
storm. T runs her hand over the coastlines of the world,
creating a wall of light. The oceans smash against the
wall, then roll back and hurl forward again and again.

The Goddess speaks. "Sky Blue! Raise Mt. Rube!"

Her order knocks fear off the radar. Habit takes
over—actions from his lifetimes as Luca's student. Sky
withdraws Time Blade from the sash at his waist.

*To open Time, aim the tip of the Blade to the Golden
Pyramid atop the Crystal Temple of Science, and the
Earth's Cycles will appear. Ask permission to reverse, stop,
or speed forward.*

Sky adjusts those instructions to fit current conditions. He tilts the Blade straight up to the top of the
Golden Dome. Earth's Cycles of Time shimmer before
him—its great wheels glowing pink against space.
Dimension shifts, bringing the Cycles close enough to
touch. His eye goes to the dot where the past crosses
over the future—the Now. He aims the tip of the Blade
into the dot. Time opens—its glowing masses of perfect impersonal intelligence filling the cosmos. A bolt of

darkness blots Sky's vision. Thunder rumbles the heavens. Dark Master swoops over Sky.

Everyone belongs to me. It's only a matter of time until I get you, Sky Blue.

The ruler whirls his cape, swishing it inside out. Sky ducks, but the daggers in the lining of his cloak slice into the muscles of Sky's right upper arm. Agony ignites fury. The carefully managed anger of all his lifetimes takes him over. He's never wielded Time Blade with his left hand, but by god he will now. He withdraws the Blade from the golden sash of his monk's outfit. *You will never get me. I will kill you first.*

Dark Master swivels his hooded head to face Sky, and laughs, a nasty mocking sound that says *I dare you.* Sky points Time Blade at the ruler's neck. *I'll decapitate you, rip your cape into a zillion tiny shreds and burn them in the fire of the sun.* His arm shakes and he wobbles on his feet. The columns surrounding the square fade in and out of view.

Look into my face, Sky Blue.

Sky recalls the old saying, to look into Dark Master's face is to see your own, and you will die of fright. The ruler's cape falls still and eerily victorious. Sky's heart drums a wild and irregular beat. He cannot raise Mt. Rube in his current state of mind. Time will not hear him. He cannot turn back. There's nowhere to go. Slowly, he touches the tip of Time Blade to the hood on the ruler's head. Easing the cloth to one side, he meets a grossly distorted version of his own face. The hungry glitter of lust sparkles in his eyes—his old fervor to kill Da'krah. The grimace of anger lines his cheeks, and his mouth twists in an expression of angst. Not normal. Panic mounts in Sky's chest. He struggles to breathe. Death threatens, but he cannot give in to it. He'd have to come back into another life and do all this over again. One thought rises above all others—clear and uncluttered. He meets the face straight on. *I forgive you.*

The ugly image dissolves, melting like wax under fire. T stands before him in Dark Master's place, smiling. "Well done, my darling child. Now get back to work. Time awaits you."

Sky touches his upper arm, where the ruler had sliced into his muscles. Nothing. No pain. In fact, he's never felt better. He is a man in the right place on the right planet at the right time. He strengthens his grip on Time Blade, and bows back into Time.

"Permission to raise Mt. Rube back to Earth."

Granted.

He sights the secret ocean beneath the planet, where Mt. Rube rests. He has to get it from there onto the newly formed island in the Pacific. He aims Time Blade into the black dot of the Now in Earth's Cycles, and twists the weapon, pushing it through the thickly twined cords of the moment—to the other side of Time—eternity. Everything in the world stops—the oceans, winds, all creatures, and everyone everywhere fall still. Sky searches his ancient jeweled memory, and there it is—the astral pattern for Mt. Rube—as seen by E'am on the day EmFire destroyed the world of Ruberah. He leans over the planet and presses his forehead to the newly formed land. The diagram with the twelve triangles sears into the ground, and the deva chorus of the ruby mountain bursts into song. The goddesses of emeralds, sapphires, amethysts, diamonds, and pearls emerge from their long exile, their jeweled bodies streaking across the cosmos, lighting up the world.

In the Holy Square, the Servers pull in the forces of their native astral kingdoms, and from the sun and the Milky Way. Gold, Lord of Love for Earth, embraces all these energies into his body, and then lifts Mt. Rube from the secret ocean at the bottom of the planet and places it on the island in the Pacific.

The mountain settles, and ruby light emanates from its base. Rivers of sparkling pink waters stream through the oceans, seeping into every country in the world, filling the ley lines beneath the planet. Ruby light paths blaze to life, and an astral disk glows on the hand of every man, woman, and child who elected to receive it. The Age of Jeweled Intelligence begins anew.

CHAPTER THIRTY-NINE

The Lezant headland towers above Sky—silent and stone-faced against time and tide. Per T's instructions, Sky stands on a rock jutting into the ocean at the bottom of the cliff. The wind howls around him, carrying echoes of excitement and discord—reactions to a world newly powered by a force beyond human control.

A sudden blaze of silver-gold light brims the horizon, and Sky's sapphire vision opens. What is far away is right beside him. Joy tempers his heart. He bows to his teacher. "Beloved Master."

"Excellent work!" Luca beams. "You have fulfilled the sacred future you wrote as E'am. I am empowered to return the Sun Heart to you."

"Return?" Sky says, his voice barely audible.

Master's golden gaze falls softly on Sky. "You come from the Sun Kingdom, Sky Blue. You returned to the human family as Rae Blue on planet Miron, because I asked you to. My contract with Time neared its end. I had to be free to work on a different plane. Earth needed a new Master. Everything you did, getting angry with me for not saving the people of planet Miron and all that fol-lowed right up to your present-day life, you did for me. For humanity."

It might confound Sky except Rae Blue's sudden loss of trust in Master has never rung true. "Asari?" he asks.

"Asari is your Sun Mate. She waits for you in the Sun Kingdom. Time is timeless there. Sun beings don't age."

"When can I be with her?"

"We will speak of that later. Come." Master takes Sky's arm. "Let us walk on the sands of the primordial. The promises you made as Rae Blue lie there. Before you go forward with your life, we will mark them done."

Sky keeps stride with Master, step-for step. The Sun Lord's crystal-beaded hair sways about his shoulders, sometimes brushing against Sky's. Nothing exists except being here with Luca. At the touch of Master's feet, the golden sands of the primordial part and a path of light spirals back from z27, the black hole leading to the Sun Kingdom. The promises Rae Blue made to mankind stretch before Sky—hand-drawn symbols etched over the face of Time.

Memory sweeps Sky back to the day Rae Blue wrote them. Emotions well up in Sky but not in Rae Blue, the man he had been. Rae Blue cherished every vow he crafted into the golden sands. The shapes of possible futures drifted around him. He saw destiny had marked him as the next man to carry Time Blade. He realized becoming Spirit Master for Earth would be a painful journey. He would find fault with Luca and suffer greatly for having done so. Twenty-First Century Earth shimmered on a distant horizon—a misty mirage, marked with a set of golden footprints and the date of his birth as a boy called Sky Blue.

Sky points to the footprints. "What are those?"

"A golden footprint represents a promise to help mankind," Luca says. "It is the only certain mark a person can imprint on the future. Those are mine. You did not see me, but I walked ahead of you all through your life as Rae Blue and as E'am and in your current life. You followed me, faithfully. Now you may erase your past and claim those footprints as your own. Go on," Luca says. "Kneel, and wipe the sands clean."

Sky drops to his knees, plunges his hands into the symbols drawn by Rae Blue, and sweeps them off the face of the primordial.

Luca dusts sand from Sky's arms, as he rises back onto his feet. "I am empowered to offer you safe passage home to the Sun Kingdom," he says, "but Earth cannot be without a man to carry Time Blade. Time asks you to stay and teach the laws of the Blade to your successor."

"I have one? Who is he?"

"Your son. The boy coming to you and Zara."

"Is the child definite?" Sky asks. "All we have is an embryo frozen in time. What if it's not viable?"

"Your son will be born. He is coming from the Kingdom of Flames, the universe beyond the Sun Kingdom. Time asked him to descend to Earth and speed up the evolution of man. Zara is the only star woman on the planet. He needs her to be his mother and you to be his father."

Sky touches Master's shoulder, trying to digest all this. "This boy will be a thousand times smarter than me. What will I teach him?"

"You will teach him how to be the man who carries Time Blade. You have already walked ahead of him. He will follow your golden footprint in Time, just as you followed mine."

Luca rests his hand on Sky's arm, and continues speaking as they amble back across the golden sands. "There will always be those who oppose astral intelligence. Some will attain positions of influence in the world and hold command over weapons that could destroy humanity. The strongest force on Earth is compassion—the ability to see the whole of another person, like you experienced with Da'krah, when you offered him an honor killing by Time Blade. A man or woman may fall far from the *I am* of their atom in Time—but that perfect impersonal intelligence still serves in the mastermind. When you look at someone through the eyes of your own *I am*, you can know the journey that led them into a downward spiral. You feel compassion, because you realize that but for the fortune of your life circumstances, it could be you. This understanding frees you from judgment and the fallen person will intuit that, because compassion is the native nature of mankind. This opens the door for change."

Sky says, "I understand, but even as E'am, living by your side, I seldom reached a true state of compassion."

"That's about to change," Luca says. "One of the rays of the Sun Heart is dedicated to the vibration of compassion. Let me restore yours before we talk any further."

With the touch of Master's hand, the Sun Heart opens at the top of Sky's head. Ten thousand rays of silver-gold light float around him, like the petals of an ever-blooming flower. The Sun Heart feels at once familiar—a lost but found treasure—a friend. A teacher. Home.

Master speaks. "To access the compassion ray, simply turn your attention to your Sun Heart and ask for it.

When teaching your son the laws of Time Blade, always center your intelligence in that ray. It's very important that he views the world through the eyes of *I am*. The beings in the Kingdom of Flames serve this universe by burning up corrupt entities that intend to harm the natural order of birth and death among the galaxies. Your son will become fully aware in his Heart of Fire by the time he takes custody of Time Blade. Then he will be able to direct a flame to anyone, anywhere in the world and erase them from existence. Without compassion for his fellow man, he could become a lethal weapon."

Shivers of unease crawl over Sky's skin. He'd imagined being a dad and a teacher to an adorable little boy, not a killing machine. "I hope I'm up for this."

Luca chuckles. "You have a saying, what goes around comes around, hmm? As a young boy, E'am thought he'd use Time Blade to kill anyone who opposed his opinions. I had to tame the killer instinct in you, back then. I usually got your attention by assuring you that you already knew everything I had to teach you. If you listened, it would come alive again in your own knowing. Remember?"

"Yes." Sky laughs. Luca had always been so patient with E'am. Hopefully, that's a side effect of working with the Sun Heart.

Luca draws them to a halt. "When your son is born the Flames in his soul will help lift the collective consciousness of mankind. The millions who perished on planet Miron will begin to reincarnate, bringing their highest jeweled awareness with them. Evolution will speed up. The Lords for the planet want everyone to transcend to the Sun Kingdom before Earth's sun star burns out."

"Do you know when that might be?"

"No technology on Earth today can match the instruments we had during the Mironese era. Back then I teleported my own intelligence into the sun, along with that of our most brilliant scientists. We had what is today called a slow-moving supernova—until, without any warning, it wasn't. So what I know is, nature is a law unto herself and man lives under the law of free will and neither is predictable."

Sky rolls his shoulders, taking that reality to heart. He will do as Time asks, but he'd like to meet with Asari first. His gaze drifts to the silver-gold ray leading to the Sun Kingdom.

"A word of advice." Luca raises his hand and blocks the light of z27. "If you visit Asari now, it will make your life more difficult on Earth. You will be a better father and teacher if you give the love you can give, rather than long for a love that awaits you in another world."

Sky doubts he could love another woman, now that he knows Asari waits for him, but he will love his son with the full measure of his Sun Heart. "Does Time ask me to stay until Earth's sun dies?"

"No, just until you can pass custody of Time Blade to your son. Then you may leave Earth at the time of your choosing."

Sky bows to the Sun Lord. "It is so."

CHAPTER FORTY

Ten years later

He comes running into Sky's studio, his thick chestnut hair swaying about his face. Simeon Sky—born seven years ago. Sky kneels, and opens his arms to his son.

"Daddy, Daddy!" Simeon thuds against Sky's chest. "Can we go into Time?"

"Yes, we can."

Sky points to the sculpture of infinity he made as a teenager, now hanging above the desk where Simeon does his studies. "What is Time?" he asks.

"It's the soul of the world. On the way into life, everyone leaves an atom of their highest awareness in Time. Time is smart, Daddy, but it's too slow. It shouldn't take so long to search intelligence and get answers."

"What do you suggest?"

"I could direct a flame into Time, burn it up, and create a faster model."

Sky tousles his son's hair, and looks at him through the ray of compassion in his Sun Heart. His awareness expands, opening up and becoming more receptive to receive his son's point of view, but his own remains firm. He says, "On Earth we need Time the way it is."

"Why?"

"Remember when you struck a match and burnt your finger, thinking the flame would remove a splinter? It didn't, did it? You got a blister and it took time to heal."

"But Time isn't skin. It's intelligence. If I set it on fire, it will come back a hundred times faster and smarter than before."

"Simeon, if we didn't have hours and minutes in the day, people wouldn't know when to go to school, or work, or when to visit with friends."

"I would know, but never mind, Daddy."

His son's eyes grow wide and tinged with sadness. The Heart of Fire glows above his head—circles within circles of flames. Simeon already perceives knowledge from the heart. He doesn't need a clock to know what time it is. The Flames guide him to be wherever he's meant to be. They've also told him he's come to Earth to take his father's place. Brave as he is, that's a lot for a young boy to handle.

Sky hugs him closer. "I will be with you for a very, very, very long time," he says. "I'll be so old I'll have to lean on your arm just to get one foot in front of the other. Now, why don't you get Time Blade from the drawer, and we'll begin a lesson?"

Glee replaces sorrow, and Simeon dashes to Sky's desk.

"Remember to lift the Blade by the handle, like I showed you."

Zara bustles into the room, cuddling Luca Ramon, the newest addition to the family. Sky lifts the baby from her arms, lays his head against his shoulder, and pats his back. Just ten weeks old, Luca is a sweet child—serene like his namesake.

"It's Saturday," Zara says, looking from Simeon to Sky. "What are you two up to?"

"Nothing, Mommy." Simeon slams the drawer closed and runs to his mom, burrowing his head into her waist.

Zara keeps strict tabs on Simeon's astral studies, as left to Sky he'd spend half the day wandering about the universe, teaching his dad what's what.

Simeon smiles up at his mom, cheeks bursting at the seams. "You're the best mommy in the whole world."

Sky chuckles beneath his breath, watching Zara. Simeon inherited her charm tactics. She knows, but it still catches her by surprise. She frowns, and a half smile quivers on her lips, as if caught between delight in this little boy version of herself and the need to rope him in.

"Just one hour with Time Blade," she says, "and then Daddy has to take Bella to ballet class."

Simeon skips back to the drawer that holds Time Blade.

"It's date night," Zara says, taking the baby back in her arms. "Don't get lost in Time, Awesome Balls."

Falling in love happened ten years ago. Mt. Rube was back on the planet, and they were on Zara's plane, flying from England to New York—the last jet-fueled flight for the Gulfstream. Sky sat beside Zara on a banquette in the main cabin. He had just left Luca, and he still looked at the world through the love in his Sun Heart. He could see the glow of Zara's star intelligence, glistening on her skin and in her eyes. They were in the same place at the same time—above the rise and fall of everyday emotion—at peace with themselves and each other.

Sky told Zara what Luca said about the child coming to them from the Kingdom of Flames. She listened with rapt attention, then spoke in that breathless whisper of hers. "He'll need brothers and sisters," she said. "Family."

That knocked Sky off balance. Zara claimed she would never marry. Her parents had fought bitterly and slept around with other people. She wouldn't chance having that happen to her. Sky sat speechless. Zara said he had reminded her of Rae Blue, as he worked on the Ruby Ring that day. He had the same poetic beauty about him—like a man who would right the wrongs of the world. "Up until then," she said, "I tended to think of you as the boy who left me ... who didn't challenge my breakup line." She sniffed. "I'm still pissed about that, but ... well ... all married people fight, so if you love me, that could be like our default argument ... a way to break up the huge rows we will no doubt have. That way we won't kill each other."

Marriage with Zara? How not to kill each other?

Zara pulled a ring from her jacket pocket and held it up to Sky. It was a gold band with a diamond so small he had to squint to see it. She said, "It was my Grandma Greta's ring, Daddy's mother. I loved Grandma Greta and she adored me. She loved Daddy with all the love he gave to me. This ring holds that vibration. I have that love in me, Sky, and I'll give it to you, if you want me."

Her essence shone through her whole expression— pure and mystical—otherworldly—like a girl whose feet had never trodden the muddy path of mortal life. Of course he loved her, but he'd long since written off the possibility of them as a couple. His mind went to Asari, waiting for him in the Sun Kingdom. He couldn't see anything beyond being true to her. Then she appeared—Asari—in her astral body of dazzling suns. She strode down the ray from the Sun Kingdom and stood in the center of his Sun Heart. "Love Zara," she said. "You need each other. When you return to me, we will be all the happier for the love you have given to her." Then she was gone, and Sky fell off the cliff of all resistance.

He took Grandma Greta's ring, slipped it on Zara's finger, and promised to love her faithfully for all the days of his life. Then he touched her cheek as if she were a priceless porcelain vase—so delicate she could break beneath his fingers, and claimed the kiss that went with being a man in love.

Zara spent the next year completing her modeling assignments, and then flew to Switzerland for the embryo transplant. It took without a hitch. She rented a chalet in the Swiss Alps. While waiting for the baby, she finalized her vision for the Simeon Bosche Foundation, and convinced twelve of her father's most powerful friends and business associates to serve on the board.

Sky lived on a triple-decker ruby airship with ten colleagues for that year. They crisscrossed the globe, trouble-shooting problems with the switch to astral energy. He visited Zara every day via SunScreen—astral dating—now a worldwide phenomenon. His global travels for Earth-Astral ended exactly one week before Zara's due date.

It snowed as he drove up to her mountain home. The Alps towered into the sky, silent, white, majestic. Zara opened the door and drew him close to her. He felt the baby stir in her belly. Her water broke. Sky piled her into the car. Simeon Sky entered the world twenty minutes after they arrived at the birthing center. Gazing into his son's eyes, Sky watched the fire of the Flame Kingdom blaze around the world. Simeon wrapped his tiny fingers around Sky's thumb, and stole his heart.

He married Zara a month later in a drive-through wedding chapel in Las Vegas—her choice. Nannymein sat in the back seat, weeping wedding tears. Simeon slept. After a visit with family in L.A., they traveled on to New Zealand. Bella Amor arrived two years after Simeon, followed by Luca Ramon.

Zara runs Third Choice, a division of the Simeon Bosche Foundation. The program offers an option—other than abortion or putting the child up for adoption—to pregnant women not ready to care for a baby. The one Zara chose, now made affordable to most women and free to those without funds.

Aside from his work at Earth-Astral, Sky teaches the Nature of Time, giving a public lecture in the local town hall once a week. As he strides to the podium, he visualizes Luca's golden footprints in Time, and places his own firmly inside them. People wander in, coming from all walks of life. For the man who carries Time Blade, there's only one way off the planet. He must find someone to take his place. Sky hopes to pass a few worthy candidates on to Simeon.

The Mironese have arrived on Earth in staggering numbers. More than half the kids in Simeon's school once lived on planet Miron. They're very smart, but humble and kind by nature. As if haunted by the loss of their once magnificent civilization, they understand no one goes forward alone. They help kids with lesser abilities than their own, and they're careful not to litter or cause harm to the planet. These are the children of Luca's legacy—the product of the ages he spent guiding the human family from its lowest, animal-like nature to the highest realms of love and compassion. They are the future—the bright shining path to the Sun Kingdom.

In the evenings, after the kids have gone to bed, he and Zara sit outside on the terrace, sipping wine. It doesn't cease to amuse them that they are married with children. Zara rolls out of bed in the mornings, climbs into sweats, and takes her turn carpooling kids to school. He gets Simeon and Bella up and dressed and makes them breakfast. Nannymein lives in a cottage on the property, enjoying retirement, but ever happy to babysit.

Fourteen years have passed since he and Zara got drunk and ran naked into the ocean and made out in the breaking waves. If Zara hadn't got pregnant that night, it's highly unlikely they would be together today. And, should the world become a better place because of Simeon, some credit should be given to a great bottle of tequila, a couple of joints, and the indomitable teenage spirit that is ours for such a brief period of time.

Zara will return to her star mate one day, just as Sky will return to Asari in the Sun Kingdom. Meanwhile, their love is more precious, knowing it's just for now—the moment at hand—the breath taken. The future is the next breath. It may or may not come, but eternity rides in the space between each breath. Time holds our hopes and dreams. Some will catch the fire of destiny. Others will fade away, maybe for lack of effort on the part of the dreamer, or for reasons known only to Time. Undreamed of dreams happen too. His life is living proof of that. He did nothing more than follow an inner drive that told him to get out into the world and let it teach him what he needed to know. In retrospect, that's easily understood. He couldn't be a leader in the new Age of Jeweled Intelligence unless he knew firsthand the conditions that needed to change.

Sky glances at Simeon, sitting at his desk by the windows. He could pass all the tests for the man who carries Time Blade today, but there's no telling how long it will take him to accept Time, as it is used on Earth. Or perhaps, the other way around—for Sky to realize Simeon has come to change Time, as it works on Earth. Either way, Sky will not take his dying breath until he sees Zara home to the stars, and until he can leave Time Blade safely in his son's hands. That's the grain of his nature—the way of the Sun Heart—the way home.

Acknowledgements

If you're reading this, then thank you for reading *Time Blade*. Let us remain connected in the causes of the novel—caring for Earth—and for each other.

I am deeply grateful to those who helped me shape this story. Jordan Rosenfeld for editing. Jana Lamb for copyediting. Maria Verez for proofreading. Scott Hale for creating the book cover. I received much more than professional services from these individuals. Each one gave me encouragement—nourishment of the soul—that which every writer needs to make it to the end of a long, long journey.

www.christinagreenaway.com

www.ingramcontent.com/pod-product-compliance
Lightning Source LLC
Chambersburg PA
CBHW062108170626
46813CB00002B/365